CHINA RISING

PAUL SANDE

Dedication

ACKNOWLEDGMENTS

Without the love, support, patience, and unwavering belief of my wife I would not be able to dedicate the time that I do to writing my novels. For this, and so much more, I am forever indebted to her.

Laura Galante is a leading authority on state cyber operations. Accomplished in her field, she gave an incredible Ted Talk on the Russian hacking of the 2016 election. I was inspired by the talk and reached out to her, asking if I could include her as a character in my novel. She graciously agreed. I then transcribed her presentation so I could fully understand it, and having gone through that exercise I realized how much I had missed by just listening to it once. If you haven't watched it, I encourage you to do so.

As you will see, part of this novel takes place on the Principality of Sealand. This micro-nation's history is worth reading about. I've been a fan of Sealand for many years and always knew that I would work it into one of my thrillers. I was so pleased when Prince Michael allowed me to use his likeness as a character in the novel and to add to the mystique of this unique place on earth.

My good friends Dan Nolan and Lawrence Ayippey both appear as characters in this novel. I have woven the characteristics that I admire in each of them into their characters, and I hope they enjoy being part of the story.

QUOTES

"China is a rising power, casting off its century of humiliation in a bid to become a force in regional and world affairs."
   – Noam Chomsky

"When all else fails, they take you to war."
   – Gerald Celente

PROLOGUE

Jang Dung let the steering wheel slide easily between his thumb and forefinger as he roared down Jinggang'ao Expressway. He'd left the fifty-lane section of highway far behind and traffic was light. With his free hand he tapped the steering wheel to the latest Chinese pop hit that pumped through his stereo speakers. The scenery barely registered; his mind was occupied by thoughts of his wife.

Her heart condition had worsened and doctors had warned them she had just months to live unless a donor could be found. A situation that would leave his two young children motherless and his burgeoning career threatened by having to care for them.

But he had good news and could barely contain his excitement. His rise to the upper middle class meant he could now afford things that five years ago would have been unthinkable.

Jang had bought her a donor.

An agency had connected him with a source that offered access to organs harvested from Falun Gong practitioners. While the practice was formally illegal, with money and silence came a solution. His wife needn't know the source of the donor or the method by which the organ was procured. It had cost a fortune, for sure, but all that mattered was that their family would be protected.

He grunted when the accelerator pulled away from his foot and slammed itself to the floor, and the electric car surged forward in response. The force threw Jang against his seat, his hands now gripping the steering wheel, his knuckles turning white. He pounded the brakes, but the pedal didn't move.

"*Tā mā de!*" he called out. There was no one to hear.

His car wove through traffic, avoiding other vehicles on the road with surgical precision. The steering wheel moved of its own accord, like a car possessed, no matter the resistance he applied.

The gate on the exit ramp ahead was closed, blocked by a police car with flashing lights. Jang's car accelerated, swerved onto the exit ramp, and deftly navigated itself around the police car. Tires squealed and the car slid ever so slightly on the paved shoulder of the road. The officer gawked in disbelief.

Jang's car raced down the exit ramp toward a convoy of three limousines. Surrendering the wheel, Jang put both hands on the dash of the car. His mouth was opened wide but he let out no sound.

The limousine in the rear swerved to block Jang's car. His vehicle slowed and fell obediently behind the elongated vehicle.

Jang took a deep breath and grasped the wheel again while stomping on the brakes. No response. "*Tā mā de! Tā mā de! Tā mā de!*" His eyes were wide.

Like a cat suddenly bolting for its prey, the rear limousine accelerated and swerved off the road, cartwheeling into a field. Jang's car immediately sped up and drew alongside the middle limousine. He could see the face of the Chinese vice president pressed against the glass. They exchanged horrified looks, Jang holding his hands in the air to show that he wasn't controlling the vehicle.

Jang's car turned hard into the limousine, forcing it off the road, then following after it. Both vehicles tumbled end over end before coming to rest in a field of wheat.

Hanging upside down in his car, his head pounding, Jang reached up to touch his forehead.

Blood.

He gasped as he glanced through the place where the driver's side window used to be. There were four black drones streaking toward the crash site. Two approached each limousine. One landed on the gas tank of each overturned car and the other navigated to the interior of the car. Each drone deposited a black disk shaped like a large hockey puck before retreating and disappearing into the sky like errant bats. A few moments passed and then each of the pucks burst into intense flame, setting the limousines on fire. Acrid smoke billowed from the burning vehicles and overwhelmed the crash site.

Clutching his head to dull the agony, Jang heard the clank of metal on metal close by. Despite the pain, he turned his head and caught sight of a drone depositing one of the black pucks on the fabric roof of his car before rising and disappearing through the shattered window. Jang reached for the puck, but his view of the world faded to black before his eyes before he could touch it.

Linda glanced over her shoulder every few feet, her long

black hair held in check by a ponytail. Look left. Look right. Look back. It was part of the ritual. No one was following her. As she picked up her pace, her sneakers silenced her steps. Making an abrupt right turn down an alley, she disappeared into the darkness.

She speed walked the length of the modern building before rounding the corner at the end and coming to a stop in front of an unpainted steel door. There was no doorknob. Raising her right hand, she rapped sharply four times on the door, startling a squirrel nearby. There was a muffled rustle, the sound of a deadbolt sliding, and then the door opened out toward her.

With a practiced step, she entered. "Hi Armando," she whispered, flashing a smile as she passed the large man. He said nothing but flashed a grin in response. He closed the door behind them like a teenage boy sneaking his girlfriend into the house at night. This was a quiet place.

Making her way down a short hall, she pushed through a door on silent hinges and entered a makeshift hospital waiting room. The Hall of Redemption, as it was known to those who waited there. The walls were painted a calming light pink. There were women's magazines arranged on each side table, and a shelf full of donated books for the taking.

This place was not advertised. Could not be advertised. Its existence was passed on in secret from women-resolved to women-in-need. A whisper secret.

Linda's work here was dangerous. Not because she was a doctor who was risking her medical license and a prison term by performing illegal abortions, but because of who she was. Her birthright made her very presence in this place inappropriate. Yet it was worth the risk. She owed the women of Alabama her skills. The number of abortion clinics had declined from forty-five in 1982 to just three, and regular demonstrations made discretion a challenge. The past three years had seen a wave of laws passed, blocked, and reintroduced that made virtually all forms of abortion illegal.

A small group had created the secret clinic during this tumultuous time, of which Linda was a founding member. They'd developed security protocols to protect the clinic's ongoing existence. Everyone who worked there was connected to someone who had benefited from their services. A rite of passage. A precursor to trust.

There were two girls in the waiting room. Both of them looked young, but Linda knew that her patient, Wendy, was different. She was just fourteen. The girl wore jean shorts that were cut off at the knee, and a baggy sweatshirt with the name of her high school emblazoned on the front. Linda made eye contact with her and smiled, motioning for the girl to follow her into an examination room.

The young girl slid onto the padded table and fidgeted with her sweatshirt. Her shoes looked like hand-me-downs, worn in but several sizes too large. Her baby toe peeked out of a frayed hole in the canvas.

Linda reached out and took her hand. She bent over so they were eye to eye and said, "You're going to be okay." Smiling, she patted the girl's hand, then motioned for her to lie down so she could begin the examination.

The girl answered Linda's questions, her voice barely a whisper. She knew the exact day she'd become pregnant, but clammed up when asked who the father was and how it had happened.

"Will I go to jail?" Her eyes welled up.

"No," Linda assured her, once again taking her hand in her own.

"They made it illegal last year. My pa said it was against the law." The word "law" was accentuated by her Alabaman accent. "My pa would kill me if he knew."

"Well, as you are aware, this place is secret. We don't keep any records, so if you don't tell anyone then no one will ever know."

The young girl exhaled. Her shoulders loosened and a smile flashed across her lips, then disappeared.

The two discussed the ideal time for her procedure. She'd planned a sleepover at a friend's house the following week, but had told her parents the meet up time was three hours earlier than it was. Enough time for her to get to the clinic, have the procedure, and recover. A volunteer from the clinic would drop her off at her friend's house for the sleepover. No one would know. Redemption.

The details set, the girl slipped off the table. She was a step out the door when she spun around, lunged toward Linda, and threw her arms around her. "Thank you so much!"

Linda hugged her back. Her smile faded as she reflected on the danger that she brought to the clinic. She was here to help, but she could never escape the fact that her birthright made her presence here inappropriate.

ONE

The roar of American dissidents drowned out the typical sounds of traffic in front of the Capitol building. The NRA had organized an event they dubbed the C2M March. An event they'd hoped would bring two million American citizens to this historic place. From Lavinia's perspective, they'd succeeded.

"So how many of these people do you figure are carrying?" Lavinia asked off-duty detective, John Miller. The two were in that uncomfortable stage where they weren't officially dating, but it was clear where things were headed.

"I think the question is how *many* weapons is each of these people carrying," John replied with pursed lips. She watched him for a moment as he scanned the crowd with a practiced eye.

A man in his twenties brushed past Lavinia, carrying a sign that read *From my cold dead fingers*. She raised a hand to protect her side. The wound from her adventure at Mount Weather four months ago had required multiple surgeries to repair the damage, with the most recent procedure just a month ago. So while she had largely healed, the area was still tender.

"It's a tough debate," John remarked, not noticing her discomfort as he was surveying the crowd. "The idea that people can print their own guns at home on a personal printer is a little scary. When they were made of plastic and capable of a single shot, that was one thing. Now that there's liquid steel and 3D printers are cheap enough for everyone to have in their home, it changes the equation."

"My country, my rights!" a crowd of protesters chanted as they swarmed around Lavinia and John. A mix of cigar smoke, body odor, and leather polluted the air.

"You knew the decision to restrict the sale of liquid steel was going to be controversial, but taking down websites that posted schematics to print guns was a bit over the line," he continued.

"That wasn't Barbara Anderson, though." Lavinia was quick to come to the president's defense. "Some rogue ISPs took down a few websites and social media exploded with the wild accusation that the president was behind it."

"Yeah, social media is out of control."

They watched as Elijah Colt, the founder of a hate-based crowdfunding site called Freemantreon, ascended the stage at the head of the crowd. Lavinia had read up on him last night. He was a follower of Cody Wilson, the man who started an organization called Defense Distributed in 2012. Their goal was to give anyone the ability to make 3D-printed weapons at home, albeit out of plastic. Back then, Wilson had enjoyed early victories against the government when they'd forced him to take down his detailed blueprints that would allow people to print their own guns.

A few years ago Cody Wilson had left the organization. Defense Distributed was again under siege, but this time they had the support of a newly revitalized NRA, and advances in 3D printing technology had made the weapons far more dangerous. Elijah Colt, who was wildly charismatic, had picked up Cody Wilson's mantle and taken the cause to the next level. He was one of the primary organizers of this event.

A roar rose from the crowd, drawing Lavinia's attention. She turned toward the sound.

"Over there." John pointed. A crowd of protesters had started shoving hard against a group of police officers holding full-height plastic body shields.

Lavinia and John made their way toward the commotion.

"There," said John, his eyes locked on something.

Lavinia saw it too. A revolver appeared in the hand of a protester, who slowly lifted it to aim at the officers. She broke into a run.

Despite her injury, Lavinia sprinted along the periphery of the crowd, dodging and pushing people out of the way as she went. John did his best to keep up with her.

A young officer in the second row behind the transparent shields spied the gun too; Lavinia caught the look of panic spreading across his face. He reached for his holster, called out a warning to the other officers, and leveled his gun.

Pushing forward, Lavinia clamped the protester's wrist with her right hand, twisted up, and disarmed him with her left hand. Holding the gun up for all to see, she popped the cylinder of the revolver open and emptied the bullets onto the ground.

John came up behind her. "Everyone, relax! Relax!" He was waving his detective badge high in the air.

The disarmed man started to protest his weapon being

taken away, but when a reporter and her cameraman came on the scene he melted into the crowd and disappeared.

Lavinia handed the weapon to the police officer behind the shield.

"You came out of nowhere!" he exclaimed. He bent over and retrieved the live ammunition from the ground.

"Just trying to help."

"Are you on the force?" the man asked.

"I'm a government agent," Lavinia said, anxious to avoid giving more detail.

"Well, glad you happened along." He turned and pointed at John. "You, I know. Strange place to hang out on your day off." It was a statement, but there was a question in his tone.

"We were on our way to lunch and decided to stop by to see how big the turnout was," John replied with a lift of his shoulder. "And we kind of got caught up in it."

Lavinia knew it was a lie, but the officer would never find out. The president had asked Lavinia to check out the rally and report back to her. John was along for the ride.

After a pause, the officer repeated, "Well, we're glad you came along." He turned his attention back to the crowd.

The reporter was readying her microphone, so Lavinia looped her arm through John's. "We should go." Before anyone could stop them, she led him back into the crowd.

John leaned in and called into her ear, "That was close."

"Yeah, we're lucky it went the way it did."

"It gave me flashbacks, seeing you rush in there like that."

"I was fine."

"The president asked you to monitor the crowd, not disarm it." A proud smile spread across his face.

Lavinia shrugged. She knew he loved the fact that she

could take care of herself. A date night often started at the shooting range, engaging in friendly competition. She was a better shot than he was, and she appreciated that he wasn't threatened by her. Quite the contrary. He enjoyed bragging about her to his friends.

He slipped his arm around her waist and pulled her close to whisper into her ear, "I worry about you."

Wincing, she snapped her hand in place to protect her injury and slipped out of his grasp. "I can take care of myself."

"Sorry, did that hurt?" He frowned.

"It's fine."

It was an awkward moment. A part of her wanted to lean in to him, accept his touch, but her recent connection to President Barbara Anderson had led her to an unexpected opportunity. She was now an agent for the Defense Intelligence Agency, the Pentagon's top spies. The little-known organization collected and analyzed intelligence on foreign militaries. Their primary mission was to prevent wars where preventable and win them decisively where not.

A relationship risked holding her back from what was sure to be a once in a lifetime opportunity. While she was a member of the DIA on paper, she reported directly to the president. An unusual arrangement, but having saved the president's life, she had her trust, and the president wanted to be able to task Lavinia as needed.

She reflected on how far her career had progressed. At nineteen she'd been recruited by the FBI in a special program designed to increase the number of women in the intelligence community. It meant that while she was at college she trained on weekends and over the summers she worked through a rotation of government jobs. Each meant to contribute to a foundation of knowledge to prepare her for life as an agent. On her twenty-third birthday she graduated to full agent status. Now a year later, here she was. The greatest opportunity of her career and this amazing guy were colliding. She wondered if she could have both.

"Why don't we get something to eat?" she suggested.

John agreed, but she could sense the disappointment in his voice.

"Come in," the president called out.

Dan Nolan, her longtime friend and chief of staff, entered the Oval Office and crossed the room to the couch. You could distinguish him a mile away by his lumbering gait and imposing six-foot-two frame. Yet despite the physicality of his presence, the former football player always brought with him a sense of calm.

Barbara Anderson smiled. "Dan, you can come and go as you please. You don't have to be announced."

"That's true until it isn't." Dan gave an easy smile. His sandy blond hair, sporting an Ivy League haircut, looked fresh and crisp.

"Well, I can't imagine a circumstance in which it wouldn't be true. Have you been watching the protests?"

"Yes, Madam President."

She chuckled under her breath. Regardless of her telling him innumerable times that he didn't have to address her that way when they were alone, he insisted on the formality. Despite herself, she found it charming.

"What did you think of Elijah Colt's speech?"

"It's what I've come to expect from him," Dan replied with a wave of his hand. "He's reinforcing the narrative that's been spreading online, that you intend to censor websites offering blueprints to print guns."

"Do you think it's just him? Or is there a foreign government meddling again?"

Dan hesitated. "The intelligence community thinks the Chinese are behind it and he's just a pawn, but there isn't enough concrete evidence to come out publicly and condemn them."

"What's the endgame if it's the Chinese government? We just had an election six months ago. Why expend the effort now?"

Dan shrugged.

"The liquid steel printers are still selling like crazy. We don't have enough support to introduce legislation to ban the printers. We've had restrictions on the import and sale of liquid steel in place for three months but the supply doesn't seem to deplete. I don't know where it's coming from, to be frank." Her dark shoulder-length hair swung side to side as she shook her head.

"The FBI's monitoring a warehouse a few miles from the Port of New York and New Jersey. I hear they're planning a raid, but I'm not sure when."

"I want someone I can trust on the ground for that," Barbara replied, drumming her fingers on the desk.

"Did you have someone in mind?"

She pushed back her chair, stood, and took a step away from the Resolute Desk. "Detective Miller. He's a good man."

Dan scribbled in the black pocket-sized notebook he always had with him.

Barbara removed her reading glasses and rubbed the spot between her eyes with a sigh. "How did this ever become a thing? The governments before me sleepwalked through the advent of social media, so it's falling on me to fix it. I need to meet with Zuckerberg again," she lamented.

"Tell him to put a stop to it."

Barbara shook her head. "You know I can't do that, Dan."

"You're the president; you can do whatever you want," he replied.

"I don't like that kind of thinking, Dan, and it's important that we guard against that train of thought. It can take a leader to dangerous places."

"You're right, Madam President. I'm sorry."

There it was again. She shook her head with a smile. "When does the vice president get back?" she asked, pacing.

"She'll be here within the hour."

"Good. Can you ask her to see me when she arrives? I want to know how her meeting with O'Donnell went."

"I'm still not comfortable with her meeting the head of the Senate unaccompanied."

The president regarded Dan. "You still don't trust her, do you?"

"No, Madam President."

"The party insisted I bring her on, Dan. She's seen as a reach-across-the-aisle politician, something that I'm not... apparently. The Republicans like her and the DNC was concerned I couldn't win the election without her help. So I have to give her some leeway to operate."

"I see her as friendly to the Republicans, if not one herself. I'd like to keep a close eye on her, if you'd allow it."

"I can't, Dan. You know what she's like. She'll squawk if she isn't allowed to do whatever she pleases, and I don't need the hassle. I have bigger problems."

"You know what they say a president normally looks for in their vice president?" Dan asked.

"Un-electability? If that's even a word."

"Exactly. She's not that. I feel like everything she says and does is an attempt to subvert you."

"Well, she's on board, so there isn't much we can do about it now. I can't fire the vice president, as you know. It's in the Constitution."

"Well, I'll keep watching from a distance, then."

"You've always got my back, Dan. Not many Democratic presidents bring on a Republican as their chief of staff, but there isn't anyone I trust more than you."

"Thank you, Madam President. You're my oldest friend; you can always believe that I have your best interests at heart." After a pause, he added, "I'll send the vice president in when she arrives."

"Vice President MacQueen. Welcome," President Anderson said a short while later, as Olivia MacQueen entered the Oval Office. "Make yourself comfortable."

After a curt wave and a half smile, MacQueen took a seat on the couch. She crossed her legs and placed her purse and Burberry laptop bag beside her, then folded her hands in her lap and waited for the president to join her.

"How was your meeting?" Anderson asked.

"Uneventful. He was noncommittal on the climate bill, waiting to see what concessions he can draw from you." MacQueen sat like a statue, her straight blond hair reaching halfway down her back and her fingernails done up in black polish.

The president nodded. She hadn't missed MacQueen's use of the word "you." "What of the protests?"

"I think he's waiting to see if he can make any political

hay from it. He seems perfectly willing to allow the online narrative that's driving the protests to manifest itself."

"He needs to understand the damage that these false stories do to all of us. They can just as easily be turned against the Republicans in the future."

"Fair."

The president hated her one-word answers. Everything that came from this woman's mouth was aimed at giving the appearance of someone in control and superior to those around her. Anderson believed the arrogant public persona concealed a deep-rooted insecurity.

"We need to contain the issue so we can get people to focus on the true narrative," she continued. "If the Republicans won't help us then we have to find a way to do it alone."

"What about the Puerto Rico policy? Your paper on the subject when Obama restructured their debt was brilliant."

A pause. The president wasn't fooled by MacQueen's moments of flattery. It wasn't the first time she'd brought that document up. Anderson rounded the desk and made her way to the back of the blue-striped couch, putting the furniture between them. "I'm not sure people want to talk about Puerto Rico right now, Olivia. They're more focused on holding on to their guns."

"Puerto Rico will be in the news soon anyway." Olivia's tone was encouraging and sweet. "Hurricane season is just weeks away and the National Oceanic and Atmospheric Administration is already watching a system in the Atlantic Ocean that could grow into a hurricane. If it does, they'll be in its path. They haven't fully recovered from Hurricane Maria, so if this one hits them too, it'll set them further back. Prime time for you to talk about doing what Obama started but didn't go deep enough on."

Anderson crossed her arms and walked the length of the couch, deep in thought. "Olivia, I appreciate the support of my writing from the time before I was president, but I'm not looking to be opportunistic about a tragedy. I believe in the strategy that I outlined on Puerto Rico, don't get me wrong, but I won't take advantage of their situation to deflect the country's attention away from another crisis I'm facing. The issue isn't that I want to take away people's guns, but that someone is leveraging social media to create this false narrative about my intentions. What I want the country to face is that we are being attacked again and again in this manner, but we aren't learning from it because one party in our divided country will always be willing to leverage it to make gains. We need to break the cycle and be united in defending our country."

"Noted."

The president was speechless for a moment. All that and she got one word back. "Well, I'm glad we agree."

A series of brown rugs decorated the length of the east colonnade of the White House. The space between rugs revealed a polished red tile laid in a chevron. Lavinia's shoes squeaked whenever she walked on the tile. She cringed inside and made a note to never wear these shoes in the White House again.

The colonnade was framed by a white wall on Lavinia's right-hand side, featuring a series of half-moon windows above historical photos. On her left, the windows were full length, stretching from the ceiling to a few feet above the ground. Lavinia reflected on the pristine view through the wall of windows. All of the country's past presidents, save Washington, had shared the same view during their tenure.

Lavinia was halfway down the length of the grand hallway when a figure appeared in the entrance at the far end. As they drew nearer, Lavinia saw that it was Dan Nolan, the president's chief of staff.

"Mister Nolan," she greeted him.

"Lavinia, how very nice to see you again. How are you?"

"I'm well," she said. "I'm here to see the president." Inside she winced at the obviousness of her words. What else could she be here for?

"She's just finishing up with the vice president. I hear she has some plans for you."

"You know more than I do, then."

His expression turned serious. "These are challenging times. I'm glad she has you on her staff. The president needs to be surrounded by people she can trust, and I know you're one of them."

"Thank you, that means a lot. We'll get through this. Good people always win."

Dan tilted his head ever so slightly and regarded her. "Well, we can hope that's true."

"It is," Lavinia replied, her jaw set. "I think January was a good example of that. There was no reason for us to successfully interrupt that plot. All of the odds were against us." Lavinia was referring to a deep cover terrorist who was bent on destroying the United States. "All of the odds were against us, but we won the day."

Dan held her in his gaze for a long time before he spoke. "Don't ever lose that optimism, Lavinia, but forgive me for being bold enough to disagree. I'm twice your age, if I had to guess, and I've got some battle scars." His tone was honest; there was no condescension in his voice. "Based on those experiences, what I'll say is this: good won't always win. There will be times when we lose, but it's important to realize that those losses are not an end point, just a step along the journey. Those losses form part of who we are and they affect how we react in the future. The hope is that those losses will help you succeed when you need it most. So maybe in the fullness of time good will win, but not always along the way."

Lavinia nodded slowly, her eyes locked on his. They were kind eyes. "Thank you. I'll bear that in mind."

"Good day, Lavinia. I'm sure we'll speak again soon." With that, Dan continued on his way and disappeared at the end of the hallway.

Lavinia paused to watch him go before she made her way to the center hall and found the China Room. There she studied the dishes on display. The new place settings were designed and hand painted by an artist from the president's hometown in New Hampshire. For the first time in US history, they'd been chosen by the First Husband.

"Welcome back!" President Anderson said behind her. Lavinia turned with a smile, pleased to see her again. "The last time we were at the White House together you could barely stand on your own." Anderson put her hand on her right side to indicate where Lavinia had been shot. "How are you doing?"

"Almost back to a hundred percent," Lavinia replied. "Three surgeries to repair the damage, but that's behind me now. So I feel pretty good, but it still hurts when I do sit-ups."

"Another reason not to do sit-ups, if there was ever a need for another reason." An easy smile spread across Anderson's face. "I'm pleased to see you again."

"Me too, Madam President."

"Thank you for coming. Please sit down." She led Lavinia across the room to a floral couch. "This room was normally free of furniture, but I like to sit here at night and read. I had this couch moved in here a few months ago. It was selected by Nancy Reagan."

Lavinia sat down, but the president crossed the room and stopped to stare out the window in silence. After a time she spoke.

"Tell me what you saw at the protest."

"I haven't seen the Park Commission's analysis yet, but if they didn't get two million people out, they were darn close. A pretty militant bunch in some places but calm for the most part. There were two distinct groups. The gun lobby and a much smaller contingent of African American community leaders protesting police violence."

The president nodded and turned to face Lavinia. "Elijah Colt called for the rally three months ago, the day I announced the restriction on importing liquid steel. He had little to no traction until two weeks ago. All of a sudden it went viral."

"Social media can do that," Lavinia said.

"Yes, particularly when it's being helped."

"Helped by...?"

The president paced the room, her hands clasped behind her back. She wore a smart navy pencil dress and heels. "Lavinia, the intelligence community suspects that China is trying to foster dissent in the United States, and they're doing it by manipulating one of the most passionate issues in America—the Second Amendment. We can't prove it's coming from them yet, but our best analysts strongly suspect it. On the one hand there are these social media accounts attacking me and organizing rallies. On the other we have this uncontrollable flood of liquid steel and cheap 3D printers. I need some concrete proof that China is behind all of it so I can call them out publicly." She stopped and held Lavinia's gaze with her piercing eyes. "To hold them accountable."

Lavinia knew what was coming next.

"I know you're just getting over your latest surgery, but I need someone I can trust. I can't think of anyone I believe in more than you."

Lavinia paused. The first thought to cross her mind was that she'd have to spend time away from John. As quickly as it occurred to her, she dismissed it. "It'd be an honor to serve my country," she replied, nodding.

"Good. When 3D printing with plastic polymers was invented, single-use firearms that were untraceable became possible. They called them Ghost Guns. Now, with liquid steel, they call them FOGGs, or Fully Operational Ghost Guns. We would completely lose control of the weapons in our country. We couldn't keep them out of the hands of people who should not have them."

"It's a divisive issue, and one that's ripe for abuse."

"I know it is. That's precisely why they chose it. I'm concerned they'll escalate it, because they've seen some success."

"In what way?"

The president joined Lavinia on the couch. "Well, we've already seen attempts to link FOGGs to the African American community. We think they're trying to build on the rift between the police and African Americans. We have proposals for significant police reform under review right now, but that process is slow. As these weapons end up on our streets, the police become nervous when they're in the community, and then..." She trailed off.

"Then things that shouldn't happen, happen," Lavinia finished.

"Exactly. Lavinia, I want you to go to China and find the people who are trying to divide us. Find them and stop them."

Lavinia nodded. The trust placed in her by the president should have been overwhelming. At just twenty-three years of age and with less than a year's experience in the intelligence community, she knew her position was unprecedented. Her actions at Mount Weather earlier in the year had earned her the president's faith and had taught her to trust her instincts.

Her father, a retired journalist, had always told her that loyalty was the most important ingredient when building a newsroom. She supposed that the same logic could be applied to any position of leadership.

I can do this!

The president interrupted her thoughts. "I can connect you with someone in Cyber Command, if you think that will help."

"I'll let you know. I think I have some friends who can point me in the right direction."

"Okay then. It's agreed. Thank you for taking this on, Lavinia. Please keep safe."

"I will, Madam President." Lavinia stood up to leave the room. "I'll be in touch."

It was an easy walk to P.J. Clarke's from the White House. While the restaurant's decor was dominated by dark wood paneling, red and white checkered tablecloths gave the restaurant a welcoming ambience. John and Lavinia were seated at a table adjacent to a faux greenhouse with metal scrollwork painted a pale green and a panel of opaque glass set behind it.

"So what do you make of these protests?" John asked before diving into his Clarke burger.

"I'm impressed with the turnout," said Lavinia. "When I read they were planning to get two million people out I was skeptical, but I guess there isn't an issue people are more passionate about than guns."

He nodded. After swallowing his first bite, he replied, "I have no issue with gun ownership. I'm just a little nervous about anyone having the ability to print their own. I mean, all we need is for some nut to make himself an arsenal and then go into a school."

Lavinia frowned. "Gun violence is not a mental health problem," she countered. "There's a lot of evidence to refute that assumption, despite the fact that whenever something happens, politicians automatically make that assumption and people believe them."

John paused, considering whether to argue the point. "So, you're saying that these people aren't crazy?"

Lavinia put her fork down and gazed at him. "People have suggested that we use technology to track those suffering from mental health issues to try to identify an attack before it happens."

"Sounds reasonable, doesn't it? Monitor their social media, track their purchases?"

"And violate their Fourth Amendment rights?"

"If it keeps us safe."

"Oh boy, Aaron and Jacob would have a field day with you!" Lavinia laughed as she stabbed a baby potato with her fork.

Aaron and Jacob were gray hat hackers and privacy

advocates. John knew that they'd become her good friends. "Yeah, please don't sic them on me." He held his hands up in mock defense. "Particularly Jacob." He let out a laugh. "How are Aaron, Jacob, and Martin doing, by the way?"

"The Disruptor is doing great," Lavinia replied, referring to Jacob Appleton. "The German government has been using him to combat social media attacks on their elections, so he's in his element. I spoke with Aaron last night. He's taken Martin in, but I can't say where for obvious reasons. He's worried about Martin. He's afraid that he's suffering from depression after his wife's death."

"I couldn't imagine," John mumbled. "I'd be a mess if anything happened to you." He could tell that she was trying to catch his gaze, but he stayed focused on his meal.

"Nothing to worry about here." She grinned, patting the holster under her arm.

"I sure wouldn't mess with you!" He gave a wry smile.

Lavinia stood, leaned over the table, and kissed him. "Good! Because I'd mess you up! Now I need to use the ladies' room."

John sat back in his chair. His hand slid into the pocket of his leather jacket and felt the velvet-covered box hidden away. He'd known Lavinia for just about seven months, but he knew she was *the one* shortly after they'd met. She was brilliant, tough, and confident. Most importantly, though, it was always easy to smile when he was with her.

Over the past few weeks he kept finding himself at Market Street Diamonds, looking at engagement rings. Yesterday, against his better judgment, he'd made a purchase. He worried that he was being premature, but his father's advice to him as a boy kept playing out in his mind: "When you get your first job, start saving up for an engagement ring. Because when you meet the right girl, you'll want to be ready."

His father was one of the police officers who had died on September eleventh, rushing into the towers. John had worked hard since then to remember as much about him as he could. Despite what some people might think about the ring, he knew his father would have approved of his purchase.

TWO

The Second World War-era airplane hangar stood at the end of an overgrown runway, long lost to Mother Nature. A parked Mercedes and two white buses were hidden under the nearby trees that had encroached on the property over seven decades of neglect.

The interior had been stripped bare by soldiers at the request of Liu Wei, the generalissimo of the PRC—the highest military rank in China and one rarely awarded. While he ran the entire military, this battalion was loyal to him and him alone. He'd spent almost two decades cultivating the specialized force, taking boys from poor families and giving them something they lacked from birth: hope.

The inside of the building had been sandblasted and refreshed, the smell of paint still strong. In the center of the facility, an eight hundred square foot area had been carpeted, and chairs placed in tidy rows facing a podium on a raised stage. The false wall behind the stage was covered in a blue vinyl wrap with the words "Economic Club of America" in white text, repeated over and over. Around the perimeter of the faux room were tables organized in precise rows, topped with sleek computers, their cables bundled into tidy snakes that ran to a power station against the distant wall.

Twenty-five-year-old Wang Juan was the sole woman under Liu Wei's command. From the side door, she regarded the finished product of the months-long project she had meticulously overseen.

The silence was broken by the screech of metal on metal. A young soldier held the heavy steel door wide open as the Chinese military leader brushed past her into the empty hangar. Falling confidently into step behind him, Wang followed as he regarded her work. Less the screeching door, everything was in place, as he had requested. She had personally seen to it, but was angry at the oversight. The door had been propped open for weeks while the renovations took place and during her many inspections, so she had never heard the noisy hinges.

When he nodded his approval at the setup inside, she stepped past him and spoke, her eyes averted. "You will have a clear view of the stage from here." She motioned with her arm to a bank of comfortable chairs off to the side. A table laden with freshly cut fruit, pastries, and cold pitchers of a variety of drinks sat behind his chair.

She was interrupted by the sound of the door opening once again. A stream of soldiers dressed in American-style suits entered the room and filled the seats in the audience. Men dressed in black t-shirts and matching jeans slipped behind the television cameras and computers around the perimeter and put on headsets.

She watched Liu Wei pick up a Western-style mini Danish and pop it into his mouth with one hand as he poured himself a glass of water with the other. Drink in hand, he strode toward the stage, taking to the podium as if it were his own. In her seat, Wang Juan folded her hands in her lap and smiled in anticipation.

"Patriots. Today we write the next chapter in the story of a revitalized China. A China who will take her rightful place on the world stage, shrugging off those who would endeavor to hold her back. We have been humiliated! Treated like a child sent to the corner of their bedroom to consider their actions." Spittle flew from his mouth as he spoke. "Did we resist? No! We negotiated agreements in fear of the impact that tariffs would have on our economic growth, pretending we didn't know that those agreements would have the same damaging long-term impact. China used to measure patience in centuries, but our cowardly leaders reacted in months. Robbing the people of this republic of their rightful wealth and prosperity. We must take back the leadership of our Communist Party from the hands of weak men. We must show our oppressors that we are not afraid to embrace our destiny."

There was enthusiastic applause. Liu Wei studied the admiring faces in the crowd.

"Our population is four times the size of the United States, yet they will not allow us to surpass the size of their economy. Never mind surpass, basic mathematics dictates that our economy should be at least four times the size—and together we will be! Together we will show the world the resolve of the Chinese people, reviving the pride in what it means to be Chinese!"

The applause was deafening. Holding his hands up, he acknowledged the crowd before descending the steps at the head of the stage and walking down the center aisle. The audience stood as one and cheered him on.

When he returned to the chair next to Wang and sat down, she reached over and touched his knee, acknowledging his performance. A subtle smile formed on her lips.

She reached into a pocket in her blue skirt and removed a smartphone. She typed a short message and a moment later the noisy door opened once again.

An American woman, dressed in a blue pantsuit and surrounded by guards, entered. Her name was Lisa Moyer. She was a middle-aged journalist who had been kidnapped a week ago. Wang had promised her that she'd be released if she cooperated with today's project. It was a lie.

Lisa Moyer was led to the podium and Wang Juan went up to meet her. "Ms. Moyer, thank you for agreeing to help us," she said in perfect English. A product of her ivy league education.

The middle-aged woman wrung her fingers while scanning the room.

"Here, take this. It will calm your nerves." Wang handed her a small white pill and a glass of water. When the woman hesitated, Wang smiled. "Please, you can trust me."

"Thank you." Lisa Moyer took the pill and the glass. After popping it into her mouth, she took a drink and placed the half-full glass on the shelf under the podium.

"Let me explain how the teleprompter works. It'll help you deliver the speech the way we practiced."

When she was finished, Wang stepped off the stage and sat down next to Liu Wei.

Lisa Moyer began to speak, reading the speech projected on the teleprompter. Wang motioned for her boss to put on the headphones that lay on the table between them. She put on her own pair, then glanced at the computer screen of the technician at the table in front of her. On the screen, President Barbara Anderson was addressing a crowd of American businessmen. Over the headphones came the voice of the forty-sixth president of the United States.

The speaker in the police cruiser crackled to life. "Reports of a man brandishing a weapon at a party in the Greenmount East neighborhood. Any cruisers in that area, please respond."

Officer Garrison hesitated before answering. Officers in their precinct always patrolled in pairs, given the neighborhood. His partner was down with the flu, which was going around, leaving the station shorthanded. As a white officer on his own in a predominantly African American community, responding gave him pause. He was planning to retire in a month and didn't need any excitement. With two police shootings in the past three months, everyone was on edge. The recent flood of 3D-printed guns had become a real danger to police officers and the public at large.

To serve and protect, he thought and reached for the button on his comm. "Officer Garrison responding. I'm in the area, over."

The dispatcher relayed the vague details that had been called in. An African American male in his twenties, walking down the street brandishing a suspicious object after leaving a party.

Turning at the next light, Garrison made his way toward the address he'd been given. A block away from his destination, he drove past a young man matching the description. He was wearing a gray hoodie and holding something in his right hand, his arms swinging back and forth to match his swagger. It was dark out, so Garrison couldn't make out what he was holding.

"Dispatch, I see a person matching the description of the suspect on East Lanvale Street heading westbound. I'm going to engage the citizen, over."

"Acknowledged. Proceed with caution. Ensure that your body cam is on."

Officer Garrison flipped the switch on his body camera without needing to look. The camera was as much for his protection as it was to hold him accountable. "Acknowledged."

Turning left into the first available driveway, Garrison was in the middle of a three-point turn when the man in the hoodie looked over his shoulder and caught sight of him. Then he turned and broke into a run.

"Suspect has taken flight," he called into the microphone.

"Proceed with caution. Backup being dispatched."

Garrison threw on his patrol lights and accelerated toward the man, who was sprinting full out. As Garrison gained on him, the guy in the hoodie broke hard to his right and ran between two homes, hopping a low wire fence with ease.

Officer Garrison pulled over and continued his pursuit on foot. The sound of an approaching siren brought comfort. Help was on the way. Despite his age, he was a marathoner and in great shape. He hopped the fence, matching his pursuer step for step. The man was already passing over the wire fence at the end of the yard when Garrison approached.

"Stop!" he called out. "Stop, and keep your hands where I can see them!"

Time seemed to accelerate as the man skidded to a stop

on the other side of the fence and spun like a gunslinger, an object in his right hand. Garrison unholstered his weapon, dropped to one knee, and fired a single shot.

There was a cry of pain and the man fell backward, clasping his stomach. The object in his right hand fell to the grass. Garrison stood, his gun still pointing forward. His jaw dropped. The object lit up as it lay in the grass. It was a phone.

While the world stood still, he was aware of two officers coming up behind him, but their words didn't resonate. He stood frozen, his gun in hand. One officer hopped the fence at the end of the yard and attended to the victim, while the other officer put an arm around his shoulder and spoke calming words into his ear. The officer placed a hand on his and pushed the muzzle down toward the ground.

Lundi Steinsson had been with OrbitTracker for just three months. Recruited from his native Iceland, he was still adjusting to life in California. The weather was the biggest issue for him because it was always so hot!

But the climate was the main reason he enjoyed working so much. In what the founders called the Radar Room, Lundi found solace. The walls and ceiling were painted matte black, and the floor was finished with two-foot-square gray slate tiles. There were two eighty-inch televisions on the wall at the end of the room, with a series of desks facing them. Best of all, they had air conditioning!

OrbitTracker was a young company that tracked ninety-five percent of the half million pieces of space debris in low Earth orbit. While NASA was a customer, they served a wide range of corporations that owned satellites. Lundi had taken a job as an analyst, reviewing projected debris collisions with their customers' satellites. Once an imminent collision was confirmed, Lundi would contact their high-paying customers with advice on how they could safely steer their satellites to avoid disaster.

His shift had ended hours ago, but the idea of enduring the seemingly endless sunlight was unappealing. As was his routine now, he hung around till evening before going out for dinner and then home to his sparsely furnished apartment. The other guy working was a manager who preferred to work in his office.

A shrill alarm from his computer made him slide his feet off the edge of his desk and sit up straight in his seat. The system had identified a potential collision.

Tapping his keyboard, he pulled up some reports and launched a three-dimensional animation of the projected collision. Frowning, he shut down the window and opened a new scan. A new animation opened, repeating what he'd seen just moments earlier. "That's impossible." The words slipped from his mouth, dissipating into the empty room.

Opening another window on a second monitor, he logged on to his client's satellite in what was known as fire-fighter mode. This gave him total control over the satellite. After entering a short explanation for taking the extraordinary measure, he was granted full access to his customer's satellite. He accessed the camera, rewound a few minutes, and watched actual footage from the vantage point of the orbital device.

Maximizing the window to fill the screen, he watched as a piece of space debris approached him from a distance. It was on a collision course, which was what had set off the alarm, when what he could only describe as a space drone appeared from a right angle and intercepted it. The craft was the size of a small microwave and had four arms extended in front of it with some sort of mesh. At first he thought it was a solar panel array, but in this case it looked almost like it was catching the space debris and forcing it into free fall in the atmosphere, where they would burn up together.

Lundi rewound and watched it again, puzzled. Was it a new technology to try to clean up the massive amount of space debris in orbit around the Earth? Surely no one could possibly consider that an efficient solution to the Earth's cloud of space junk. There were over three thousand dead satellites orbiting the planet and approximately thirty-four thousand pieces of debris larger than four inches. The smaller the debris you measured, the more of it there was. While there was some science being done to find ways to clean up low Earth orbit, the paradoxical problem was both the sheer quantity of junk and how far apart all of it was.

Companies like OrbitTracker had come into existence because it was easier to track the things flying around Earth faster than a bullet than it was to collect it all. What he was witnessing was an incredibly inefficient and expensive way to address the problem. The craft didn't have any identifying markings on it, so it was impossible to assess its origin before it burned up in the atmosphere.

With a series of staccato keystrokes, he recorded a video of both screens and saved it to a file. Following the protocol he'd been taught on his first day, he opened an email and attached the file. He entered the email addresses of the two owners, then added the address for their contact at NASA.

THREE

Pulling onto the fourth floor of the Rhode Island Avenue-Brentwood parking garage, Lawrence Ayippey coasted his vehicle toward the spot at the farthest corner on the top floor as instructed. He backed in, then killed the lights on his car and folded his hands in his lap. He noticed that half the lampposts on the top floor of the lot didn't work.

He wasn't crazy about the venue, now that he saw it. An African American man sitting in a car on the roof of a darkened car park after midnight—he could imagine the conversation. *Yes, Officer, I'm waiting to meet the chief of staff to the president of the United States.*

That would be believable.

It wasn't long before he heard a car coming up the ramp at the other end of the garage. After a beat, headlights came into view and the driver parked at the far end, across from him.

A Caucasian man exited the vehicle and walked toward him. He was lost in the inky darkness at first, but Lawrence could soon make out the man's tall form as he approached.

Exiting his vehicle, Lawrence crossed the short distance

to the electrical room in the corner of the garage closest to him. He waited for the man to join him.

"It's good to see you again." Dan Nolan offered his hand to Lawrence when he arrived. The two shook with vigor. "Follow me." Removing a keychain from his pocket, Dan unlocked the heavy door protecting the electrical unit and motioned for Lawrence to enter. "My brother-in-law works for the city." He held up the keychain. "This was a favor."

He didn't speak again until they were both inside and he'd closed the door behind them. "Please don't say my name, in case we're being monitored," Dan warned.

"Cloak and dagger," Lawrence replied. He glanced around the small room. They were in almost total darkness, but the indicator light on a smoke alarm provided a surprising amount of illumination. "Is it coincidence that the lights on this floor don't work?"

"No, not a coincidence," Dan replied. "I've had the timers set to turn the lights off in this section between midnight and one in the morning every Friday."

"So this is your meeting place?"

"Created just for you and I, Lawrence. What was it your mother always told you?"

"I can find sunshine in a black hole." Although he could barely make out his friend's face, he could tell he was smiling. His mother's expression was meant to say that he could find the good in every situation, but in this dark room it took on new meaning. "What do you need, Dan?"

"I need you to surveil someone for me."

"Electronic surveillance? Hack their email and social media?"

"No, the old-fashioned kind."

"Who's the target?"

"Olivia MacQueen."

Lawrence let out a quiet whistle. "The vice president? Are you serious?"

"I'm serious."

"I love you like a brother and all, but my dad didn't move here from Ghana before I was born so I could spend my adult years in prison. My wife and daughters would not be happy."

"I know, I'm asking a lot. That's why I want you to keep tabs on her the old-fashioned way. So there are no digital footprints traceable back to you. That way you're safe."

"Unless I'm caught." Lawrence ran his teeth over his lower lip, considering. "What are you looking for?"

"I can't give you anything specific. It's more of a gut feeling. I think she's trying to undermine the president. I'd like you and your team to follow her and keep tabs on who she sees, when, and where."

"That's all official record, isn't it? The vice president's schedule?"

"When it's official, it is."

"Do you want me to record conversations?"

Dan hesitated, as if he were about to cross the Rubicon. "If you can do it without getting caught, then yes."

"Is the president aware that you're doing this?"

There was a noticeable pause. "No. She expressly forbade it, actually. Which is why we're meeting here."

Lawrence rubbed his chin. "This will require at least one member of my team. I can't do this for free..." he began.

"I've got that covered." Dan reached into the breast pocket of his jacket and removed a bulky white envelope.

"Cash?" Lawrence asked, taking the envelope from him and feeling the wad inside.

"Cash. Unmarked bills. They can't be traced back to me. I can't tell you where the funding came from, but there's no limit. Whatever you need to spend, I'll reimburse you. Let's meet here at the same time on Fridays. Before you come, drive by my Washington apartment an hour before. If you see more than one lamp on in the window then it means it's not safe to come and I'll reach out to you via other means to set up a new meeting place. Does that make sense?"

"I think so. Pretty straightforward."

"Are we good?"

Lawrence reached out and shook Dan's hand. "Yeah, we're good."

Returning to his drab Washington apartment, Dan spun the deadbolt on the door and slid the chain into place. His late night adventure meant that he'd missed his evening video call with his wife, a lawyer in Portland. Their daughters had grown and were forging their own lives. His wife hadn't wanted to give up her place in her firm to move to Washington, given how short the average tenure of a chief of staff was. So after accepting the job working for the president, Dan had rented a modest bachelor apartment off the train line just outside of the city.

He dropped his keys and wallet on the dark maple side table he'd picked up at a street sale the weekend he'd moved in. Crossing the room, Dan dropped into his chair. His stomach growled, but his mind wouldn't let him answer its call.

Why did he distrust the vice president so thoroughly? He wracked his brain, trying to put his finger on it. She was a well-respected politician, having won every political race she'd ever entered. A gifted orator and writer, she had everything going for her.

Was it her ambition that irked him? A former mentor had once shared with him an old axiom: be careful about whom you let on your ship, because some people will sink the whole damned boat just because they can't be captain. He smiled at the memory of the man. He'd passed away a few years ago.

Dan and the president had joked today about the importance of a vice president not being electable, but there was truth in that political axiom. There was, in reality, no tangible reason for his discomfort.

But there it was. She made him uncomfortable.

Having her surveilled was risky, but Dan couldn't shake the feeling that she was maneuvering in the background. There was no other way to allay his fear. To protect the president, he had to disobey her. His challenge now was to keep it secret in a town not known for keeping secrets.

Olivia MacQueen was up to something. He would bet his life on it.

———

Lawrence eased his Oldsmobile around the parking garage's tight corner, then accelerated down the ramp. He loved the feeling of gravity pressing him against the seat.

He'd been driving an Olds since he was twenty. People kidded him for years that it was an old man's car, but it offered him two benefits: the engines were powerful, allowing him to indulge his love of fast cars, and police rarely pulled him over. As a young African American man, driving his father's Mercedes meant that he was constantly being pulled over. When he'd scraped together enough money, he bought an old Toyota, thinking that he wouldn't attract attention. However, the police always found a reason to pull him over in his scrappy old car. The Oldsmobile seemed to strike the right balance for a middle-aged African American man in America. He went largely unnoticed.

Reaching the ground level, he pulled out onto Washington Pine and turned right. Traffic was sparse at this time of night, so it was easy to weave through the few vehicles that were on the road. He glanced at the envelope full of cash on the passenger seat. At the next light he reached over and put the package in the glove compartment. He didn't need a cop pulling him over and asking what was in the envelope.

He was going to surveil the vice president of the United States. He never would have predicted that was going to be Dan's assignment for him. Was it legal? He'd known Dan for fifteen years and held him in the highest regard. He'd never known a man to be more ethical. So if Dan was willing to take the risk, then there had to be a good reason for it.

The problem with twenty-four-hour coverage was that he couldn't do it alone. While he trusted his team, the fact of the matter was that the more people who knew something was happening, the greater the risk it would leak.

Lawrence glanced at the glove box again. He sensed that the contents of that envelope were going to bring him trouble.

The beat to "The Message" by Grandmaster Flash and the Furious Five broke the silence. It was the ringtone for Lawrence's phone. Reaching over, he tapped the green button on the Apple CarPlay screen to accept the call.

"Lawrence."

"Hey, Lawrence, it's Tyrone. Sorry to bother you so late."

"No, man, what's up?"

"I was wondering if you could come over. There's something strange going on here and we could use someone with a law enforcement background to help us out. But one that won't shoot us, if you know what I mean."

"Yeah, I've got ya. Is everyone safe?"

"Yeah, man. Nothing like that. It's an online thing. We could just really use your advice."

"You want me to swing by now?"

"If that wouldn't be too much trouble. I know it's late."

"No, no trouble. I'll be there in fifteen minutes or so."

"Thanks, Lawrence. See you shortly."

His curiosity piqued, Lawrence turned his attention back to the road.

FOUR

Macau was known as China's City of Dreams. Here architecture was like candy, a delight to the senses that could be found everywhere. Its crown jewel was the Morpheus Hotel, a glass building wrapped in a concrete exoskeleton that looked like something from a sci-fi film. The view of the port town from the restaurant on the twenty-first floor sky bridge was stunning, with the water still as a mill pond, except where broken by the progress of a pleasure boat.

President Xiu Ying Zhang strode toward his table, shoulders back and head high, maximizing the impact of his stout frame. As he rounded the corner, his security detail in tow, he saw that a table for four had been made up for him and his guests. The table was flanked by a white sculpted structure that looked like a pair of dinosaur ribs coming off a thick spine. Covering the outside of the structure like the scales of a dragon were a series of sculpted wooden plates, which were placed row upon row until they reached the ten foot mark. It created a unique visual and acoustic barrier, providing the diners within uncompromised privacy.

Already sitting at the table was Liu Wei, one of

China's brightest military minds, and his chief economic advisor for the armed forces. Liu Wei was a massive, barrel-chested man, standing six foot four, with fists that could've rivaled Thor's hammer. The intimidating frame housed a brilliant mind that was solely responsible for transforming China's military over the past thirty years from pauper to one that could rival the United States. He was well-regarded within the Communist Party and revered by the military. With the assassination of the Chinese vice president, Liu Wei was angling for a promotion.

His military knowledge he'd inherited from his father, a brilliant tactician in his own right. However, as a young man, Liu Wei was a prodigy of economics. He understood the need to balance a growing economy with the construction of a world-class military. His intellect made him an asset as much as a threat. While the position of vice president was mostly ceremonial, it would allow him to build relationships that could be dangerous to Zhang in the future.

President Xiu Ying Zhang allowed his aide, Fangqing, to adjust his seat for him as he sat down. The man then took his own seat beside the president. Both deaf and mute since birth, he was the president's most trusted ally. The man attended every meeting the president had, not to open doors for him and adjust seats, but because he was wired to record both audio and video. The cameras and microphones were cleverly concealed in his glasses and traditional clothing. His birth defects and lack of education made him even more valuable, as despite his presence, he knew nothing of the president's business.

Liu Wei was the first to speak. "Good day, Mister President."

Zhang gave a curt nod. It was important to keep Liu Wei in his place until he knew he could trust the man.

"I have come from our military research center, the Commission for Science, Technology, and Industry for National Defense. Our scientists are making great strides in handing us the military of the future. Soon we will have suits that will allow our marines to carry thousand-pound loads and fly to the tops of buildings. You must visit, as our progress is nothing short of miraculous."

"COSTIND, I believe you call them. I'm not sure what good flying marines are when we face a growing number of nations that have nuclear weapons. Or if we were to go to war against any country and the United States disapproved, how could we withstand their pressure, political and financial? I'm afraid, Wei Xiānshēng," he used the formal Chinese version of *Mister*, "that contrary to your reputation, you are not investing our funds wisely."

"An interesting conclusion, Mister President. I believe we must address the issue of American influence, and perhaps I am the only person that can do it."

The president tilted his head slightly to the side, as if to lend his ear.

"As you are aware, we have just implemented the second phase of our social attacks on the United States," Liu Wei continued. "The student graduates loyal to me who have returned home have been invaluable in helping bring authenticity to our online messages. Having flooded the United States with 3D printers sold well below the cost to make them, we are now smuggling vast supplies of liquid metal into the country. We have begun to encourage African Americans to print their own weapons for self-defense against the American police, who have been militarized and are out of control. We're waiting for the first serious incident so that we can turn the temperature up and turn them against the police and government."

"This will not dull their influence around the globe. It's a distraction." Zhang had allowed Liu Wei's pet project to go ahead because he thought it would preoccupy him and contain the threat he represented to his own power. Besides, surely the Americans had learned after the debacle in the 2016 election, and a social media attack would fail.

"No, Mister President, it's not just a distraction. It's something to keep them occupied while we put the pieces in place to destroy American hegemony."

"Those pieces being?"

"Today the Americans control the money markets around the world, and because of this they have global influence. They do it in two ways. First, they control the movement of money with the Worldwide Interbank Financial Telecommunication system. The second is the petrodollar. This is why they can impose their will, by cutting off countries' access to currency and by imposing sanctions."

"I've thought of replacing the petrodollar, but it's a fool's errand. Too expensive to actually implement, and look what happened to the leaders of countries that tried to stop using it. In Libya, Kaddafi was beaten to death and his body dragged through the streets. In Iraq, Saddam Hussein was humiliated and hung! Is this what you want for me?" Zhang's voice rose as he spoke, sending droplets of spittle onto the table in front of him. He began to stand, though he hadn't even eaten yet.

With one of his large hands, Liu Wei motioned for the president to stay. His expression remained neutral as he spoke. "On its own, yes, but as a part of a two-step plan, it can work. In fact, it must work." He paused for effect.

"Explain." The president dropped back into his seat and leaned back, but his shoulders remained tense.

"We will strike a deal with the Russians and the European Union. The way the previous administration used American control over the global financial infrastructure to impose tariffs and attack their economies during the trade war damaged relationships. They will be willing partners. They're hungry for ways to immunize themselves against future actions." Liu Wei leaned in, stabbing at the air to emphasize his point. "We will provide it. First we'll introduce a new system for tracking financial transactions using state-of-the-art block chain technology. Then we will set the renminbi as the base currency. The Iranians will be the first to sign on. Every country that the United States has offended in the past five years will join us."

"So we first control the infrastructure, then the currency. The flaw in your plan is that if we use the renminbi as the world's currency, then the value of our currency will appreciate against the US dollar and our manufacturing will no longer be competitive. The value of the US debt we hold will plummet and bankrupt us! No, your plan has no merit. You came here to negotiate a promotion, to become vice president. But you've proven yourself too small a thinker!" The president was exaggerating his anger because this man's ideas scared him. He'd bankrupt the country and start a third world war. *Madness!*

Liu Wei reached into a laptop bag that sat on the floor next to the table. He removed a tablet and put it on the table in front of him. He cued up a video, then handed it to the president. "You saw the video our intelligence officers discovered of the American president promising to make Puerto Rico a state?"

The president nodded. Taking the tablet, he adjusted his glasses and watched the video play. The clip he'd been shown yesterday was only a few seconds long and didn't capture his interest. These days photos and video clips could be falsified so easily, who could believe anything online?

On the screen was Barbara Anderson at a podium. She stood in front of a blue backdrop with the words "Economic Club of America" printed in bold white letters, repeating row after row. The Chinese president listened to Barbara Anderson's words:

"We must give Puerto Rico a chance to recover. The steps we have taken to date in terms of debt forgiveness have been woefully inadequate. We must forgive all of Puerto Rico's debt. The more than one hundred billion dollars of debt must be eliminated! How am I going to do that? Will Americans be willing to fork over that kind of money? No. No, they won't. Instead, China will pay! We will forgive Puerto Rico's debt dollar for dollar by cancelling our debt to China. They have taken advantage of us for decades by manipulating their currency and stealing our intellectual property. No president before me has been able to deal with this issue. It's time we take control of the situation and make China pay!"

President Zhang failed to suppress an audible gasp. He touched the screen and scrolled through the video. It was just over an hour long, with the president hosting a question and answer session where she came out from behind the podium and engaged with the crowd.

This is real!

President Zhang stopped the video, the American president's image frozen with her left hand raised and her finger pointing to the audience. "I haven't seen this in the media!"

47

"It was a secret meeting in New York. One of my international students stole the video from his friend's laptop."

The president leaned back hard in his chair, his black combover slipping out of place. The chair creaked in protest.

"Mister President, we must strike the United States economically before they strike us. This is a new form of war!"

The president exclaimed, "Our economy will be destroyed! We raised 650 million people out of poverty over the last thirty years. Much of that progress will be lost if they do this. It's madness!"

"Make me your vice president, and I will negotiate with the Russians and the European Union. I will put the pieces in place, and we will strike before the American president can strike us!"

"This is the path to war." The president shook his head and wagged a finger in the air. "We cannot win, not with the size of their nuclear arsenal."

"What if I told you that COSTIND could nullify the American nuclear threat? Our military could defeat the United States in a conventional war, you know this. As long as we are not seen as the ones who started it, the world will be behind us."

The president leaned forward on his elbows, the table bending ever so slightly under his weight. "How will our scientists eliminate the American nuclear deterrent?"

Also leaning forward, Liu Wei made his final point. "When the time is right, I'll show you the technology. I promise, you will agree that it is miraculous."

"I want to avoid a war. If you can nullify the American nuclear deterrent, then you're right, we can implement the

48

financial changes that you suggest and reduce their influence around the world. But we need to avoid a war!"

"They know that our conventional forces could repel any attack on China. We will weaken them and we will not start a war. But if they were to choose to attack, then we would defend ourselves and we would win."

The president eyed Liu Wei and let out a deep breath. "Congratulations, Mister Vice President."

Wang Juan hurried her step to keep up with Liu Wei, swinging her long, straight black hair to the side. "Did he believe the video?"

Without breaking his stride, Liu Wei smiled. "Yes. Yes, he did."

"I was concerned. That was the most sophisticated deep fake we've ever created. To replicate the likeness of the American president behind a podium was academic. But the forty minutes of video where she took questions and roamed the stage were nothing short of brilliant."

Liu Wei regarded her for a moment, the smile still tugging at the edges of his mouth. When he'd recruited his personal army, the focus was always boys who had just reached puberty. Boys he could mold. Wang Juan had been special; the only time he'd taken a girl. He'd kicked in the door of her family's home himself, interrupting their dinner.

Her father was an invalid, paralyzed from the waist down. An injury in a poorly run mine. Wang Juan, then just ten years old, had sprung to her family's defense. She grabbed her grandmother's walking stick and put herself between the general and her family, her expression as fierce as a provoked tiger.

He could still remember the words he'd said to her: "Little one. Do not fight me. Come with me, and I will make you one of China's greatest warriors."

"I'm a child, not a warrior. The purpose of my life is to care for my family."

"Spirit knows no age, child. Your family will enjoy riches they cannot imagine...if you will join me. I will educate you. I will teach you to wage war with your mind. To help China achieve its destiny."

The young girl seemed to consider this. After a heartbeat, she lowered the walking stick.

Wang Juan had been his most loyal soldier ever since. She'd gone to a private military school in Beijing where she spent her days learning English and getting the finest education the country could offer, and her evenings learning hand to hand combat and how to handle all manner of weaponry. Then she'd enrolled at Princeton where she took a double major in political science and technology. Political science was a timeless study, and computer systems were the future. Just as he had foretold, the ten-year-old girl had grown into China's greatest warrior; the world just didn't know it yet. But soon they would.

He returned to the present. "Your work is admirable, Wang. Time and again you prove yourself to me."

She blushed a little, but kept her cool. "Thank you, sir."

"When we achieve our mission, you will realize the full value of the rewards promised to you."

"You already kept your promise to me, sir. My family escaped poverty and suffering, by your generous hand."

"You have been my most loyal soldier, Wang. Soon, all of China will know your family's name."

"I will always be by your side, sir. I am honored to serve."

On the sky bridge once again, he stopped and turned to gaze upon the nighttime view of Macau, its skyline an ocean of colored lights. He sighed with pleasure. "It's begun, Wang. It's begun."

On the outskirts of the ocean port city of Guangdong, the eighty-year-old proprietor surveyed the new shipping containers coming off the line at his factory. He'd begun to manufacture shipping containers as a young man, and had stuck with it his whole life.

The peculiar trend in the West of using containers to build homes or backyard pools had led to a surge in business in recent years. And then a few months ago the Chinese military had placed the largest order for containers in his company's history. It was almost an entire year's worth of production!

He chuckled to himself. The woman they'd sent to negotiate was a fool! What was her name again? Ah, yes, Wang Juan. She was a kid in her twenties, and was unable to hold her own against a man with his life experience. He'd told her that no one would be able to get the steel to manufacture the containers as quickly as the military needed them, so he'd need a much higher price. She'd agreed to provide the steel for manufacturing and still pay him his normal price as long as he could deliver them on time. He'd signed the contract before she could realize that he'd taken advantage of her.

After a lifetime of hard work, he would finally achieve financial independence for his family.

FIVE

The Cyber Command headquarters in Washington was the yardstick by which others defined "futuristic." All doors within the building slid open of their own accord as you approached, based on the access assigned to the badge you wore. There were no thresholds between rooms; instead, the floor was a seamless polished concrete. The intern assigned to Lavinia explained that the building designer wanted to create an environment where the brilliant computer technologists who called this place home would never be distracted, even by the slight bump of a threshold between rooms.

"The exterior window frames are lined with copper, turning the building into a giant faraday cage. The only data that can come in or out of the building comes from the satellite dishes on the roof," the intern enthused. It was obvious that she loved her job. "The interior walls of every workroom are painted with Black 3.0 paint to make it impossible to record conversations using the Buran eavesdropping system."

Lavinia had learned of that method of eavesdropping

during her FBI recruit training. It'd been invented by a Russian KGB officer in 1947. You could read the micro-vibrations off a wall from great distances using his device.

She'd also read about Black 3.0 paint, which was invented by the artist Stuart Sample. It absorbed virtually all visible and ultraviolet light, rendering a laser-listening device useless if it was painted on the targeted wall.

"Lev Sergeyevich Termen's device was used to measure vibrations on windows and convert them to speech before it was used on walls. How do you protect against that?" Lavinia asked.

"All of the exterior windows in the building are connected to transducers that pipe heavy metal music onto the glass."

"Wow!" Lavinia was impressed.

"Black Sabbath, I'm told." The intern grinned. "Supernaut."

She led Lavinia to a waiting room outside the office of Admiral Connor O'Leary, the head of Cyber Command. "The admiral will be right with you, Ms. Walsh. Is there anything I can get you?"

"No, I'm okay." Lavinia flashed her a smile.

The girl paused, her hands folded behind her back.

Lavinia smiled again and raised her eyebrows.

"Are you Lavinia Walsh, the one who stopped the terrorist attack earlier this year?"

"I'm her."

"If you don't mind my saying, you're the one who inspired me to join the intelligence community."

"I was in the right place at the right time." Lavinia shrugged. "I did what any American in my place would have done."

The girl leaned forward and whispered in her ear, "You kick ass!" With that she turned and was gone.

Lavinia folded her hands in her lap. It was nice the girl felt inspired, but Lavinia's goal wasn't to build a following. It was to do her part and represent her country well in completing the mission. The phrase sounded trite, but it was true. With few exceptions, the people in the intelligence community were committed to the goals of their departments above all else, particularly self.

It would be another thirty minutes before the square-jawed admiral emerged from his office to greet Lavinia.

"Ms. Walsh." There was the hint of an Irish accent in his greeting. "Apologies for the wait. I had to rearrange my schedule on short notice to meet with you."

Lavinia noted his broad shoulders and firm handshake. "Thank you for making the time, sir."

"The president has asked me to grant you my full cooperation, Ms. Walsh. Tell me, how can I help?"

"Please, call me Lavinia," she began. "The president has asked me to go to China to find out who is behind the social media attacks on her and to find the source of liquid steel and the method being used to get it into the country in such large quantities."

"It's strange, sending an agent from the Defense Intelligence Agency for an assignment like this, isn't it? Aren't you folks supposed to work covertly to avert wars?"

"Usually we do, sir. But today I'm doing this."

The admiral let out a hearty laugh. "I deserved that, I suppose. Look, I can provide some assistance with the first of those objectives. But I'm afraid my team won't be much help with liquid steel. You'd have to reach out to the FBI for help with that."

"Of course. I'll take whatever assistance you can provide."

The admiral led her down a corridor, glass doors sliding open and then closing behind them as they progressed. He spoke while they walked.

"We have almost seventeen thousand soldiers, civilian employees, and contractors working for the US Army Cyber Command across four states. This is our headquarters, the crown jewel, if you will." He motioned broadly with his arms. "Our capabilities increase by leaps and bounds every year, although that's true of our enemies as well."

They paused in front of a pair of frosted glass doors, which did not open automatically this time. The admiral stepped up to a retinal scanner on the adjacent wall and leaned in.

When the doors opened, Lavinia followed him inside. The room was built like a theater, with platforms descending toward the front wall. It featured row after row of tables littered with computers, monitors, and all manner of electronic equipment. The expansive front wall was a series of projected monitors displaying maps, videos, and statistics. A dizzying array of information. As if to build atmosphere, the side walls were masked with camouflage netting.

"Our command center." The admiral came to an abrupt stop, clicking his heels together. "This is where everything comes together." There was pride in his voice. Turning, he led her up five metal steps to a landing made of serrated metal tread. A steel handrail ran the length of the room, a few feet in front of a floor-to-ceiling glass wall. On the other side of the glass wall was a conference room.

Following the admiral inside, Lavinia chose a seat at the

expansive maple table. She waited a moment while the admiral sent a text from his phone. Almost immediately, four other people in military garb entered the room. The admiral introduced each of the soldiers and explained Lavinia's presence.

The woman to his right spoke first. She was focused on an iPad in front of her. "We've been tracking this man." An image appeared on the screen. "His name is Liu Wei. He's the most decorated general in the Chinese military, and he's been building a team of soldiers loyal only to him. A faction called the Blood Dragons."

A chill ran down Lavinia's spine. The man's eyes were cold and calculating.

"Two weeks ago, the Chinese vice president was assassinated. We believe he's angling to fill the vacant post. He's well positioned and respected in the Communist Party and we know that he's ambitious."

"The intelligence comes from boots on the ground?" Lavinia asked.

"This information was gathered from our methods, not the CIA." Her answer was both vague and specific at the same time. Like a pilot guiding a drone from thousands of miles away who was both eyes on target and remote. Lavinia guessed that at Cyber Command, they were both in the target's room and thousands of miles away.

"We know that the Blood Dragons have a sophisticated team of programmers and hackers, so if anyone is behind the social media attacks, we'd guess it's them."

"Do you have evidence of that?"

"Not yet. They're very sophisticated and good at covering their tracks."

"So..."

"There's more." The woman interrupted, flashing the

image of a man dressed head to toe in Chinese military attire. "The Blood Dragons have enlisted this man, Wu Zhao. He goes by the Western name American Jack."

"I see how he got that." Lavinia seemed to be the only person in the room to find humor in her sarcasm.

"He's the creator of some of the best deep fake software available on the internet."

"Deep fake." She twisted her mouth. "Is that where you can put your face on another person's in a video and make it look like you're talking?"

"That's a rudimentary example. These days you can take a video clip of Brad Pitt in an interview and create your own clip entirely and make him say whatever you want."

"But you'd have to have someone imitate the voice."

The woman put away her iPad and opened a laptop. Taking over the screen, she pulled up a piece of software and opened a new document. She typed in the phrase, *Lavinia, I order you to stand down.* Over the speaker system in a stern tone came the voice of Barbara Anderson. "Lavinia, I order you to stand down."

Lavinia's mouth dropped open.

The woman continued. "Wu Zhao, aka American Jack, lived in the United States for ten years. He went to MIT and is a gifted software engineer. He's done some of the most advanced machine learning research in the field. Six months ago he returned to China and became a Blood Dragon. We're concerned that he's working on next generation deep fake technology."

Lavinia chewed on her lower lip. "That would take what's been happening since the 2016 election to a whole new level, wouldn't it?"

"There's been a degree of fake news fatigue over the past year," the admiral said, "so we're concerned this may take it to the next level, yes. It'd be hard to convince people that what they see and hear isn't real."

"How do I find him?" Lavinia asked.

Admiral O'Leary folded his hands on the table. "We don't know. However, we can set you up with a contact in the Chinese government. His name is Tungya Kato. He's the equivalent to our secretary of state and will be your envoy."

"I would appreciate it if you could arrange for him to meet me in China."

"When do you leave?"

"I can leave tomorrow."

"We'll set it up. Provide your contact and arrival information and we'll arrange the details."

"Thank you, Admiral. I appreciate your support."

"You're welcome." Everyone in the room stood. The admiral addressed her again. "And Lavinia?"

"Yes?"

"Watch your stern." The naval reference was clear to Lavinia. "Liu Wei is a dangerous man."

The exterior of the Cyber Command building was a mix of gray stone, glass, and solar panels. The $500 million building was Lavinia's backdrop as she waited for John to pick her up. Removing her phone, Lavinia selected the number of a good friend.

"Hello?" came a familiar, if tentative, voice.

"Can I speak with The Disruptor, please?"

"Lavinia? Oh my, it's you, isn't it?"

"It is, sir. How are you doing?"

"I'm great! Where are you?"

"Well, actually, I'm standing in front of the US Army Cyber Command building."

"What?" His voice dropped an octave.

Lavinia laughed out loud. "Yup, I just met with—"

"Don't tell me you just met Admiral O'Leary?"

"You know him?"

"Yeah, we go way back, the two of us. Waaayyy back!"

"Seriously, Jacob, I need your help."

"I'm listening."

"The president has asked me to go to China to see if I can find out who is behind the social media attacks against her."

"You're telling me this while you're standing in front of the NSA's cousin?"

"Jacob, seriously, I need your help. There isn't anyone I trust more with this than you."

There was a pause. "Well, if you neeeed me..."

"Jacob?"

"Okay, seriously. How can I help?"

"I'm heading to China. They're going to arrange for someone in the Chinese government to be my envoy, but I need to be ready. I need to understand which questions to ask and what to look for."

"Why don't you come to Germany first? It's on your way."

"On the way? I'll bring a map with me."

"Stay a couple of days. I'll introduce you to some friends and we'll help you prepare."

"Your friends?" She snorted. "This will be an experience."

"They're hackers. You'll love them; they know how to party. Much more fun than the prudes you're hanging out with at US Cyber Command."

"Prudes? They carry guns, Jacob."

"Guns? You should see what I can do with a computer!"

Lavinia laughed. "Okay, Germany it is. Let me arrange my travel and coordinate with Admiral O'Leary and I'll get back to you. It'll be soon, though. Maybe even tomorrow."

"I'll be waiting."

"With bated breath, I'll bet."

"Bated!"

John saw Lavinia pocket her phone as he pulled up in his Ford pickup.

"Hey!" she exclaimed after opening the door.

John smiled back at her. "Hey, how was your meeting?"

"Informative." She stepped on the running board, slipped in, and pulled the door shut.

John nodded as he turned the wheel and accelerated away from the curb. "I passed an Indian place on the way in. Do you want to stop for lunch?"

"Sounds great." Lavinia sat back, apparently lost in thought.

John glanced at her every few minutes, but she was silent. Finding the restaurant, he parked the truck and took her hand to lead her inside. They were seated and after they'd ordered, John reached across the table and took her hand in his.

"So, how about we get away for a while?" he suggested.

Lavinia frowned. "The president has asked me to go to China for her."

"When?"

"We haven't set the dates yet, but soon."

"What about next week? We could go to Harrisburg for

a few days, check out the state museum. Stay at a nice Airbnb and enjoy some good restaurants."

"I might be leaving tomorrow." She grimaced. "I'm sorry."

John withdrew his hand and picked up the dessert menu. He pretended to study it to hide his frustration. "How long will you be gone?" His eyes were glued to his menu.

"I'm not sure. At least a few weeks."

He paused for a long time. "Okay."

"John, I've been home for months and we haven't done anything. I'm sorry I have to go away now."

"No, I understand, it's part of the package."

Lavinia paused. "You don't look like you understand."

John dropped the menu and smiled. "I'm good, okay? Don't worry about me. Can you tell me anything about your mission?"

"No, I can't. I may go to Germany first to see Jacob."

"Computer stuff?"

"Computer stuff," she confirmed. "That part of it is a little out of my league, so I need to get up to speed."

"I can understand that. There's no one better than him. Maybe when you get back, we can plan a vacation."

Lavinia reached across the table and took his hand in hers this time. "I'd like that, John. I really would. I'm sorry that my work will take me away again. I know that this thing between us is new and it needs time and attention. I want it to work as much as you do. But the reality is, the work that I do is going to take me away a lot and I need you to be okay with that."

John half stood and leaned across the table to give her a peck on the lips. "I'm okay with that. Part of the total package, and if getting you means that I have to be without you now and again, then I'll take it."

John smiled as he held her hand. Yet inside he couldn't beat the disappointment. He'd finally decided that he was going to propose. It'd have to wait a while longer.

SIX

The light yellow walls made the office of the Speaker of the House bright and airy. Bradley Tanner, lost in thought, sat in one of the antique armchairs next to the marble fireplace. He glanced up when the most senior advisor on his staff, Margot, entered. She had long, straight black hair, wore a white blouse buttoned low, and a black skirt. She approached him with a confident step. Tanner stood and motioned for her to sit in the chair adjacent to him.

"Did you read the headlines today?" she asked as she crossed one shapely leg over the other.

"Yes, the gun rally was a huge success." He smiled, his eyes lingering.

"It achieved what we wanted," she agreed. "It'll be interesting to see how the president responds."

"How the president responds? She shouldn't even be president. She lost the popular vote and won the electoral college by a margin smaller than Hawaii's allotment! She doesn't have the House or the Senate! She's as illegitimate a president as there ever has been."

"I can't agree more." She folded her hands in her lap.

Her milky white skin stood out against her black skirt. "Which is why we're doing what we're doing. Do you think the vice president can hold up her part in this?"

"I think she can, and she will. She's more ambitious than anyone else in this town, and that's saying a lot."

"She'll be more Republican-friendly once we've demonstrated President Anderson is unfit for office and removed her. We can get a lot done with MacQueen in control," Margot said.

A sinister smile spread across Tanner's face. "Well, don't get too used to that idea."

Margot returned the smile and tilted her head a few degrees. "What are you planning?"

"I've learned some information that's very interesting and I think will be useful."

"Some information about the president?"

"No, some information about the vice president."

"But we need her, don't we? She's the one who's going to stick the dagger in the president's back and invoke the Twenty-Fifth Amendment."

"You're right, we need her. Until she's done her part. But it takes all of Congress to convene to approve the appointment of a new vice president. What happens if she's suddenly removed?"

Margot's eyes opened wide. "What would happen to her?"

"I've become aware of some information that would prove Olivia MacQueen is unfit to assume the presidency."

"Which would mean you would assume the powers of the presidency?"

"Yes, and then Congress would appoint the new permanent president. And we control both the House and Senate."

A smile spread across her face. "I learn from you every day!"

"Stick with me." He let out a hearty laugh. After a moment he continued., "We need this secret meeting at the United Nations with the vice president and the newly announced Chinese vice president to go off without a hitch. Have you arranged the room for us to meet in? We need the agreed-upon talking points that the three of us will share with the media when asked what was discussed."

"Yes, everything is ready. These are the talking points." She reached across the gap between them and handed him a monogramed presentation folder that contained a single sheet of paper. Her top was loose enough to expose her white lace bra.

A smile tugged at the edges of his lips. Removing the document, the Speaker of the House perused it and suggested some edits.

"Looks good. Make those changes and put it on my iPad, so I can share them with our two guests." Tanner stood, signaling that their meeting was over.

"Exciting times, sir," she said, reaching out to shake his hand.

"Exciting times indeed." The father of three looked deep into her eyes as he took her hand.

Melanie pulled up to One Observatory Circle, the vice president's Washington, DC residence. The home had been built in 1893 on the grounds of the US Naval Observatory in Washington for its superintendent. The three-story building's white-painted brick exterior preserved the classic

look of the home, but the interior had been extensively reno-
vated and updated.

In her role as the vice president's primary aide, Melanie
knew the woman better than most...which wasn't saying a
lot. She'd never met a person more secretive in her life.

Melanie began the process of turning every light in the
residence on, because Olivia MacQueen didn't like to enter
dark rooms—ever! It was one of her many peculiarities.
After completing the main floor and upstairs, she went
down to the basement. She made quick work of the rooms
downstairs before she pushed open the door to the not-so-
secret bunker, which had been dug out in 2002. Melanie
flipped on the switch and the small room lit up. It featured a
desk in front of some bookshelves, a couch, a television, a
two-piece bathroom, and a small kitchenette.

What the Secret Service didn't know about was another
secret door at the back of the bunker. Melanie crossed to the
desk and sat down. Reaching inside the central drawer, she
felt around the back until her fingers brushed against a wire
loop. She gave it a firm pull. There was an audible click
behind her. Getting up, she slid the chair back under the
desk and turned to face the bookshelf. She grasped one of
the shelves and pulled it toward her.

The book shelf swung inward, as if on rails, to reveal
an underground tunnel with rough-hewn wooden walls
and ceiling. Conduit ran along the ceiling and about every
ten feet was an exposed lightbulb. Who built it and how
far the tunnel went Melanie didn't know, but it curved to
the right off in the distance. Her job was to ensure that
the bulbs were on before Olivia MacQueen arrived,
period. The vice president had entrusted her with knowledge of the secret tunnel on the grounds she would never
enter it. If not for the vice president's apparent fear of

dark rooms, she would not have been given this information. It was passed down from vice president to vice president.

Returning to the main floor, she ensured that she hadn't missed any lights. Satisfied, she went to the lounge she had been instructed to stay in whenever the vice president returned for a meeting with Rasha Brown, her longtime friend and life coach.

It was another of the vice president's strange routines. She always went to pick up Rasha Brown and bring her back to the residence. Upon their arrival, Melanie would wait in the lounge until they holed themselves up in the garden room, where MacQueen had set up her makeshift home office. Once the two women were locked away in her study, Melanie would normally leave for the night. Today, however, the vice president would be leaving for a trip so she'd asked Melanie to stay and turn off all of the lights after she'd left.

A Secret Service agent entered the front door and strode past the lounge. His presence signaled that the vice president would soon arrive. Melanie turned her attention back to her book.

The agent completed his search of the home, then disappeared through the front door. A moment later Melanie heard two women's voices.

"Rasha, thank you for coming."

"Always a pleasure," Rasha said. Her voice gushed. "I never tire of how beautiful this house is."

"Thank you. Let's talk in my office, as usual."

Melanie imagined MacQueen leading Rasha through the reception hall and sitting room to the stunning garden room. An old-fashioned rolltop desk against the wall had a long rustic harvest table adjacent to it, forming a large Lshaped workspace. The guest seat was a leather armchair on the far side of the room.

Melanie tried to focus on her book, but the vice president had opened the door between the sitting room and the garden room a crack, probably to improve the airflow. Melanie could clearly hear the women talking.

"So what did you want to talk about, Olivia? The last two years have been kind to you."

"There's more at play than this," Olivia replied. "This place is nice. The title is nice. The pomp and circumstance, all nice."

"But?"

"But the vice president doesn't *do* anything." Olivia's voice rose in pitch. "I don't want to fly around and smile while people take my picture as I wait in case the president is assassinated. I'm not royalty; I want to achieve something!" Her voice was becoming shrill.

"Olivia, this is a process. Getting yourself to this spot was itself a process. Becoming president will happen in due course. You need to bide your time and create your opportunities."

"I agree with that last part."

"What does that mean, exactly?" Rasha said.

Melanie could hear footsteps and guessed that Olivia had begun to pace. "I've been doing this for a year, Rasha. I can't do this for three or seven more years. Particularly for that...woman."

"So what do you want?"

"You know what I want."

"Olivia, we've talked about this. If you can't say it out loud then you aren't ready to take it on."

"I want to be president."

"So what are you going to do about that, if you aren't willing to put in the time?"

"I'm afraid to talk in this house. It's a government building. It's not a safe environment."

"So, where would you like to talk? A restaurant? My place?"

"No, your place might be watched. Rent an Airbnb, somewhere secluded, and send the address to my SIGNAL account. Let's meet on Friday night."

"How would that be any better, Olivia? The Secret Service goes everywhere but the bathroom with you."

"I'll handle that. It'll have to be late at night. After midnight."

"Whatever you need, Olivia, I'll support you. You're my oldest friend, you know that. We've been together all our lives."

Melanie heard stomping, then the front door open and slam shut, followed by silence. She waited another ten minutes before emerging. Melanie hurried about turning off all of the lights before she let herself out.

———

Hidden amongst the trees of Upper Ridge Road, Lawrence crouched, watching the street. He shifted his weight to his left leg and stretched the right one out. Reaching up, he rubbed his neck and let out a yawn. Due to the sensitivity of the assignment, he could only trust one of his guys with the fact that he was surveilling the vice president. That meant twelve-hour shifts seven days a week. For today's mission, however, he had help.

Headlights came into view so he raised his binoculars to

his eyes. Once the car turned he got a good view of the driver and saw that it was his target behind the wheel.

Dropping his binoculars into his backpack, he tossed it over his shoulder and threw the tarp behind him to the side to reveal his black Kawasaki Ninja. Swinging his leg over the seat, he started the bike and took off in pursuit of the car. Keeping back just far enough not to lose her, Lawrence followed the woman onto the highway. From his headset he notified his other investigator that they would be passing his exit shortly.

The black Tesla came into view in Lawrence's mirror. He relayed the details of the target's car and then accelerated and pulled in front of her. She drove for eight miles before she exited, the black Tesla following her. Lawrence raced to the next exit and took the off ramp. He pulled over on the shoulder at the top of the exit ramp and removed his black biker's jacket, turned it inside out, and slipped it back on. The red jacket would make him look like a different motorcyclist when he passed her car again.

"Where are you now, Clifford?" Clifford provided his location and the two continued to tag team so they could follow the car.

Lawrence slowed as she turned down a side street. He continued on past the intersection, pulled over, parked, doffed his helmet and jacket, then backtracked on foot. Turning down the side street, Lawrence kept to the opposite side of the road. She pulled into a driveway and turned her car off. Noting the address, Lawrence continued his walk.

Tomorrow, phase two began.

———

The man's fingers flew over the keyboard. He'd been working for months to find a vulnerability and two days ago he'd gotten a break. He'd redirected a shipment of office supplies going to NASA's headquarters in Washington, and had them delivered to a post office box he'd rented. Bringing it to his apartment, he opened the packaging for all of the thumb drives and installed his invisible malware on them. He then sealed them in new packaging, put the box of supplies back together, and re-shipped it to the original address.

It had seemed to take forever, but last week he started to get some hits. Most people seemed to be taking them home for use, because all he was getting was access to kids' computers full of games and homework. Yesterday, however, a user with access to the server that he needed had used the drive and he'd gotten access to the network.

Since gaining access he'd worked twenty hours straight. He'd copied the satellite's code to his computer. The code was written in C++ and then compiled to machine code, so he had to reverse the compiling procedure and then figure out which modifications he needed to make. With a satis-fying tap on the *Enter* key, the updated file was sent to the satellite.

His target was not a military satellite. It was scientific, so the security protocols were weak. The symptom his code created would seem to be a mere irritant to NASA scien-tists. To China, however, it was integral to the Blood Drag-on's plan. It was integral to China's future.

SEVEN

West 40th Street in New York City was a narrow one-way road where two lanes of traffic had somehow been squeezed in. With rising towers crowding each side of the street as far as you could see, it would be easy to feel claustrophobic. Yet for Lavinia it was one of the things that she loved most about the city. There was an order to it, like being in a labyrinth where you could discover new paths and new places each time you visited.

During the day, cars would be lined up and you'd have to weave between them, but it was mid evening and things were quiet. A light breeze lifted Lavinia's long brown hair from her shoulders before placing it gently back in place. Stepping onto the road, she made her way to the coffee shop. From the text she'd received moments ago she knew that her friend, Samantha Patel, was already there. Samantha was a senior reporter for the *New York Minute*.

Before Lavinia even reached the far curb, her friend's signature braided hair came into view on the other side of the glass wall. The jet black braid stretched to her waist and swung back and forth as she glanced around, probably looking for Lavinia.

Pulling the heavy glass door toward her, Lavinia entered, snuck up behind Samantha, and gave her a hug from behind.

"Oh my, it's so good to see you again," Samantha said, turning in Lavinia's grasp. "I've missed you. You look like you've fully recovered."

"Almost a hundred percent," Lavinia said. "I see you've been promoted! I read your articles all the time."

"Yes, thanks to you!" The smooth brown skin around her mouth creased with a smile.

"Well, it was reciprocal." An article Samantha had convinced her editor to print on Lavinia's behalf had helped avert a national disaster. Samantha had quipped to Lavinia weeks later that her article was evidence that the pen can in fact be mightier than the sword.

"So what are you up to these days? I know you left the FBI."

"Left isn't quite the right word." Lavinia flashed a wry smile. "Although the president assigned me to the Defense Intelligence Agency after I was removed from the FBI."

"Really? What do they do?" asked Samantha.

"Our job is to stop wars, basically. Military intelligence."

"Like the NSA?"

"Sort of like the NSA, CIA, and FBI all rolled into one. With a focus on foreign militaries."

"So more than just passive surveillance, then."

"Yes."

The two women lined up and ordered drinks and a light dinner. They found a table in a quiet corner of the busy shop.

Samantha asked, "How can I help?"

"I'm working on an investigation into the manipulation of social media in America."

Samantha frowned. "That doesn't sound like something the DIA would look into, based on what you just described."

"It is and it isn't. You've probably both read and written stories about what I'm investigating. What began with the 2016 election has only gotten worse. It seems there's an effort to further divide our country."

"You mean pitting the police against the African American community?"

"Yes, that's one aspect of it."

"Combined with the flood of 3D-printed guns and the fact that the police have become trigger-happy because they think everyone that isn't white is now carrying?"

Lavinia frowned. "I'm sorry, but I can't give you too much detail about what I'm looking into. What I was hoping you could do is educate me about social media manipulation. How is it being used to cause chaos in America?"

"Well, to continue with the example about the police being pitted against the African American community, I can give you a good example. These bad actors will create memes or images with controversial messages and circulate them on Facebook. They often contain one element of truth, but then twist the logic to come up with a conclusion that supports their narrative. Or they just create fake headlines that they know will support the worldview of certain voters so there is a high probability that they will circulate it."

Lavinia bit her lip. "Give me an example."

Samantha pulled out her phone and did a search.

"Here, look at this ad." It looked like the headline from a legitimate news site that featured an image of Hillary Clinton with her hand over her mouth, looking shocked. The headline said, *Wikileaks confirms Clinton gave weapons to ISIS*. "So that's an example of something that is patently false, but people who hated Hillary Clinton would share it. Other like-minded people would see it and share it as well. It pops up so often that people begin to believe it."

Lavinia raised an eyebrow. "That actually works?"

"You'd be surprised. That's just one example, though. Back to my earlier one with the African American community. Let's say there's a police shooting involving a black man. Something we've seen a lot of lately, by the way. These people will create fake Facebook pages claiming to organize an event. They put all kinds of garbage up there to rile people up. At the same time, they organize an event with a competing group for the same place at the same time."

"So they release the ball at the top of the hill and let gravity do the work."

"Good analogy."

"So how do you investigate this? How do you find out who's doing it?"

Samantha shook her head. "It's really hard. You can engage these people by joining their page and messaging them. You can usually tell from their responses that they aren't legit, but if you try to set up a call or a meeting, they won't engage. So you can identify the fake sites with some work, but finding out who they are is virtually impossible. I have a friend who's an expert in this stuff, though. Her name is Laura Galante. I can set up a call or meeting if you'd like."

There was the screech of tires out in front of the coffee

shop that made both women stop and look outside. A Ford Mustang, its windows down, gunned its engine and roared down the street. A pair of handguns emerged from the rear passenger window.

While Samantha ducked, Lavinia pulled a Sig Sauer from her shoulder holster and raced outside. Half a block down, two officers were sitting in their parked police cruiser. There was a series of staccato explosions as a hail of bullets struck the police car.

"Police!" Lavinia screamed as she broke into a run. As the car began to turn the next corner, Lavinia stopped, aimed her pistol, and squeezed off a shot, hitting the front passenger side tire of the car.

The stress of the hard turn combined with the speed and being hit by a bullet made the tire burst, and the driver lost control of the car.

Lavinia broke into a sprint. As she passed the patrol car, she glanced inside and saw one of the officers taking care of the other while talking into the dash-mounted microphone. Continuing her pace, Lavinia rounded the corner and saw the Mustang a hundred yards up the road. Racing up to the vehicle, her gun in front of her, she found it empty.

On the sidewalk beside the car were three automatic weapons. All of them FOGGs.

Melanie was reading *Eat, Prey, Love* while she stood in line at Starbucks. When it was her turn, she ordered a Grande vanilla latte without looking up. Tapping her credit card, she took her drink and was searching the packed restaurant when an African American man lifted his backpack out of the seat next to him to make space for her.

"You can sit here," he offered with a charming smile.

Melanie noticed his gorgeous eyes and chiseled cheekbones first. She flashed her sweetest smile back. "Thanks, you're so nice!"

She took a seat and set her phone down next to her purse, while continuing to read. Blowing on her mug with her eyes glued to her book, she tried to sneak a peek at the handsome man who had offered her the seat. A thrill ran through her when she caught him looking at her.

"Good book?" he asked.

"I've read it five times," she admitted, snapping it shut and putting it facedown. "How about you?"

"How about me what?" he asked. "Have I read it?"

Her face flushed and she let out a flirty laugh. "Sorry, I don't even know what I'm saying. Let me start again. So, do you have a favorite book?"

He raised a corner of her book and peeked at the cover. "Yeah, not that one."

His smile was back and it made her stomach twirl.

"*The Hate U Give*, by Angie Thomas," he said. "Great book. Very timely, given what's going on these days."

Melanie nodded with a broad smile, but had no idea what the book was about. "So, are you from around here?"

"No, just passing through for business. I'm in sales."

"Oh." She couldn't contain her disappointment. "What's your name?"

"I'm Lawrence," he said.

A guy on the other side of Melanie stood and tried to slip between the tightly packed tables and knocked hers, spilling her coffee. The man named Lawrence reached out and scooped up her purse, saving it from getting wet, but it slipped from his grasp and dropped to the floor.

"Oh, I'm sorry, let me get that." The stranger who'd knocked her table bent over.

"It's okay, I've got it," she assured him, bending down to gather the things that had fallen out of her purse. When she reemerged, Lawrence was holding her phone above the tabletop and sopping up the spilled coffee on the table with some napkins.

Melanie slung her purse over her shoulder and grabbed her napkin and helped clean the table. Lawrence put her phone down next to his and borrowed a napkin from his neighbor. Together they cleaned up the mess while the stranger muttered his apologies and disappeared.

"Thanks for your help. I can't believe this."

"That's pretty much your entire coffee," Lawrence said. "Let me buy you another one."

"No, I should get going." Melanie glanced at the lineup and then her watch, picked up her phone, purse, and book, and hurried out of the coffee shop. She muttered to herself, "What an embarrassing mess!"

Lawrence picked up Melanie's phone. His assistant investigator had played his part perfectly, knocking the girl's coffee over. He was waiting for Lawrence in the van in the parking lot with the equipment to install software that would allow him to track her movements and to control the microphone and camera without her ever knowing. He needed to work fast, before she discovered that she had taken the identical phone Lawrence had purchased instead of her own.

Lavinia leaned all of her weight against the black chain-link fence of the octagon. Her sparring partner came at her low, looking to knock her off her feet and bring the fight to the mat.

Pushing off the fence, she feigned to her right, then dodged left to avoid a takedown. Lavinia was more of a kick-boxer than a wrestler, so she tried to stay off the floor as much as possible. The site of her last surgery was still a bit tender and made wrestling more difficult.

Throwing a series of jabs, Lavinia tried to create an opening against her opponent. As the woman came at her again, Lavinia threw a kick to keep her at bay. The two combatants circled the enclosure, looking for opportunities.

There was a loud bang as the heavy steel side door to the gym slammed shut. Lavinia glanced in the direction of the sound for just a second, but it was enough time for the woman to attack and throw her to the floor. She put her forearms up to block as the woman pounced and started to rain blows down on her. Lavinia wrapped one leg behind the woman's back and slipped one in front of her. Before the woman could react, Lavinia flipped their positions so she was on top.

As Lavinia raised her hand to attack, the woman tapped out.

Collapsing onto the mat beside her opponent, she rolled onto her side and curled into a ball with a groan.

"Lavinia, what happened?" the club trainer, who also owned the gym, called out.

"I'm fine." She held up a hand to wave him off. "Aggravated my injury a bit, I think. Just need a second." Rolling onto her hands and knees, she stayed on all fours and controlled her breathing.

"I thought I had you when the door slammed shut," said her sparring partner.

Lavinia glanced at her and smiled. "I did too."

"Nice flip. You okay?"

"Yeah, just need a minute."

The woman left the octagon while Lavinia took a few more minutes to catch her breath.

"You okay?" The trainer entered and leaned over her with concern. His hands were on his knees. The five o'clock shadow accentuated his chiseled facial features. "I was wondering if you were ready to spar yet. You looked good in there." He paused. "Till you won."

Lavinia got up and left the octagon and dropped onto the bench a few feet from the door. She hung her towel over her shoulder, then bent over and put her elbows on her knees. The trainer followed, his hands on his hips.

"I'll be fine. I need the exercise if I'm going to regain the strength in my core. I just tweaked it when I flipped her."

"Yeah, that was a nice move. You executed it smoothly."

She smiled.

"Why don't you hit the showers? You can come back tomorrow and work out."

"I'm traveling tomorrow, actually. I'll be gone a few weeks, which is why I came in today. Wanted to get something in before I left."

"You know, I've seen a lot of people come through this gym. Not many take to MMA like you have."

"I like to push myself to learn new things. You can always be stronger, you know what I mean?"

"Have you ever thought of competing?"

"No, that's not why I'm doing it. There are other things that I want to learn to stretch myself, like parkour or motocross."

"I've never met a woman who's such an adrenaline junkie." He let out a laugh. "Well, take care of yourself there." He pointed to her side. "Make sure you let it heal completely before you fight anyone again, okay? I know this was your first sparring session since your injury, but coming back too fast will put you out longer."

Lavinia nodded as she rose to head to the change room. "Will do."

She had a quick shower and changed into a comfortable pair of black jeans and an army green t-shirt. After lacing up her classic Doc Martin boots, she stood and slung her purse over her shoulder.

When the black Toyota Camry pulled up in front of her, Lavinia pulled the door open.

"Lavinia?" the Uber driver asked.

"Yes," she confirmed and dropped into the back seat. As they pulled away from the gym, Lavinia removed a brief from her bag and read about the woman she was to meet.

Laura Galante was a self-made woman. She'd started a firm called Galante Strategies in 2017 after distinguishing herself as a cybersecurity expert. Her services were in demand around the world. Galante had addressed the United Nations Security Council, directed analysis for the 2019 Ukrainian Election Task Force to develop a security framework, and graced the Ted Talk stage with a cerebral and oft-watched presentation on cybersecurity. She was considered the de facto expert in the field. Glancing at the headshot in her folder, Lavinia reflected that the woman was proof that intellect and beauty were not mutually exclusive.

The Italian-themed restaurant was packed with patrons, as evidenced by the pleasant din of conversation and clinking glasses that greeted Lavinia when she opened the door. A black marble countertop with subtle gray and red veins sat atop a reception desk with clean lines that picked up on the color scheme. A young woman in a form-fitting white dress stood in stark contrast to the dark backdrop.

"Hi, I'm here to meet someone. The table is booked under Galante Strategies."

A smile formed on the woman's narrow face. "Oh, you're here to see Ms. Galante. Follow me."

"She's a regular here?"

"She is." The woman glanced at Lavinia as she led her to the table. "She's a special customer. My mother owns the restaurant and is a big fan. She had a special table created for her. One that affords a little more privacy for her meetings. When the original restaurant was built there was a dead space between the kitchen and the seating area. My mother opened it up and finished it just for Ms. Galante."

The woman led Lavinia to a nook at the back of the restaurant. It was an oddly shaped cutout, with the wall done up with faux white brick that was partially covered with stucco to make it look like an aged building. A four foot section of harvest table seemed to emerge from the wall, cantilevered in place. The kind of table that you'd imagine on the back patio of an Italian vineyard used to host the entire extended family. Four leather-backed chairs surrounded the table, with the head of the table left open.

A woman sat in one of the seats, an embossed folder done up in red at the top and fading to black at the bottom lying in front of her. She held a sheaf of papers and studied them, her lips pressed together and her eyes focused.

As the hostess approached, Laura Galante looked up and locked eyes with Lavinia. A smile spread across her face as she stood to shake hands. She was tall, with elegant black hair and charismatic eyes. Meeting her gaze, Lavinia felt drawn in, as if at that moment she was the most important person in the room to the woman. It was the same effect she'd read that Bill Clinton had on people when he spoke with them face to face.

"Hi, I'm Laura Galante." She shook Lavinia's hand. Firm. Confident.

"Lavinia Walsh. Thanks so much for meeting me, Ms. Galante."

"Oh please, call me Laura."

The two women sat down and reviewed their menus. Laura pointed out some of her favorites and they both placed their orders.

"Samantha tells me you're a spy." Laura leaned in, her eyebrows arched playfully.

Lavinia laughed. "I worked for the FBI but recently moved to the Defense Intelligence Agency. Not a lot of people know who they are, but—"

"I've done some work with them," Laura interrupted. "Some incredible people there."

Lavinia nodded. She had to remind herself that this woman wasn't a model, but was as connected as you could get in intelligence circles.

"I understand you're a personal friend of the president," Laura added.

"Friend is probably not quite the right word. I have her trust, might be a more accurate way to put it." Lavinia smiled. "As I'm sure you're aware from media reports, there's been a lot of negative information floating around social media about the president."

"Yes, it's coming from China."

Lavinia stopped mid speech, taken aback. "How do you know that?"

"The intelligence community's assessment has been unanimous. This is a hangover from the trade war in 2019. They fight their battles over a much longer time frame. We've moved on from it, of course—we're already a dozen major international events past that period—but for them it's still fresh."

"Do you know who specifically?"

"No. From what I understand this is a fresh assessment, but the various intelligence agencies are starting to marshal their resources. I assume that includes you."

Lavinia lifted her glass of wine and took a deliberate sip to buy herself a moment. While she'd grown a lot over the past year, she was still just twenty-four and this woman made her feel it. She found her both intimidating and charming. Lavinia's father, a once-famous news anchor, had always told her to listen twice and speak once; to never assume you're the smartest person in the room because there's something you can learn from everyone.

"I'd like to understand how these social media attacks work. What makes them effective, because from what I've seen they don't look overly sophisticated."

"The best one's aren't."

"Flashing ads that are blatantly false to people who already share your worldview? It seems like an inefficient way to achieve a goal."

"Is it?"

Lavinia folded her hands in her lap and listened.

Laura continued. "How does a country get revenge on another nation?"

"You go to war."

"Is that efficient?" Laura crossed her arms on the table and leaned in. "It's expensive, messy, and destructive for both sides. No one really wins, one side just loses less. So what do you do if you want to make a point? To take your opponent down a peg?"

"Buy ads on Facebook?" Lavinia frowned, unable to hide her skepticism.

"Let's start with the goal. If you're going to attack a democracy, you hit it at its most fundamental point. You need to get the people who are the very foundation of a democracy to start to question the system. Do you remember the movie *Inception*, with Leonardo DiCaprio?"

"I do. That was a great movie."

"Remember DiCaprio's character said that an idea is the most resilient parasite? That it's highly contagious and almost impossible to eradicate once it has taken hold. Inception, in the film, was to plant an idea so deep in someone's subconscious that it takes hold and becomes their own."

"Yes, I recall that now."

"Well, information attacks on a democracy work just like that. You turn your target's most powerful asset, an open mind, into their greatest vulnerability. Make the idea occur in people's own minds that democracy and its institutions are failing them. That their elite are corrupt puppet masters and the country they know is in free fall. Make them question the truth."

"That sounds so abstract."

The waitress returned with fresh drinks and set them on the table. "Your meals will be up in a moment. Do you want your appetizers with your meal or before?"

"With is fine," Laura replied with a smile.

"That sounds so abstract," Lavinia repeated. "What does it look like in real life? How do you make inception happen?" She grinned at her reference to the movie.

Laura smiled and took a deep breath. "My favorite example is from February, 2014, a few weeks before Russia invaded Crimea. A phone call leaked on YouTube of two American diplomats discussing the situation in Ukraine. In it, two American diplomats sound like they're trying to play kingmaker there, and worse, they curse the EU for its lack of speed and leadership in resolving the crisis. The media covers the phone call and the ensuing diplomatic backlash leaves Washington and Europe reeling. This creates a fissured response and a feckless attitude toward Russia's land grab in Ukraine." She sat back in her chair and raised her wine glass. "Mission accomplished." She took a sip.

"So by releasing a phone call you split two groups that should be allies and make them fight, so when you do something your adversaries should be united on, it goes unnoticed. Or at least the response is divided. Is that the idea?"

Placing her glass on the table, Laura leaned back in. "In Russia they call it reflexive control. It's the ability to use information on someone else, so that they make a decision on the record that's favorable to you."

"So it doesn't have to be, if you'll forgive the term, fake news. It can be true information."

"Sure. It can be true, it can be true but shown out of context, or it can be totally false. It's there to distract from the true goal."

"With respect to what's happening in the United States right now, then, we're seeing the scabbed wounds between the police and African American community being picked apart. You're saying that it's being done to distract us from the true threat?"

Laura sat back in her leather chair and raised the glass of wine to her lips and paused. "Exactly. So the question is, what is the true threat?" She took another sip.

Lavinia sat back in her chair as well and let out a deep

breath. Maybe her mission wasn't about stopping a misinformation campaign after all.

The waitress arrived with a platter balanced on one hand. She lowered it to the table and began to distribute the appetizers and main dishes.

Lavinia picked up her utensils and stared at her plate. She was suddenly not hungry at all.

John Miller glanced around to make sure no one was watching him before he risked rubbing his eyes. At the request of the president, he'd flown into New York late last night. One of the senior agents planning the raid targeting a suspected liquid steel distribution point had taken him for a midnight tour of the area, a tour that had taken far too long. The Port of New York/New Jersey was huge, basically a twenty-five mile radius around the Statue of Liberty. The six hundred and fifty miles of shoreline was one of the largest natural harbors in the world; the port was the third largest in the United States and the busiest on the east coast.

The complex multi-agency task force had met at six o'clock in the morning to ensure that everyone knew their role. John was a ride-along at the president's request, but the agent in charge had rolled with it and included him in the action. He would be part of the second wave to enter the building. If there was no action upon breach, he and his partner were assigned a section of warehouse to search. The intelligence from inside the warehouse was just three days old, so with recent imagery there should be no surprises.

They were minutes away from go time. John sat in the front passenger seat of a black Ford Explorer with his gun loaded and safety off. The Kevlar vest added a lot of bulk, but given the unknowns they were about to face, it was necessary.

"All officers converge on the property," a voice ordered over the speaker system. The officer driving the vehicle jumped on the gas and they surged ahead. The building was just two blocks away. They covered the distance in seconds.

Six vehicles converged on the entrance to the building. Officers appeared on the rooftop of the building across the street, guns poised, providing overhead cover. John exited his vehicle along with a dozen and a half officers and agents, their guns drawn. Two officers swung a heavy steel battering ram and the door flew open on the first blow. John and his driver followed behind the first group of officers through the door, their guns leading the way.

John broke to his right, while his driver kept left. Overhead lights snapped on, triggered by motion sensors. The blueprints they'd studied earlier that morning had shown a large open bay with an office at the back of the building. There were six shipping containers filling the bay area.

Eight officers had streamed inside along with John. He motioned for two to follow him as they moved toward the two containers on the far right. The three men ran up to the farthest container and leaned their backs up against it. John motioned for one man to check the left side while he checked the right. The third would provide cover as needed.

John peered around the corner. He saw nothing, so with his gun pointing in front of him, he moved along the length of the container. The exterior cinderblock wall made for a narrow hallway. He would be trapped if someone suddenly appeared at the other end of the container.

"Clear! Clear! Clear!"

Voices began to ring out as the other officers moved along the length of their containers. John reached the end and rounded the corner without incident. "Clear," he called, parroting the others. Two officers had entered from the rear of the building and had already searched the office.

The officers regrouped at the entrance of the containers, each of which was locked.

"Let's see what we've got," the lead officer bellowed. "Maybe we've captured a monstrous supply of liquid steel and saved some officers' lives."

One by one they cut the chains and opened the containers to inspect their contents.

Every single one was empty.

EIGHT

The waitress at Charlie Palmer Steakhouse led Bradley Tanner to the private lounge at the back of Washington's most popular restaurant. His team had arranged the private fundraiser for him.

Gray soundproofing panels lined the walls, highlighted with wall sconces to add a touch of class to the privacy the room afforded. The lounge seated thirty-six, but the extra tables had been removed to accommodate their party of eight guests. Six of them were very high-paying guests, so the cost of booking the entire room would not be a problem.

Tanner always arranged it so he was the last person to arrive for meals such as this one. The liquor flowed early, enticing his guests to be on time, so his late entrance gave an air of importance to his arrival.

"Gentlemen, gentlemen, so good to see you." Tanner shook hands with each of the men, making eye contact as he did so. All of them were CEOs of the largest military contractors in the country. He flashed his Southern smile and grasped each of their hands in his as he worked his way around the table. *Firm handshakes,* he reminded himself.

"Please sit, please sit. Has everyone ordered?"

"Yes, sir," Margot answered. "I ordered you the full cut double ribeye steak, served with creamed spinach and truffle and bacon twice-baked potato."

"You take good care of me, Margot," he enthused, squeezing her arm.

She smiled in return, putting a hand ever so briefly on his chest before pulling it away.

Appetizers and wine arrived in short order and conversation began to flow easily. There was discussion about how well the economy was holding up, despite President Anderson's destructive policies. Everyone agreed it was a travesty that she was president at all, given the trifecta of having lost the popular vote, the House, and the Senate.

"Our founders didn't foresee that possibility when they wrote the Constitution," one CEO opined.

"I hear she's anti-gun," said another. "She's just too afraid to come right out and say it. This liquid steel issue is a disaster. Why shouldn't I be allowed to print my own guns? Imagine what I'd make selling blueprints to Americans. It's one hundred percent profit, no material cost!"

"You'd have to be able to control people sharing the blueprints."

"It's all in the go to market strategy," the man replied with a wave of his small, fat hand. "Just wrap the document in DRM, the same way the music industry does. Single-use blueprints."

As dinner gave way to dessert and then coffee, the wait staff disappeared and conversation turned to the real business at hand.

Tanner stood to address the group. "Gentlemen, thank you for taking the time to come out here tonight and meet with me. As you all know, the Democrats are no friend to your industry. They're too weak to take a stand on the global stage. This president in particular!" He stabbed at the air to emphasize his point.

"We live in dangerous times, when nations like China, whose population is four times that of the United States, are on pace to be outspending us on military hardware within a decade. Their military spending is growing at a rate of ten percent per year, while ours is stagnant!" He stared down each of the CEOs in mock indignation.

"China's military budget is double that of Russia. Double!" He waved his hands over his head, feigning disbelief. "Of Russia! What do the Chinese plan to do with the world's second largest military? Why are they investing so much? For show?"

Tanner began to pace the room. "While our Democratic president is focusing her energy on banning 3D printers, our military equipment is aging. Do you know how much we spend each year to take care of our 1950s-era nuclear arsenal? What we spend in one year on maintenance, we could use to replace the entire system with modern equipment!

"Gentlemen." The Speaker of the House dropped his voice, taking a serious tone. "Gentlemen, our country is in danger. We need to step up our investment in our military, that much is clear. We need to upgrade our equipment and our capabilities before we become vulnerable to China."

"How do you propose we do that?" one of the CEOs piped up. "It isn't on our current president's priority list."

"The threat of war with China is coming, gentlemen. I have access to intelligence that tells me in short order we will need to respond with investments in our infrastructure. The country is going to demand that we reprioritize how we spend our tax dollars. The need for our collective defense will jump to the forefront of the political agenda."

"But is our president going to understand the need?"

"Let me share a secret with you. I believe that information is going to come out in the coming weeks that is going to send Washington reeling."

"Is it Wikileaks again?"

"No. No, sir. Nothing like that." He shook his head, smiling. "I believe we're going to learn things that will make it impossible for President Anderson to continue on as president. The good news is that we have a vice president who is sympathetic to our cause. However, to make sure things stay on track, I'm going to need your support. Support like you've never provided before. But I can promise you one thing. One true thing." He wagged a finger again for emphasis. "If you support me now, you will be rewarded ten times over."

There was silence for a moment as his words sank in. Then one by one, each of the CEOs stood and began to clap.

Classical music, which seemed familiar but Aliyah could not name, streamed over the speaker system in the background. The music was calming and the volume was low, so it tugged at you and brought relief like a gentle breeze on a hot day. Aliyah sat as still as a stonefish with her left leg crossed over her right and her arms hugging her torso. The clinic she'd been told to visit was literally in a back alley. The fact that she had to visit late at night after her mother went to bed was a blessing, because she could do it without being missed, but it also made the entire thing seem sketchy.

A woman with long black hair and smooth white skin approached her with a welcoming smile. "Hi, I'm Linda." She held out a welcoming hand.

She bit her lip. "I'm Aliyah—"

"No last names, Aliyah," the woman interrupted her.

"I'm sorry, I forgot." She paused and looked at her feet. "I'm nervous."

She felt Linda put a finger under her chin and tilt her head up so she was looking into the woman's eyes. Linda smiled again. "We all are, honey."

All of the dread and stress drained from Aliyah's body. She'd been terrified of this visit all week, since a stranger had confided its existence to her and given her the secret phone number. She'd been stocking shelves at the department store, lost in the bowels of the four-story building. A customer had happened across her and seen the tears streaming down her face. For no good reason, she'd told the stranger that she was pregnant and was terrified to tell her boyfriend. He was the star fullback at his high school and was being scouted by professional teams. He didn't need a scandal.

Aliyah told the woman that she loved him and didn't want to do anything to hurt him. That at seventeen she was too young to have a child. Her mother barely had the resources to keep the household afloat as it was, with her father being in prison.

The lady had taken her into her arms, and Aliyah had buried her head in the stranger's shoulder. Tears streamed faster. She could still remember the *sh, sh, sh, sh* gently whispered into her ear and the comfort it had brought. Then the whispered secret. *"The Hall of Redemption."* She'd made Aliyah commit a phone number to memory.

Ordered her to never write it down and to never reveal its secret, unless to another woman in similar need.

As a seventeen-year-old in Alabama, she knew it was illegal for her to seek an abortion without consulting her mother. A new controversial law had resurrected the spirit of Bill 1566, meaning that she also had to get the permission of the father to have the abortion. Neither of those were an option.

She followed Linda to a small treatment room. The doctor explained the procedure in a way that Aliyah could understand, and ended by asking if she was ready to make her decision. Did she want to proceed?

Aliyah took a deep breath. "Yes."

The camera face was disguised as a rivet head in the steel frame holding the ceiling-mounted track of the examination light. From the back of the camera a cable snaked above the drywall to an empty room three floors up. Empty save for the computer that recorded the video and transmitted it. Video of a doctor performing an illegal abortion.

Shannon Coleman stared at the data on her computer and furrowed her brow. Dumping the file, she reset her criteria and kicked off the SQL query to run again.

She'd been studying the Lunar Reconnaissance Orbiter's diagnostic files and noticed that it'd developed a blind spot on the far side of the Moon. Given that the satellite had launched in 2009 and originally had a three-year mission life, this wasn't unusual. Any data they got after the three years before equipment started to fail was a bonus.

The satellite had been in orbit almost a decade longer than its scheduled life. If it had launched in 2009, the technology on board was from 2006 at the earliest. So it was old. Over fifteen years old. But a blind spot was odd. Why not complete failure?

She'd analyzed all of the satellite's systems to see if she could trace it back to some causal factor, but had found nothing. Then last night she'd had a crazy idea. There were three other American satellites orbiting the Moon. Were any of them experiencing a similar problem? Surely not.

The data she'd just dumped showed that *all four of the satellites* were experiencing blind spots on the far side of the Moon.

As the mainframe extracted her data files, Shannon looked up at the ceiling, lost in thought. The common name for the far side of the Moon was the misnomer *the dark side of the Moon*. If you were an Ozzy Osbourne fan, that was gospel to you. If you were a scientist, you knew that with the Moon's orbit matching the Earth's, we on Earth always looked at the same face of the Moon. If you lived on the Moon, each face of the Moon experienced about two weeks of daylight and two weeks of night. So the far side of the Moon was "dark" to us because we couldn't observe it from Earth. Not because it was actually dark. So as of right now, the dark side of the Moon was in its sunlit phase.

Maybe the solar wind was doing something to these satellites? A large solar flare?

Nothing seemed to make sense to her.

Shannon resolved to spend some more time on the problem in another week, when the Moon moved to its next solar phase. She smiled to herself. It wouldn't do to raise the specter that little green men on the Moon were trying to hide their existence by shooting death rays at passing satellites.

Her computer beeped. Rather than look at the data again, she dumped the file and made a note to try it again in a week.

NINE

Pulling her carry-on suitcase behind her and with her laptop bag slung over her shoulder, Lavinia made her way through the expansive Berlin-Tegel Airport toward the exit doors. Known as the airport that wouldn't die, its replacement had been announced in 2006, and after a very un-German decade of delays was set to finally open. Lavinia took in the history of the building; with its glass on gridiron construction and polished cement floors it still looked modern after almost forty-seven years.

Pulling out her Blackberry 7290, she called Jacob. The device was ancient by modern standards as it lacked the features of today's smartphones, but that was also the reason it was difficult to hack. "Hey, I'm here. Just walking out of the arrivals door."

"I'll be right there. I pulled over on the shoulder of the road a mile away."

"They use kilometers here."

"Once American, always American." Jacob's voice was cheerful.

A few minutes later a black BMW 3-series pulled up to

the curb, with Jacob behind the wheel. She recognized his familiar straight black hair cropped short on the sides and back, but long on top. His pale skin betrayed his solitary profession as a gray hat hacker.

"Why don't you get a real phone like normal people?" Jacob complained when she'd dropped into the seat next to him.

"Because I don't want the government following me everywhere I go. I thought of all people, you'd appreciate that."

"I thought you worked for the government."

Lavinia rolled her eyes. "I'm not concerned about *my* government; I'm concerned about all the rest."

"Has anyone told you that your fears are misplaced?"

"Drive!"

Jacob kept his eyes on the road as he spoke. "I'll get you a real phone, my dear. And I'll teach you how to use it."

Lavinia laughed. "I've missed you, Jacob. I'm staying at—"

"The Ellington Hotel. Got it."

"How did you know that?"

Jacob smiled knowingly. "Your password is my password."

"I'm getting a new phone." Lavinia held the device up and pretended to study it, turning it over and around.

"And I'll show you how to use it," he finished.

They caught up during the twenty minute drive to the Ellington. Jacob dropped her out front and went to park the car. Lavinia had checked in by the time he returned. He took the handle of her bag and pulled it for her as they went up to her room. When she'd opened the door, he raced in and jumped on the bed, stretched out with his feet crossed and arms behind his head.

"You know no social limits, do you."

"None. That's what makes me so charming."

"Charming—is that what you're being?"

"Isn't that why you reached out to your favorite hacker?" His infectious smile was back.

Lavinia sat on the bench across from the bed. She started pulling things out of her bag, including her laptop. "Have you been keeping up on what's happening back home?"

"Of course. What a mess. The government asked me to help last year, so I did for a minute. But the people in charge there don't know what they're doing, so I stopped joining the calls. It was a waste of my time."

"That's too bad. It's causing a lot of chaos."

He clucked his tongue. "It's going to get worse."

"You know that, or just opining?"

"It's obvious. This isn't a four hundred pound guy from New Jersey sitting on his bed. This is clearly state sponsored."

"What are the fingerprints?"

"Pervasiveness. Getting something to go viral isn't easy. It takes thousands upon thousands of attempts to get one really significant hit. The fact that we're seeing it everywhere means that the number of actual attacks is in the millions."

"Can you prove where it's coming from?"

He grimaced, shaking his head. "That's hard to do these days, if the people behind it are technical. Anyone can buy a VPN and make it look like their computer is in Bulgaria or Romania or any country that ends in *IA*. Plus, using an onion router like TOR makes it virtually impossible to trace the person's origins."

"The president believes it's coming from China. She's

asked me to go out there to look around. Do you know anyone there who can connect me?"

Jacob rubbed his chin. "No one comes to mind. It's a bit like hiring a hit man in Italy. You don't just walk up to the doorman at your hotel and ask who you should use."

Lavinia threw hear head back and laughed. "Right. I'll be more subtle, then."

"We can begin some detective work here. Many of the attackers have fake Facebook accounts. If you can get them to engage with you, sometimes you can get a hint at their background from the way they write. From their broken English, I mean. You can also study their followers, like who signed up first. Often they have other false accounts follow them so they're sharing each other's posts."

"But if you can't find out where they're from and who they are, what good is it?"

"Agh, because if I try to reset their password it'll enforce secondary authentication. Facebook will show you a partially masked phone number, with two real digits at the end of the phone number."

"But what good is two digits in a ten-digit phone number? That's still millions of combinations."

"Yes, but what else do they show you?"

"A bunch of hashtags."

"A bunch of hashtags in the format of the phone number. A format that is different for many countries."

Lavinia's jaw dropped. "I would have never thought of that!"

"Unless they're using a burner phone. But if you find enough of these accounts—of which there are probably thousands—and plot the phone code formats, well, then there's a chance that the real country will emerge."

"Incredible. Let's get started!"

"No, not yet. Is that your computer?" He pointed to the Lenovo Thinkpad she'd set on the dresser next to her.

"Yes, that's my work laptop."

"Okay, let's find a locker at the public train station and we'll store it there."

"For how long?"

"Forever. That's useless to you. Let's go shopping." Jacob hopped up, grabbed her arm, and dragged her toward the door.

Despite her international flight, the excitement of what Lavinia had learned from Jacob had given her a second wind. They returned to her room after a three-hour shopping trip to take an inventory of their wares.

"So why the used laptop?"

"Because you're not registered with the manufacturer as having bought it. That's why—" he held up a mini screwdriver set and selected the appropriate one "—we bought this."

Opening up the bottom of the laptop, he removed the hard drive and tossed it across the room at the garbage can, missing by a good foot.

"I think you just took a chunk of the drywall next to the garbage can out," Lavinia observed.

"Whatever. Pass me that new drive."

Lavinia handed a small box over. Jacob opened it, removed a new drive, and inserted it into the computer. He also added extra RAM. Turning the machine on, he plugged in a USB drive and began to install some software.

"Are you putting Windows on it?"

Jacob looked pained. "No, Linux. Mint flavor, if you

care, because it's the easiest to learn. Most importantly, though, no licenses required. Untraceable."

After the setup was done, Jacob booted the computer up and showed her the basics of the operating system.

"I'm going to download something called TAILS."

"As in cute things that tell you when a dog is happy?" Lavinia knew that would irritate him.

"No, as in software." He didn't look up from his screen. He was so engrossed that the question barely registered. "TAILS is an OS that's contained on a USB stick. You plug it into any computer while it's off, turn it on, and you boot up a virtual computer. You can surf the Net, send messages, answer email, and as soon as you pull out the USB stick, everything is wiped. There is absolutely no record of what you did. It's the only way to truly compute anonymously."

"And does it use the TOR browser?"

"Yes; let me show you."

Once he'd trained her on TAILS and TOR, he sat back, away from the screen. "Okay, now let's talk passwords."

"I use a ten-digit password."

"Yeah, that's sad. Maybe ten minutes for a sophisticated government to hack that passcode."

"How many characters, then?"

"At least fifty."

"Fifty? How am I supposed to remember that?"

"Easy, just pick a long sentence that you can remember. For example: the queen mum is a sexy bitch and I'd love to put her over my knee and spank her Tuesday."

Lavinia fell on the bed laughing.

"That's sixty-nine characters ignoring spaces...do you see what I did there?"

Lavinia shook her head, smiling. "Hackers are so funny."

"Charming. We're charming. So you come up with a long sentence, then you drop all of the spaces and pick two letters that you replace with special characters. For example replace the letter *I* with an exclamation mark and the letter *O* with an ampersand. Now you have a code that will take even the most sophisticated hacker a decade to solve. If ever."

Lavinia nodded, impressed. "That's really smart. I'm glad I came here first."

"If you're going to China, Lavinia, you're going to war with some of the world's best hackers. You need to be really careful."

"I will," she promised.

"Okay, now phones. I can't believe you wanted another Blackberry. It's like a decade newer than yours, but a Blackberry? You have brand loyalty issues."

"You know I'm loyal, Jacob."

"Whatever. This is your phone. The WiPhone." He held it out to her. "It was a kickstarter project that was funded in 2019."

She looked it over, frowning. "It looks like a regular phone. All I can do is calls."

"No. This is the ultimate hacker phone. Watch."

Jacob pulled out the screwdriver and removed the back of the device. He switched to a cross-legged position and dumped a small plastic bag of components he'd bought at the store. He started to work on the phone, his eyes focused.

A big yawn split Lavinia's face. "I'm exhausted. I'm going to have a nap."

"You do that."

"Are you going to move?"

"It's a queen-sized bed."

Lavinia rolled her eyes. Slipping under the covers fully clothed, she was asleep by the time her head hit the pillow.

Lavinia sat bolt upright in bed and came face to face with Jacob. He was still sitting on the bed and was holding up a large piece of plastic and exclaiming, "It works, it works!"

As the cobwebs cleared, what Jacob was holding in his hand came into focus.

"What is that?" Lavinia exclaimed.

"This is your phone." He held it in his right hand and made a dramatic motion with his left. "I call it—"

"Ugly?"

"We're going for function here, not form."

The bottom third of her bed was littered with electronic parts, tools, cables, and Jacob's laptop. Lavinia slipped out from under the covers and stretched her arms above her head. "Okay, let's see what you've got."

Lavinia could best describe the device as the phone version of a Mr. Potato Head.

"On the front, you have a standard-issue phone. Old school, except that it's a VOIP phone so you get free phone calls worldwide. I've programmed this button on the side to cycle through ten different phone numbers. You have ten SIM cards in this baby, so you don't need to buy multiple burner phones."

"That's cool. But how do I text when there's just a number pad?"

"Voilà. Flip it over and you have a full-sized capacitive touchscreen. This will give you a basic browser, email, and texting with a built-in VPN. No one will know where you are in the world or who you are. The phone number is masked and untraceable."

"Jacob, that's incredible, thank you. It's..." She paused as she turned it over in her hands. "Quite possibly the ugliest phone ever made."

"Thank you." Jacob slipped off the bed and took a bow. "Now, if you're rested up, why don't I introduce you to some of my friends at the Chaos Computer Club?"

"A computer club?"

"Oh, this is no ordinary computer club. Don't bring anything electronic. Except your new phone. That you can bring."

Lavinia and Jacob had returned from shopping and gone to their respective rooms to rest. Lavinia had lay on her bed for almost two hours, unable to sleep, when there was a knock at her door. The next thing she knew, she and Jacob were leaving the hotel.

"So where are we going?" A breeze played with Lavinia's long brown hair as the double glass doors of the Ellington Hotel slid open upon their approach.

"To a crypto party. It's a meeting of the Chaos Computer Club. They have them all over Europe, but this is the one I go to. The bar's called C-Base."

After a fifteen-minute cab ride, they were dropped at an unmarked street adjacent to a power station. The buildings were clean and middle class, but unremarkable in every way. Jacob led her through two courtyards and an unmarked door and they were suddenly transported, if not in time then certainly in space. The entrance to C-Base looked like a spacecraft from a post-apocalyptic movie. Like the Earth was doomed and they had an hour to throw together a spaceship to save the seeds of humanity. It was a combination of exposed metal and bright red lights, with some yellow light along the floor where you would normally have floorboards. A jumble of cables ran across the ceiling and the walls.

"We're here."

"This is a bar?" Lavinia pointed at the entrance.

"Sort of. You can drink here. Legend has it that a space-craft crashed here and is half buried under Berlin, with evidence of the craft strewn about the city. Our computer club meets here," he motioned with his arms. "It's built like a maze, a series of concentric Cs, each slightly off center so you have to find your way through to the different levels."

Lavinia thought the interior decor was, well, spacey. They passed a tiny green-lit room with what looked to be the statue of a grotesque alien inside it. Jacob led them through the maze to the fourth and outermost ring. At the end of the room there was a metal stairway going down to a platform with a table, some chairs, and a random strip of seats you'd normally see at an airport gate. The room was lit in a garish yellow light. Eight men and one woman were seated there. Lavinia followed Jacob down, her eyes on the steps as she descended.

A bean sprout of a man was the first to stand and shake her hand. He was dressed like the doorman from a high-end hotel and wore an excessively tall top hat with an LED screen circling it.

"What's the screen for?"

The man reached into his right-hand pocket and pulled out what looked like a phaser from an old *Star Trek* movie. He pointed it at one of the other men in the room and a series of four digit numbers began to scroll across his hat.

"Hey, cut that out!"

"His credit card number. The fool keeps it on his phone."

The man whose data was stolen threw an empty french fry boat at the bean sprout.

"I'm Kevin," the bean sprout introduced himself.

"Nice to meet you, Kevin." Lavinia shook the hand that didn't have the phaser in it. "Please point that somewhere else, though," she said with a smile.

They made introductions around the room and Jacob introduced Lavinia as his friend from America.

The other woman in the room wore a shiny black leather bra, high-waist matching panties, black fishnet stockings, and a pair of platform high heels. To finish the look she had long black gloves and a black leather English driving cap. "I'm Modesty."

"Of course you are." Lavinia smiled, taking the hand that was lavishly presented to her.

"Don't let her sexy attire fool you; she'll take you for all you've got if you let her close to you," said Jacob.

"She's worse than me," Kevin added. "At least I tell you I've stolen your data."

"I would never hurt a woman. We girls have to stick together, don't we, Lavinia?"

"We sure do! I like your shoes, by the way."

"Oh, those aren't shoes," Kevin said.

Modesty plopped into the nearest seat and slipped her heels off. She put them on the table, a smile stretching ear to ear.

Lavinia cringed at the thought of stockinged feet on this floor.

As if it were a Chinese puzzle box, she worked an area close to the footbed and a small piece of the midsole popped out of place. Moving her fingers to the back of the heel, she applied pressure in a second spot and a second piece of midsole slipped out of place, and then the entire sole separated from the rest of the high heel, revealing three cavities jammed with equipment. Modesty began to pull things out and call out a running inventory. "Lockpick set, USB keystroke recorder, a wireless router, a retractable ethernet cable..."

Lavinia's jaw dropped. "That is amazing," she said.

Modesty shrugged. "Girl tech."

The group sat together and Jacob called for another round of beer.

"Show them your phone." Jacob smirked.

Lavinia removed the monstrosity from her pocket and placed it on the table.

"That's incredible!" One of the men reached for the chunky device.

Modesty slapped his hand before he reached it, then used her index finger to turn it over. "I love it. You have to make me one, Jacob."

"One of a kind original. Sorry, Modesty."

The beer arrived, more people joined the group, and they caught up on the latest goings on in tech. The majority of what they were talking about was gibberish to Lavinia. She heard words that she knew here and there, but they were surrounded by talk about protocols, bandwidth, and blockchain.

"So Lavinia is on her way to China," Jacob revealed.

"Some talented hackers there," one of the men added.

"You'll meet some amazing women down there," said Modesty.

"Just be careful which crowd you connect with. There's a sophisticated network of organized crime and you can find yourself in a lot of trouble really quickly," someone offered.

"Does anyone have any contacts down there?" Jacob asked. "Anyone who could help her connect?"

"It would help if we knew what your interest was."

Lavinia decided to take a chance. "I'm trying to connect with a group that calls themselves the Blood Dragons."

At the mention of the name, the room went completely silent. All eyes were on Lavinia.

"Did I say something?"

"Why would you want to connect with them? Who are you?" Modesty asked, taking a step back.

"I'm no one. No one important."

No one seemed convinced by this. Her question ignored, conversation pivoted, although Lavinia could sense an underlying nervous energy. A short while later, people began to excuse themselves, and pretty soon Lavinia and Jacob were alone.

"Blood Dragons?" He raised an eyebrow at her.

"Yeah. I guess that hit a button."

"I have no idea what just happened." Jacob held his hands up in the air. The table was covered in beer bottles still half full.

It was dark out when Jacob and Lavinia got out of the cab in front of the Ellington Hotel.

"Sorry I broke up the party," Lavinia repeated for the fourth time.

"It's okay. I'm sure someone will reach out and tell me what happened in there."

"Your bag of stuff is still in my room."

"Yeah, that's right. Let me grab it and we can regroup tomorrow."

"Miss Walsh?" A woman in a white dress shirt and gray skirt called from behind the counter as the two entered the hotel. "There's a message for you."

"A message?"

She handed Lavinia a piece of paper.

"What does it say?" asked Jacob.

"It says, *If you want to find out more about the Blood Dragons, meet me at Monsterkabinett Tuesday at 7:00 p.m.* What's Monsterkabinett?"

"It's an artists' collective. It won't look safe at night, but it's probably the safest place in Berlin for a private meeting. Who left it? Did they sign it?"

"No." She flipped the piece of paper over. Following the lady back to the desk, Lavinia addressed her. "Excuse me, but who gave you this note?"

"It was given to one of the doormen to pass on to me."

"Which one?"

"He's left for the evening, I'm afraid."

Lavinia returned to Jacob. "How does everyone in this city know where I'm staying?"

"I think it's your Blackberry."

TEN

Dan invited Detective John Miller into the Oval Office with a wave of his arm. As the man approached, there was an expression on his face that Dan recognized.

He leaned in as John passed him. "Awe-inspiring, isn't it?"

John smiled and nodded.

"It never wears off," he whispered.

"Madam President," John greeted Anderson formally.

"Thank you for joining us, John. We're going to get Lavinia on a secure line in a moment, and we can all get on the same page."

Dan closed the door and went to the president's side as she dialed Lavinia's private number. They waited while it rang.

"Hello?"

"Lavinia, it's the president. I have Chief of Staff Dan Nolan and John Miller here with me."

"Hi everyone," Lavinia said.

"Lavinia, I want all of us to update each other on what's

going on so that we're all on the same page. It's important we work as a team."

"Of course, Madam President."

"Dan, why don't you start by updating us on what's been happening stateside?"

"Of course, Madam President. Last week an African American youth was shot and killed by a police officer. By all accounts it was an accident. The officer involved is on suicide watch, but the public outcry has been tremendous. There have been more protests around the country and we continue to see fake social media campaigns popping up, trying to incite violence. Lavinia, as you know, there was a drive-by shooting of two officers in a parked cruiser. One officer was wounded but will survive. The other wasn't injured, although both have been badly shaken. We believe the police shooting was a response to the earlier incident."

"Thank you, Dan. Detective Miller, can you tell us about your raid on the warehouse?"

"Yes, Madam President. A raid involving approximately eighteen officers on a warehouse in the Port of New York/New Jersey was executed five days ago. We secured six cargo containers and a lot of equipment, but all of the containers were empty. They were obviously tipped off and had moved the supply of liquid steel to another location. We're currently investigating where the containers came from, but it doesn't look good. It may be a dead end."

"Are there any other leads that the New York State Police are following up?"

"I'm afraid not, Madam President."

"Lavinia, how have you fared so far?"

"I've really just begun. I'm in Germany and Jacob Appleton is preparing me for my trip to China. He's trained me on some new equipment and he's educating me on social media hacking. I did have someone reach out to me through my hotel concierge, anonymously requesting a secret meeting. I'm going to meet the person tomorrow evening, actually, to see what it's about."

"Are you going alone?" Dan said.

"No, Jacob is going to accompany me."

"Make sure you keep safe, Lavinia. Have you checked in with the US embassy?"

There was a pause. "I'm sorry, Madam President, I haven't. I'm six hours ahead of you so the embassy is closed now, but I will first thing in the morning. That was an oversight."

"It's for your own safety, Lavinia," Dan piped in. "If anything happens to you when you're in a foreign country, the embassy is a resource. But they can only help you if you reach out to them."

"Yes, sir."

"When do you leave for China, Lavinia?"

"I'm going to see what this meeting brings, but unless it's something significant, I'm ready to leave the next day. Admiral O'Leary over at Cyber Command has a government contact for me when I arrive. Oh, and Cyber Command did give me one tip. Apparently the new Chinese vice president is the former head of the military there and he has a faction in the military that is loyal only to him. They call them the Blood Dragons. I don't know if that means anything or not, but that did come up."

"Have you heard of that before, Dan?"

"No, Madam President. I'll reach out to the head of the CIA and Homeland Security and see what they know."

"That's fine, but let's keep this circle small for now. People are tired of hearing about other countries manipulating our social media. When we have something more actionable we can involve the rest of the government's machinery. For now, let's gather information."

"There is one more domestic issue that we need to keep an eye on," Dan said. "The National Weather Service has issued a warning for Puerto Rico. Looks like a storm that could surpass Maria is forming and it could be headed their way."

"That's terrible," the president lamented. "Dan, please have FEMA prepare an update for me. I want to be briefed on how they would respond if something does happen."

"Yes, Madam President."

"John and Lavinia, thank you for your time. Lavinia, when you have an update from China, please schedule time with Mr. Nolan. John, if you can call in as well. Dan can arrange for you to have a secure phone."

"It'd be my pleasure, Madam President. Bye, Lavinia; keep safe!"

"I will. Goodbye, everyone."

When they were alone, Barbara Anderson made a steeple with her fingers and leaned back in her chair. "Dan, I've been thinking about Puerto Rico." She paused and pursed her lips.

"Yes," Dan said, prompting her to continue.

"I've been thinking about them since the Weather Service briefed me on the start of storm season. I want to make sure that they're supported this time, not left out in the cold, so to speak."

"What did you have in mind?"

She looked up toward the ceiling of the Oval Office, at the plaster presidential seal in the center. "Can you get me a brief on the impact of Obama's debt relief for Puerto Rico? I want to understand how much of a difference it's made. Also, after Hurricane Maria, what was the infrastructure that was most vulnerable? I want to ensure that we have supplies available to replace them. We should begin moving them to Florida so the travel time isn't as long once the storm passes. Whether it's food or cell phone towers, we should know in advance what they need and have it ready to go."

"FEMA should include that in their brief, actually. I'll make sure they begin to mobilize whatever hardware is necessary. Let me check your schedule this afternoon and I'll get the director to share his plans."

"I want the people of Puerto Rico to know that we have their back, Dan. I want this time to be different."

"I understand, Madam President."

"I wish that the rest of America would focus on real dangers and not those being drummed up by our enemies. They're trying to divide us, Dan, and they're succeeding." She stood and began to pace behind the ornately carved Resolute Desk. "They're pitting Americans against fellow Americans. It's been getting worse and worse over the past five or six years, and I want it to stop on my watch. I need Lavinia to find out who is doing this and get me definitive proof." She stabbed at the air to emphasize her point. "Then we can begin to focus on the real problems."

"Like Puerto Rico?"

"Yes, like Puerto Rico. And income disparity and health care and racial equality."

"Those are all important objectives, Madam President. If I can caution you on one thing."

"Yes, Dan?"

"I caution you on making Puerto Rico *the* major issue.

We need to be seen as dealing with national security threats and protecting America. If the Chinese are behind this, then that has to be our number one focus."

"I'm not trying to make hay with the plight of Puerto Rico, Dan. This isn't about politics. They're part of our country and my responsibility is to protect all Americans."

"They're a territory, Madam President."

Barbara Anderson was staring out the window of the Oval Office, across the lawn. "Yes. Yes, they are."

Dan watched as Lawrence emerged from the shadows of the parking garage to join him. He wore all black, right down to his sneakers. Without a sound they once again entered the electrical room, engulfed in almost perfect blackness.

"So, any updates?"

"Not a lot yet, but I expect to have some news soon. The vice president has referred frequently to an old friend named Rasha Brown. They go way back, apparently. Brown is a life coach."

"What's a life coach?"

"I had the same question. According to her website, which is thin on substance by the way, she helps people set professional and personal goals and then plot a path to achieve them. Sounds like a rich person thing to me, but I don't judge."

Dan smirked. "So they met? Were you able to hear anything?"

"No, I wasn't able to hear anything. Not yet, anyway. Brown is impossible to track down; she's like a ghost. So I decided to follow the vice president's aide home to learn her routines. I arranged to bump into her the next day and was able to install some software on her phone that allows me to track where she is and to turn her microphone and camera on without her knowledge."

"That could be helpful."

"Yeah. Her aide is always with her. Next time MacQueen meets with Brown, I'll be able to get more details for you. If anyone knows what MacQueen's up to, it's Rasha Brown."

"Anything else? Any strange meetings?"

"No, not really. I used a blacked-out drone to drop a camera in the backyard of One Observatory Circle, and one in a tree out front. So we have surveillance of the front and rear entrances for about the next two weeks."

"Is there any danger of the Secret Service finding them?"

"My cameras are pretty discreet. I doubt they sweep the outside property for bugs. You'd have to be a certain level of paranoid to do that."

"Right, because what are the chances someone might go to that trouble?" Dan chuckled. "High, I suppose."

"How about you, anything that might help me?"

"No. She and the president don't talk a lot. I don't think they like each other very much. Mutual distrust, although the president downplays it. MacQueen was forced on the president by the party, pretty much. We've been pretty tied up with the shooting last week and the drive-by shooting of those two police officers."

"Oh, about that. When you and I last met, I got a call on my way home from a friend. He runs a community group in town. Nothing fancy. Some meetings at the local church; they run events for the youth to keep them busy. Educate them. That kind of thing. They have a Facebook page and a pretty active following. Well, after that shooting, a new group popped up online and started recruiting kids. Encouraging them to protest and cause trouble."

"There's been a lot of that lately."

"Yeah, so I used his son's account and tried to reach out to them, find out who they are."

"Did you have any luck?"

"Sort of. We had a little bit of back and forth that night. His English was off, like he was foreign. Hard to place where he was from. At first I thought they were a gang or something."

"What made you think that?"

"He said we couldn't meet up because I wasn't a Blood Dragon. Then he cut off communication."

Dan felt beads of sweat break out over his entire body. In the darkness he grabbed Lawrence's arm. "What did you say?"

"That he couldn't meet me because I wasn't a Blood Dragon."

"I need to meet your friend."

ELEVEN

Lavinia looked around as she and Jacob exited the taxi, and she couldn't help but wonder if they were in the right place. It was difficult to tell if the buildings had been defaced with graffiti or if it was purposeful art. The paint on the buildings appeared to be old and peeling, but upon closer inspection, Lavinia wondered if it was meant to be that way.

"I'm not sure if I would describe this place as decrepit or artistic."

Jacob's head was on a swivel, taking in the complex paintings and sculptures that could just as easily be mistaken for trash someone had set out that had never been collected. He too looked unsure of what he was looking at. "I've been in Germany for four months and I've seen a lot of things, but nothing like this," he said. "I've been meaning to visit because it's one of those places everyone mentions."

They passed through the alleyway, which featured wrought-iron bars over windows, cafe doors that had writing of all kinds scribbled all over them, and strange sculptures of grotesque beings. Finally they arrived at what appeared to be the entrance to the Monsterkabinett. There were four steps up a metal staircase littered with strange art and built to a post-apocalyptic building code. A small A-frame sign announced *Monster Kabinett Show In*: with the hands pointing to a broken analog clock set to eight thirty.

They both stood before the sign, unsure of what to do.

"Do we buy tickets?" Lavinia finally asked.

"I guess."

The two mounted the steps and walked along the porch to a doorway. Inside on the left was a restaurant of sorts, and to the right was the theater. They agreed to get something to eat and wait for their mystery guest. They'd arrived ten minutes early, so they both ordered a coffee and a pastry that looked nothing like a pastry, before taking a seat.

Right on time, a middle-aged man of Chinese descent wearing a jean jacket with the collar turned up entered. He had straight black hair that was long in the back. He looked around and recognized Jacob right away. He made his way over.

"Hi, Jacob. Lavinia." He took a seat without shaking their hands.

"Chen?" Jacob's eyes lit up. "Lavinia, this is Chen. He's a member of the Chaos Computer Club. He's a gifted hacker. Done some amazing work in deep learning."

"We shook hands; I remember," Lavinia said.

"I started out scripting. I loved to automate things. Anything someone could do, I could automate and have it done millions of times faster."

Jacob jumped in. "He built some of the first brute force cracking tools." He was leaning so far forward as he spoke, he almost tipped his chair.

"That was fun, but Jacob taught me how to be invisible online. That made it possible to apply my skills in all sorts of places."

"Lavinia works for the US government, by the way."

"All sorts of bad places," he added. "I just hack bad people."

Chen and Jacob held each other's gaze for a beat before they both broke into fits of laugher.

"I know who you are, Lavinia. Every hacker in Germany knows you're here."

"Because Jacob warned all of them?" Lavinia wasn't sure she was comfortable being the butt of a joke.

"No, your phone."

"My phone? What about my phone?"

"The American government wraps them with a really distinct security protocol. The moment you hit a German data network, every hacker in the country saw it and wanted to get into your device."

"And did they?"

"Is your battery charged? Oh wait, let me check." Chen pulled out his phone and stabbed at the screen. "Forty-three percent."

Lavinia hesitated. If she waited till later, the battery would drain and she'd never know if he was right. Pulling her phone out of her pocket, she turned it on. "Seventy-nine percent!" A smile broke across her face. "You two are jerks!"

Both men burst into fits of laugher.

"I'm sorry, I couldn't resist," Chen apologized.

"Why are you carrying both phones?" Jacob admonished her.

"Because the president might call me. Okay, let's get serious, guys. Chen, you invited us here. What's going on?"

"You brought up the Blood Dragons at C-Base yesterday. No one talks about them publicly. No one messes with them online."

"Why?" Lavinia asked.

"Because they're dangerous. They aren't ordinary hackers. They're part of the Chinese military. A fanatical and dangerous faction in the military that's loyal to one man and one man only."

"Let me guess. Liu Wei?"

Chen's jaw dropped. "How do you know of him?"

"His name's come up a lot lately."

"Don't go near them online. If they find out who you are, they'll destroy your life."

"She's flying there tomorrow," cut in Jacob.

Chen gawked. "If you value your life, you won't go. Remember what I said about your phone hitting the network? There, it will be true. They'll spot your American phone number and before you get your luggage they'll know who you are. The Blood Dragons won't take kindly to an American spy being in their house."

"I built her a phone and got her a clean laptop," Jacob said.

"That'll help. I mean, you're going to stand out, for obvious reasons. There are other Americans there, but they don't hunt down hackers. You'll be in instant danger if you do there what you did here in Germany."

"How do you know all this?" Lavinia asked. "How do you know so much about the Blood Dragons?"

Chen paused, then turned his head to the right and revealed the back of his left earlobe. On it was the tattoo of a red dragon, curled in on itself. "Because I was one."

Both Lavinia and Jacob gasped.

Conversation stopped while this news sank in. Lavinia asked Chen if he'd like a coffee and he nodded. She got out of her seat and crossed the little cafe to get him a drink. She returned and set a cup of coffee in front of him before taking a seat to his right. Jacob was across the table, leaning forward and watching Chen intently.

"So, tell me about the Blood Dragons," Lavinia coaxed.

"I was born in a remote part of China. We were poor but happy. We didn't have any modern conveniences, but of course we didn't know what we were missing. Blissfully ignorant of what people call the civilized world. One day a convoy of military Jeeps rolled into our village. Soldiers armed to the teeth were suddenly everywhere and then the door of one of the Jeeps opened and this man got out."

"General Liu Wei?"

"Yes. He got out of the Jeep and he seemed larger than life. He was taller than everyone else and to a ten-year-old like me, he seemed a giant. They rounded up all the boys in the village and inspected us. The ones deemed acceptable they took."

"Your parents didn't try to stop them?" Lavinia asked, her eyes wide.

"One woman tried to keep a soldier from taking her son and she was shot dead right there. What could my parents do?"

Jacob shook his head. "Man, I'm so sorry. I never knew."

"What happened next?" asked Lavinia.

"We were taken to a camp in the jungle. I was too young to understand what was going on. They began training us to handle weapons, but they couldn't keep me away from their computers. I'd never seen one before; I was mesmerized. One of their soldiers took a liking to me and pretty soon I was the resident techie."

"They had a tech department in the jungle? What did they use computers for?"

"The Chinese military were on the cutting edge of hacking. Light years ahead of anyone else in the world. The foundation of my hacking skills was learned in the Chinese countryside."

"How long did you stay? Weren't you part of the government's military?"

"It wasn't a question of staying. More of escape. I was there for five years. They told us that we were an elite arm of the military, but we weren't paid a salary. Child soldiers are illegal in China, but Liu Wei had total control of the military. He was building his own private army off the books. We were really hostages, not government soldiers. I mean, for many of the boys taken it was an improved life-style and a sense of purpose, but I missed my family and wanted to get back."

"How did you get out?" Lavinia gripped the edge of the table with both hands. Her eyes were focused on him.

A smile snuck across Chen's lips. "I wrote some code that overclocked the CPU on their main server so the fans would go on full, then suddenly stop. Then once in a while it'd force a random reboot."

"You made it look like the servers were failing?" Jacob slapped the table. "You hacked your way out! That's brilliant!"

The smile was impossible to miss now. "I volunteered to make the trek into town to steal a new server from a government building. I asked them if I could bring one of the young soldiers with me. So I brought along a young boy. He was probably ten. We broke into an office building and I stole one of their servers. I found a petty cash drawer in the office and I used the money to bribe the boy to tell them that we were caught and I was killed while he managed to escape."

"Wow." Jacob slapped the table again. "My life is boring compared to yours." He shifted in his seat.

"It wasn't that exciting, to be honest. It was really hard. When I escaped I had nothing. I starved for a time. Eventually, I hopped a train and traveled to Beijing. At first I found work in a computer repair shop. The owner was a man who had never married. After a while he took me in and raised me. When he died I traveled for a while, and then I settled down here. Germany has the most vibrant hacker community in the world. It's an easy place to feel at home."

"That's an incredible story." Lavinia put a hand on his. "What can you tell me about the Blood Dragons? What do I need to know?"

"You need to know that you have to avoid them if you want to stay alive." He pulled his hand away.

Lavinia sat up straight in her seat.

"I'm sorry, I don't mean to be defensive. But you have to understand that I was just a kid. Some of the things I saw were—well, hard to describe. Beyond words."

Lavinia pursed her lips. "Did you ever see your family again?"

Chen averted his gaze. After a long pause he replied, "Beijing wasn't my first stop. I went home first."

"What did you find?" Her voice was a whisper.

"Nothing. There was no one left. The entire village was empty. It was like everyone just stood up and left all of a sudden. Food in homes had long since rotted away. There were the remains of meals on tables that families never enjoyed. I went to the next village and they told me what happened."

Chen drew in a deep breath, held it, and exhaled. "After they took us away, a bunch of the soldiers rounded up the entire village and took them out to the fields. Then they shot everyone. No witnesses left behind."

Lavinia gasped and Jacob's jaw dropped.

"I'm so sorry," Lavinia said slowly. She put a hand on Chen's fist. He didn't resist this time.

"The Chinese government has done amazing things over the past forty years." Chen set his jaw, clenching his hand on the table. "There are a lot of great people in the government, but Liu Wei is a cancer lying in wait. He just became vice president and is more powerful than ever."

"He's just one man." Lavinia shook her head. She thought back to the terrorists she and Jacob had faced not so long ago. This situation couldn't be worse.

"Lavinia, I don't know you, but you seem like a good person. On the lives of my parents and sisters, don't get involved with these people. You can't achieve anything."

"Can't is a strong word."

"They have no rules. You do."

A chill ran down Lavinia's spine.

Jacob turned his gaze to Lavinia. "I'm going with you to China."

Lavinia met his gaze. After a moment, she nodded.

TWELVE

Lawrence spun the wheel of his Oldsmobile and accelerated smoothly out of the turn. He checked that the iPhone was secured in front of the air vent on his dash, and followed the directions to a secluded two-story home. Gliding past, he went to the end of the street and turned right. Cruising the neighborhood, he searched for a good place to park where no one would call the police to report a suspicious vehicle. An African American man sitting in a parked car in a rich white neighborhood might attract attention, Lawrence thought wryly.

Circling around, he drove past the building again and went left at the end of the street. The road continued for a hundred yards and then things changed. The ground had been cleared for a new development. The only thing finished was a freshly-paved asphalt road with dirt on either side. Streetlights were in place but weren't hooked up yet and four orange cones blocked the road. Lawrence maneuvered his Oldsmobile onto the dirt shoulder and drove around the cones.

His headlights broke the inky blackness as he crawled

along, trying to find his way to the back of the target home. He lost track of where he was in relation to the home he was to surveil, so Lawrence stopped and shut down his car. Turning off the overhead light, he opened the door and went to his trunk. He removed his drone, placed it on the ground, and grasped the controller.

When he flicked a switch the rotors spun to life and the small craft took off in a cloud of fine dirt. Lawrence turned on the night mode camera and navigated a few hundred feet up. After he got his bearings he realized that he needed to go three houses farther. His car was all but invisible where it was, so he set out on foot, piloting the drone and landing it on the roof of the house across the street from his target.

A pair of yellow Caterpillar backhoes were parked in what would one day be the driveway of a home. He slipped off his backpack and climbed into the open-air cab. The yellow-framed cage offered a bit of protection from prying eyes. Surveying the property, Lawrence was offered a perfect view of the back of the target house. The lower level was obscured by a wooden fence, but he could see the second story clearly.

Sitting back, Lawrence unfolded the iPad keyboard case and plugged the device into a backup battery. He placed it on the dash in front of him and then rummaged through his backpack for his phone. Turning it on, he popped his wireless headphones into his ears. He reached over to the iPad and turned on the app that streamed HD video from his drone.

Leaning back in his seat, Lawrence settled in to wait.

It was an hour and at least four false alarms before a woman dressed in black leather pulled a motorcycle into the driveway of the Airbnb. She kicked her leg back and dismounted, sliding the kickstand into position in one smooth motion.

Peeling off her riding gloves, she made her way to the front door of the Airbnb and entered. Her helmet was still on as she closed the door.

That is the elusive Rasha Brown, Lawrence thought. The vice president and her aide must have arrived before he did, because according to the aide's cell phone location software, she was already in the house when Lawrence got there. The two almost always traveled together. The lack of Secret Service detail meant that the vice president had indeed been able to give her security team the slip. How on earth that was possible, he didn't know.

Reaching for his phone, Lawrence opened an app and selected the aide's phone. He once again enabled the microphone on her Android phone with the swipe of a thumb.

He closed his eyes and listened. The app would drain her battery relatively quickly, unless it happened to be plugged in. He wanted to make sure he only had her microphone on if something important was going on.

Olivia MacQueen's voice filled his headphones. "Melanie, why don't you go in the living room and watch television." There was a pause. "Yes, Madam Vice President," she said.

There was some scuffling as Melanie left the room. Lawrence held his breath, hoping that the girl didn't take her phone with her.

"Cut that crap out," the vice president's familiar voice came across the wire. "Being vice president to a healthy fifty-year-old woman isn't an achievement, it's a sentence. I'm suffocating under that bitch."

"Remember, Olivia, it's a process. You're setting yourself up for the next step. Better things are to come. You're immensely popular amongst both Democrats and Republicans. The president won by the narrowest of margins, and many would say you were the one who swung the balance."

"I'm just wasting my time. I have things to achieve. I don't have time to play second fiddle to her."

"Now, now," soothed an unfamiliar voice.

Lawrence leaned forward in his seat. He had no idea who was speaking now.

"You know that we have a plan, Olivia dear."

"Is that you, Cathy?" Rasha asked.

"Yes, dear. Now, Olivia. You must be patient," she chided. "A crocodile captures its prey by lying in wait until the time is right. But he prepares himself first by finding the perfect hiding spot. You're in your spot now, my dear."

"What's your plan?" asked Rasha.

"We have a meeting at the United Nations next week with the Speaker of the House and the Chinese vice president."

"What for?"

"The goal is to replace the president by..."

There was a burst of static and the sound went dead. Lawrence tapped his headphones a few times. Grabbing his phone, he did a hard reboot. He stared at the screen, willing it to finish its boot-up routine. Quickly entering his passcode, he reopened the spying app and turned the microphone on the aide's phone on once again.

"...tension in the South China Sea. She'll focus on her domestic agenda because she doesn't understand foreign policy, and it'll further alienate her."

"Do you think that'll be enough to get the Cabinet on board?" The vice president was curt.

"Yes, dear. Trust me. We need to..."

The voices disappeared again. *Are you kidding me?*

Lawrence repeated the reboot process, but the aide's phone didn't respond. He went through the process again, and finally picked their voices back up.

"The meeting at the United Nations is the key, dear. Are you sure you can trust the Speaker of the House?"

The vice president laughed. "Yeah, we're covered there."

"That's it, then," Rasha concluded.

"That's it," Olivia MacQueen agreed.

"Make sure you're ready for the meeting," the motherly voice urged. "You only have one chance at this, or you'll be waiting seven and a half years."

One by one the lights in each room were turned off. He looked back at his iPad as the front door opened. The motorcyclist was back. She was accompanied by the aide. The woman in black mounted her bike, revved the engine, and disappeared into the night.

The aide waved as the motorcycle disappeared. Lawrence watched the motorcycle go, and by the time he turned his attention back to the house the aide had slipped behind the wheel of the car and was backing out.

He cursed himself for not seeing the VP get in the car. But there was just the one vehicle in the driveway and they always traveled together, so she must have also left.

After a twenty minute wait with no sign of activity, Lawrence approached the fence at the rear of the property. Peering between the fence boards, he gazed at the back of the house.

He was wary, as he'd heard three distinct voices in the house in addition to the aide, but he thought only three people had left. Someone must still be in the house.

Scaling the fence like a cat, he was over it in seconds.

He dropped to the ground, fell to a crouch, and pricked his ears. Silence.

Stealing to the back door, he stayed low while crossing the yard and crouched beside the doorknob. He peered through the bottom of the nearest window, scanning the room for movement.

Nothing.

Reaching into his back pocket, he removed his lockpick set. It took him a few moments to pop the consumer lock. Sliding the door open an inch at a time, he braced himself for squeaks. Luck was on his side. The door opened on well-oiled hinges. After a momentary pause, he slipped through the door and closed it behind him without a sound.

Lawrence found himself in a darkened kitchen. Staying low, he searched the first floor room by room.

Empty.

Turning on his phone's flashlight, he searched each room with care, but there was nothing out of place. The house looked unoccupied. He made his way up the stairs, easing his way up one step at a time, testing for creaky steps. He found three empty bedrooms and two bathrooms upstairs.

Standing erect, he turned all the lights on upstairs and searched each room thoroughly. The beds were all made, awaiting guests. The hand towels in the bathrooms were all dry.

Heading back downstairs, he went to the refrigerator. Empty. The dishwasher and sink were both empty and dry.

With a clue nowhere to be found, Lawrence stood in the dark with his hands on his hips. They'd rented an entire house for a twenty-minute conversation. Odd. And who was the third woman and how had she left the house? Had he missed both women traveling with the aide? His drone would have stored the video, assuming he hadn't used up his allotment of storage in the cloud.

Lawrence retraced his steps to the backyard. Pulling the door closed behind him, he heard the *click* as it locked. He crossed the yard and hopped the wooden fence. Landing in a crouch, he was about to stand up and head to his car when there was a spitting sound in the distance. Lawrence jerked when the fence board next to him splintered.

THIRTEEN

It was nerd prom for rocket scientists. The entire staff of OrbitTracker was gathered in the Radar Room, and the chatter made it hard to hear yourself think. Bowls full of chips and popcorn were on every surface, and a folding table at the back of the room was stacked with pizza boxes.

Lundi Steinsson held a plastic cup full of beer as he stood in a small group including two of the company's owners.

"SpaceX has a launch next month to take supplies to the International Space Station," one of the men commented.

"No Moon mission," another observed.

"The Chinese space program has grown by leaps and bounds. They say they'll put the first Chinese person on the Moon within ten years."

"Yeah, and NASA can't get out of low Earth orbit. How many experiments can they possibly run on the space station? We had Skylab in the 1970s. We aren't progressing."

"NASA needs to step it up and take us to Mars."

Lundi pointed to the screen. "There she is."

The men gawked.

"She's huge!" said one.

"Turn up the volume," one of the owners commanded.

The news commentator came on: "Now that the Chinese government has given permission to begin our video feed, we in the West are getting our first view of this magnificent rocket ship, the *Tao 1*. She stands four hundred and ninety feet tall, seventy-five feet in diameter, and can carry a payload of up to five hundred and fifty tons. The rocket is carrying a lunar lander that will drop down to the surface much like the US landers *Spirit* and *Opportunity* on Mars. The landers will set on the dark side of the Moon, which ironically gets two solid weeks of sun every month."

"That ship is much bigger than the rockets that carried our Mars probes."

"It's probably carrying a military satellite."

"To the Moon? To attack...what, Neil Armstrong's footprint?"

"Oh, countdown has started!"

The entire room joined in for the final countdown with the commentator.

"Four, three, two, one, blast off!"

The room exploded with a round of cheers as the craft lifted off and shot into the blue sky.

The control center at Chinese Space Command was silent as scientists monitored the progress of the most ambitious space project in the country's history.

The director of Mission Control sat in a special chair in the middle of the theater-style control room. He stared unblinking at the video feed until the rocket had left Earth's atmosphere. Then he stood with military precision, spun on his heel, and headed up the theater to a conference room at the top. Two scientists noticed his move and followed.

The three men gathered around a computer screen in the conference room.

"The takeoff was flawless."

"As expected," the director snapped. "I want to review the landing sequence."

One of the scientists touched a screen and tapped through a menu till he found what he was looking for. An interactive model of the spacecraft appeared.

"We'll separate from the second stage of the rocket here," he tapped the screen, "which will put us in orbit with the mother satellite and the lander. Here we'll jettison the exterior panels, which will expose the lander. Once we initiate the break, the lander will be piloted to the surface. The lander has two stages. The rover is on the ground level; the top level houses the Nest."

"It's imperative that the landing is gentle enough that there is no damage to the Nest."

"It's Chinese designed and built, sir. It will work flawlessly."

The director nodded his approval. He reached up and rubbed his left ear. The tattoo of a red dragon was barely visible on the back of his lobe.

FOURTEEN

Lawrence turned to his left, away from where he thought the shot came from. Running in the dark was difficult, given the uneven terrain of the unfinished construction site. A bullet kicked up dirt in front of him to his left. The sound of an electric motorcycle engine screaming behind him forced a burst of adrenaline through his veins.

As the sound of the bike got closer, Lawrence looked to his left, at the row of fenced backyards. Two houses up was an inexpensive, low-lying wire fence. Pumping his legs and arms like an Olympian, Lawrence vaulted himself over the fence, hitting the ground on the other side in full stride. He cut through the yard and made a beeline for the street.

Reaching into his pocket, he pulled out his phone and glanced at the screen as he sprinted. He activated his drone and set it to "follow" mode.

Lawrence's legs burned. He hadn't sprinted since college. He was a distance runner now and his body was screaming in protest at the sudden burst of anaerobic activity.

The sound of the motorcycle slipping in behind him

broke the stillness of the night. The windshield of a car parked beside him spiderwebbed as the motorcyclist let off another shot.

Lawrence made an abrupt cut to his left and lurched across the street. Running blindly between two houses, he cut through the backyard, hopped a fence, and continued on between two more houses to the next street. He came to a stop, panting, in the middle of the road.

The headlight of the motorcycle came into view, lighting him up. He faced the rider directly, standing like a deer transfixed by the headlights of a car. The bike passed under a streetlamp, its engine screaming, and the rider extended a gun.

With the swipe of Lawrence's thumb across the screen of the phone in his hand, his drone dive-bombed, hitting the rider right in the mask and throwing her off balance. She flew off her bike and skidded along the road, while the motorcycle tumbled like an out of control football.

Lawrence stood transfixed as the woman skidded to a stop, lying prone on the road. She didn't move.

The motorcycle had come to rest on the front lawn of a home to his left. There was a moment of total silence and then the battery burst into flame, waking him from his stupor.

His body newly inspired, Lawrence broke into a run, clearing the two blocks back to his car in record time. He fired up the engine, dispensed with the paved road, and roared across the flattened earth, throwing up clouds of dust as he went.

The woman in black pushed herself up onto her elbows and

shook her head, her snug helmet holding tight. Getting up on her knees, she glanced over at her motorcycle, which lay wrecked on the front lawn of a two-story McMansion. She grimaced.

The smell of smoke wafted inside her helmet as she stood and started to walk down the road. She unzipped her black leather jacket and reached inside for her phone.

The sound of screeching tires made her spin. The Oldsmobile came into view as it rounded the corner on the way out of the subdivision. Raising her phone, she snapped a series of photos in quick succession of the back of the car.

FIFTEEN

Given the volume of people that had to go through Chinese customs, Lavinia was impressed with the efficiency. She noted the seemingly endless number of video cameras mounted on virtually any surface that would support one. Jacob had educated her on the plane about the surveillance state that China was building. It was put in place partly to support a newly instituted citizen rating system. Using facial recognition, the government could track every person's movements in any city. If someone jaywalked, the software would identify who did it and decrement their citizen score accordingly. Litter? You're downgraded. It made the NSA's activities pale in comparison.

The two passed through a pair of sliding doors with their luggage in tow. Jacob always wore black jeans and a black long-sleeve dress shirt, so his luggage was mostly electronic equipment. Lavinia was the opposite.

"Who are we meeting again?" Jacob's nose was buried in his phone.

"Tungya Kato. He's the Chinese president's most trusted ally. Intelligence reports say that he's been with the president since he entered politics," Lavinia said. "He goes by the short-form Tung."

"Tung. I can remember that." Jacob grabbed her arm and pointed. "Hey, look at that."

"I don't see anything."

"Guy in the gray suit. He's holding a sign with your name on it."

Lavinia recognized him from the file photo. "I see him." She led them through the crowd. The man was almost six feet tall, about Jacob's height. He was unusually tall compared to the other local men around them. He looked young, but Lavinia knew he was fifty-five years old.

"Tung," Lavinia said with a smile. "This is my colleague, Jacob."

"Miss Lavinia, and guest." He bowed slightly.

Lavinia and Jacob parroted his move.

"Welcome to China. I trust that your travels were smooth."

"A little tiring, but yes, thank you."

"Please, this way." Tung motioned for them to follow him. He led them through a parking structure to a Chinese-model sedan that could have been a knockoff of an Audi. They all piled in and he whisked them away.

"Is this your first time in China, Miss Lavinia?"

"Yes, it is. Everything seems very organized here," she observed, looking out the window. It felt similar to being in New York City, except that most of the skyscrapers were newer and the sidewalks pristine. She wondered if Tung was taking her along a route that was guaranteed to give her the best impression of the city.

"This is the new society. Created by China for China. Tell me, Miss Lavinia, what brings you here?"

"To be honest, the president sent me to try to find the source of online attacks against her."

"Surely you don't believe that the Chinese government would engage in such activities."

"I'm just here to find the truth, Tung."

"Then I wish you luck with your endeavor." His eyes remained on the road, so Lavinia couldn't search them to adjudicate him.

"How long have you known the president?" she asked.

"Fifty years."

"So, since you were children?"

"We were neighbors growing up." A smile spread across his face as he spoke about the past. "He was different than the other children. Inquisitive and insatiable. He would question his teachers till they could no longer answer his questions. Then he would ask them why they didn't know."

Lavinia smiled. "A prodigy."

"Prodigy. Yes. He was promoted through the school system and indoctrinated in the Party. A master pupil, and everyone knew it was a matter of time before he rose to lead China."

"And he brought you with him? His most trusted childhood friend?"

"Yes, he did." Tung turned to hold Lavinia's gaze for a moment. "I am fiercely loyal to him and would protect him with my own body."

"He's lucky to have such a trusted ally. We should all be so lucky."

Tung turned his gaze back to the road. "What about you? Who do you serve?"

"I serve my country."

"Not the Constitution? Americans love to say they serve the Constitution."

"I defend the Constitution; I don't serve it. I'm loyal to my country."

"And your president?"

"President Anderson is a great leader, yes. I'm loyal to her, after country."

"I love the word 'loyalty.' It forces people to commit their name to something. But you can only evaluate their loyalty when things go wrong — based on how they react, you can judge who they are by those actions. To claim loyalty is one thing. To demonstrate it is another."

Lavinia wasn't sure where the conversation was going. Just idle philosophical banter? Or was there a message?

"This is your hotel." He pulled into the drop-off area at the front door. "Can I interest you in dinner, or are you tired from your flight?"

Lavinia glanced at Jacob.

"I'm exhausted, to be honest," he said. "I think I'm going to head to my room to sleep."

Lavinia regarded Tung. "I'm up for dinner, if you don't mind waiting for me to check in to my room and put my bags away."

"It would be my honor."

Lavinia and Jacob checked in and rode up in the elevator together.

"So what do you think?" Lavinia asked.

"He says a lot without saying a lot."

"Yeah, I was thinking the same thing. You going to bed?"

"Hell, no. I'm going to set up my command center."

"With the Radio Shack store you packed?" She snorted. "I thought the guy at customs was never going to let you through."

Jacob grinned.

The two went to their rooms. Lavinia dropped off her bags, brushed her teeth, and headed back to the lobby.

"Hi Tung, I'm ready."

Tung bowed, then spun on his heel to lead her back to his car. He held the door open for her, then got in behind the wheel and navigated his vehicle to the highway. He drove with the needle pinned to the speed limit.

"In the United States people aren't so religious about the speed limit."

"Obeying the speed limit is our social responsibility. It's what all good citizens do."

At first the two shared polite conversation on the drive to the restaurant, before Tung began to talk politics. For an American it was taboo to talk politics with a stranger.

"The Chinese political system proved resilient over the past seventy years. We've lifted 850 million people out of extreme poverty since 1981," he said.

Lavinia thought back to the brief she'd read on her flight. She recalled the poverty rate being reduced from eighty-eight percent to under one percent. That achievement, however, was misleading, as the definition of extreme poverty was living off less than the equivalent of $1.90 US a day. Almost sixty percent of the population lived off of between $2.00 and $10.00 US a day. In comparison, only three and a half percent of Americans were in the same daily spending bracket. Given China's current population of almost 1.4 billion people, they had 13 million living on less than $2.00 a day.

"China's economic growth over the past thirty years has averaged just over nine percent, which is a pretty impressive run," she acknowledged. "It's been fueled by a lot of debt, though. Some say that's a big risk for China's economy."

Tung smiled. "Last I checked, the United States has more than thirty percent of the world's debt."

"And you own most of it," Lavinia replied, laughing. "I'm not going to debate you on economics. I'm a spy, remember?"

He pointed through the front windshield. "That's our restaurant there."

They were in an old part of Beijing. The entire building was painted red with yellow trim and boasted impressive woodwork with a curved, sloping roofline. Inside, the traditional restaurant featured ornate tables and chairs adorned with matching carvings.

Their meal was served banquet style. Bowls of rice, fish, and vegetables were all laid out for them to share. Lavinia enjoyed the foreign cuisine. She'd never tried authentic Chinese food before, and the meal was incredible.

"Tell me about President Xiu Ying Zhang." Lavinia wiped her fingers in a cloth soaked in lime juice. "What should I know about him that I wouldn't learn on CNN?"

"There is nothing you've learned about him on CNN that is accurate." Tung smiled. He folded his hands in his lap. "Xiu Ying Zhang is determined to continue the vision of former President Xi Jing Ping. China, with its population of over a billion people, is four times the size of the United States. So the Communist Party believes the Chinese economy should be four times the size of the United States'."

"And your military four times the size?"

Tung laughed, spreading his arms wide. "Where would we put it all? The United States is determined to stop China from achieving its rightful place in the world order. This is clear. The sanctions your former president put on China slowed down what is inevitable, but did not stop it."

"Some people see that as a threat to the United States."

"It is not a threat — rather, it does not need to be. Our societies can coexist with mutual respect. But respect is not earned staring at the barrel of a gun — or rather, a trade war."

"I know that period in our countries' relationship was rocky, but we have a trade deal in place now."

"Your former president's actions did lasting damage, for sure. American companies had to adapt their supply chain during the protracted trade war, and it will take time to recover. However, there is a difference in our way of thinking. Americans look for an instant win. Something they can send out on Twitter to make it look like they've won a battle. But in China, our wars are fought over centuries. We are patient, and we get what we want because what we want doesn't change every time our government does. That is the central strength of the one-party system."

Lavinia thought about that. It was true that in their first term, a president always focused on getting enough policy wins to get reelected. Then the moment they won a second term they were a lame duck and all they could hope for was to find a way to secure their legacy. The fixed term presidency was a byproduct of the concerns of America's founders and their patent dislike for the monarchy. Like every system, it had its good points and its weaknesses. However, she felt that with a one-party system, the people never had a choice.

They were interrupted as the waitress brought their second course. She placed a series of round wooden containers with wicker tops on the table, along with a wooden platter loaded with flatbread and greens. Tung removed the lids and set them aside. Lavinia noticed the age spots on his hands as he scooped a helping of rice with shrimp onto her their plates.

"What kind of meat is that?"

"Peking duck," he replied, his eyes glowing. "It's fabulous."

The kind man continued to portion out the meal until their plates were full. "Please enjoy."

Lavinia picked up the chopsticks, deciding to give them a try. She studied the way Tung operated them before attempting to eat. "What does Xiu Ying Zhang think of President Anderson?"

"They've met just once, at the United Nations. He's intrigued by her, but it seems as if, in her first year at least, international relations will not be a priority."

"She's had a lot going on domestically, as I'm sure you're aware."

Tung nodded, his gaze fixed on her. "So, your embassy asked me to be your guide. Tell me, how can I help you?"

"What can you tell me about the Blood Dragons?"

For the slightest moment the man's eyes went wide, but he regained his composure. "I've never heard of them. Tell me what you know, and maybe it'll jog my memory."

"Not much. I know they're a military group that has expertise in hacking and some of them might be involved in the social media attacks we're seeing stateside. I was hoping to set up a meeting."

"I'm not aware of this group, but I urge you to be careful when engaging with unofficial elements."

"Careful?"

"Yes, careful."

Lavinia decided to try another tack. "My condolences on the assassination of your vice president. The country must have been shocked."

"He was a great loss to the Communist Party. A great mind, no doubt."

"Have they found the people behind the assassination?"

"Not yet. The new vice president has made this his highest priority. The nation is outraged and their rage must be served."

"I don't know a lot about the new vice president, Liu Wei. He's a military legend, from what I understand."

"Yes, he grew up in a military family. He rose through the ranks and distinguished himself. He's credited with rebuilding our forces post-World War II. Within the military he's revered. Would you like to meet him?"

"I'd like that very much," Lavinia said.

"There's a dinner on Friday evening. I'll see that you're invited."

"Thank you, I appreciate that. Will the president be there?"

"Yes, it's our equivalent to a state dinner. The president actually asked me to invite you. He wants to meet you."

Her eyebrows rose a little in surprise. "Why would he be interested in meeting me? I'm not a politician. No one special."

"You are a friend loyal to the president. That makes you special."

Lavinia enjoyed the rest of their meal together and the drive back to her hotel was uneventful. Tung was easy to like and she felt herself wanting to trust him. Maybe that was why he'd been assigned to greet her. She knew she'd better keep her guard up.

Lavinia waved to Tung as he pulled away from the hotel.

The lobby design seemed to be inspired by an Antarctic desert. White ceilings, walls, curtains, and floors were broken only by a bronze-colored reception desk and a few matching planters. The result was majestic. She made her way to the bank of elevators and selected Jacob's floor. When she reached his door she rapped three times.

"Before you may be allowed to pass through this doorway, you must answer these questions three."

"Jacob, seriously?"

"What is your name?"

"You know my name. It's Lavinia."

"What is your quest?"

"I seek the counsel of the great and powerful Disruptor."

"What is your favorite color?"

"Red."

"You may proceed." Jacob opened the door to let her in. Lavinia punched him on the shoulder as she entered.

"How was dinner? Did you bring me leftovers?"

Lavinia shook her head as she passed him. "Remind me why I brought you." He started to respond but she cut him off. "Never mind. Dinner was good."

"Did you learn anything?"

"What is all this?" Lavinia surveyed the room, her hands on her hips and her mouth agape. Jacob had assembled a satellite dish the size of a dinner plate and had it pointed through his window. There were computers and iPads set up on multiple surfaces and little boxes with antennas pointing in different directions."

"Want me to set WiFi up on your laptop?"

"WiFi is included in my room."

"Yeah, but it's more satisfying if you steal it."

Lavinia laughed. "The satellite dish?"

"Bringing my disruptor skills to China. I've never done it on their soil before. I've uploaded video to the public

CCTC cameras of the president jaywalking to take down his citizen score."

"Don't get arrested. Actually, you can get arrested, but don't get me arrested."

"Okay, come on, tell me what you learned."

Lavinia sat down on the edge of his bed. "Not a lot. He was really guarded. I think he's evaluating whether or not he can trust me. I mentioned the Blood Dragons to him and I could tell he knew the reference but he played dumb."

"Why do you think that is?"

"I don't know for sure. Either he's connected to them or he's afraid of them. He did invite me to a government dinner on Friday night. I'll get to meet the president, and the new vice president will be there, so I'll get a chance to meet him as well."

"If he's connected to the Blood Dragons, why would he introduce you to Liu Wei? Based on what Chen told us, the guy's dangerous."

"You could interpret it two ways, I suppose. Either he's also connected to them and he wants Liu Wei to meet me so they can decide if I'm a risk, or he's afraid of them and this is his way of helping me while he's deciding if he should trust me."

"This sounds dangerous, Lavinia."

"Yeah, it could be. I'll have to stop by the embassy in the morning to get a gun."

"Won't do you much good at a government dinner if you're wearing a dress."

She rolled her eyes. "I'm an American woman, Jacob. I could conceal and carry in a negligee."

Jacob raised an eyebrow.

Tung regarded his dinner companion the way he did all Americans, with suspicion. Yet she appeared forthright and transparent, like an honest broker. He found himself wanting to trust her, but held back. She'd caught him off guard by mentioning the Blood Dragons. Created by Liu Wei, they bordered on being a secret society within the Chinese military. The president feared them, and for good reason. Tung believed they were behind the assassination of the former vice president, but he lacked proof.

Perhaps Lavinia could help him find evidence. Perhaps she could become a trusted ally. A rare commodity in Chinese political circles...an American you could trust.

SIXTEEN

Dan rang the bell and took a step back from the door. He glanced around the partially closed-in porch, noting the peeled paint. A basketball parked on the opening of a size fourteen athletic shoe. A baseball bat and tennis ball lay next to an under-inflated football. Your average American home. Obsessed with sports.

The neighborhood was definitely below middle class, but not quite poor. He could see pride in the American flags that adorned almost every home, even if the occupants couldn't afford to maintain the exterior. There was still pride.

A scraping sound caught his attention and the door was pulled open wide. A tall African American man poked his head out, his face long and thin. A graying beard hugged his jawbone, hinting at his age but giving him a dignified look. "You must be Lawrence's friend," the man said.

"I'm glad he considers me a friend." Dan smiled.

"Come on in."

Dan stepped inside, careful to remove his shoes. He cringed to see a hole had formed at the big toe on his right foot. Sliding his foot backward with his sole firmly on the ground, he tried to slide his sock down to hide it.

From the kitchen Lawrence appeared, wearing the larger than life smile that always seemed to dominate his face. "Dan the man! Thanks for coming." The two embraced like old friends seeing each other for the first time in years. "This is my good friend, Henry."

The two shook hands. After a beat, Dan spoke up. "I don't want to take too much of your time. I was hoping you could show me the Facebook account you found."

Henry motioned with his arm for Dan to go downstairs. "Right down here, Dan. Our computer is on the table in the corner of the living room."

The basement was finished with panel board that had been painted white to brighten it up. The computer was set up on an old kitchen table that had been relegated to the basement when the family had bought an upgrade. A band of indented steel ran around the edge of the table, and the top was white with the image of a bowl of fruit covering much of the surface.

Henry passed him and sat down at the machine. "I'm no computer wizard, but this here is where we maintain our community Facebook account. We run programs for the neighborhood kids. All volunteer based, you see."

Dan leaned forward with his hands clasped behind him and watched.

"We came across this Facebook page. It was advertising a protest after that shooting twelve days ago. They were trying to act local, but things didn't add up." Henry brought up a page that featured a photo of the boy a police officer had shot. As he scrolled down, there were images with sayings on them and text posts that supported a violent response to the shooting. There was a link to purchase a 3D printer and instructions on how to order liquid steel on the dark web.

"Can you show me the messages that you exchanged?"

Henry clicked in the top right-hand corner for the Messenger feature and a box opened up that contained the conversation, like a series of texts.

"Can I sit down?" Dan asked.

"Sure, be my guest." Henry stood to allow Dan to slide into the seat.

Dan read through the exchange. The person had tried repeatedly to convince Henry to buy a supply of liquid steel. Henry had pushed back, insisting they either meet or have a video call. It was clear that he was trying to find out if the person he was chatting with was truly from the African American community. The chat became more and more combative and culminated with the imposter's final message: *I don't meet people that aren't Blood Dragons.*

Opening a new window, Dan went to Google and created a new Gmail account with a fake name. He didn't want to share his real name and address with someone who might be a hacker. Jumping back to the Facebook page, Dan logged out and created a new account with his new fake name and email address. He navigated to the Facebook page for the suspect community organizer and entered a message.

I wanna buy some liquid steel. Like, a lot of it, if you know what I mean. Where can I score some? Dan tried to sound young and brash, although he honestly didn't know how young people talked these days. He added his new email address and hit *Send.*

"So you haven't heard from him since?" Dan looked away from the screen as he spoke.

"No, not a word. He stopped updating his page after we

challenged who he was. Although he did have the posts we made to his page deleted."

"This was really helpful, Henry; thank you. If he responds to you again, could you reach out to me?"

"At that email address you just created?"

"Yes, that'd work."

"Alright, then."

Dan thanked the men and made a hasty exit. Once outside, he hurried to his car and dropped into the driver's seat. With the door closed, he started the engine and stared out of the window. He was playing a dangerous game.

Richard placed his chipped MIT coffee mug back on his desk. He could order a new one online, but he'd bought that mug on move-in day for his first year of college. Nothing could replace it.

Turning his attention back to his computer, he reopened INTROS, which was short for Integrated Rocket Sizing Model. The software was written for NASA to design the appropriate sizing of the launch vehicle.

Looking at the notepad where he'd written down everything he could find on the Chinese rocket, he transcribed the information into the software. He took another sip of coffee as he watched the progress bar make its way across the screen. When it finally cleared and brought up the results, they confirmed what he'd got the first two times he'd run the model. There was no mistaking it. The Chinese rocket, which was unmanned, was an order of magnitude larger than it needed to be to carry even an advanced lander to the Moon.

Giving it some thought, Richard changed the inputs

around and executed a fresh analysis. When the computer displayed the results, he jotted down the maximum payload the rocket in use could carry.

Jumping over to his browser, he logged in to the portal for DARPA, the military organization that worked on advanced research projects. He searched the catalog for projects by weight and scanned the thumbnails. Nothing made sense. Changing his tack, he cleared the search criteria and entered a one-word search: *Moon*.

The screen cleared and one result came up, dated in 1959. *LBEBS*. The *Lunar-Based Earth Bombardment System*. It was an Air Force plan to establish a lunar base with nuclear missile silos that could hit a target within five miles.

The idea seemed crazy. Particularly with today's technology and understanding of the dangers of nuclear weapons. Were the Chinese going to install a nuclear missile base on the Moon?

Crazy.

His computer beeped to signal a new email. Switching to Outlook, he scanned his new messages. He'd been avoiding the *NASA Tip Box*, which his boss had punished him with. It was full of nonsense from pseudo scientists around the country who suggested ideas as crazy as a Moon-based nuke.

Scanning through the long list of outstanding messages, he replied to as many as he could right away. *Thank you for writing NASA, your feedback is invaluable...* Yada, yada, yada.

The first message to catch his interest was from a fellow NASA scientist. All four American satellites in orbit around the Moon had developed a blind spot when they passed around the dark side of the Moon. His first inclination was to write it off as some sort of solar flare, but that would last ten to twelve hours. When he read through the long message with more care, the scientist claimed that she had observed the behavior over a period of weeks.

Clicking on the *Forward* button, Richard assigned the question to a member of his team. "That one could be a valid concern," he mumbled as he hit *Send*.

He moved on to the next submitted tip. It came from a member of OrbitTracker. A respected NASA partner. An image and video was attached so Richard brought both up at the same time on separate screens. The image showed what looked like two satellites colliding. When he clicked *Play* on the video clip, it showed an animation.

It started with a large chunk of space debris in orbit. After a handful of seconds, a device came into view. It looked almost like a drone that you'd see a teenage boy flying so he could take video of the girl next door sunbathing, except that it was based in space. The drone had a long pipe in front of it. Suddenly the pipe opened up into four arms connected by some sort of webbing. The drone attached itself to the space debris and engaged a thruster on the back, which sent the two tumbling out of orbit and into the atmosphere.

Interesting. Someone had developed a method to try to clean up the space junk orbiting Earth. It was an expensive way to do it, given there were an estimated thirty-four thousand pieces of debris in orbit that were ten centimeters or larger. That number soared to 128 million if you considered objects less than a centimeter. Even small objects could take down a satellite or rocket if they hit one in the right place.

His thoughts turned back to the idea of the Moon base, suddenly connecting it to the blind spot developed by all

American satellites. Had the Chinese hacked their satellites so they could build some sort of military base on the Moon?

Richard shook his head. Surely he was going crazy.

Turning his attention back to the Inbox, he tried to concentrate on catching up on the tip line. But a thought nagged at him. What if there was something to this and he didn't tell anyone? Then he thought of September 11. Were there signs that people missed that could have prevented the tragedy?

Tapping the table with the end of his pen, Richard came up with the perfect person to confide in. He picked up his phone.

Dan jogged up the two flights to his apartment. He was puffing when he reached the top. *Desk jobs!* He placed his keys and wallet on the side table and made his way to the computer set up in the living room.

Opening Outlook, he created a new account and entered the credentials for the fake name he'd created for himself. It would make checking the Inbox easier by setting it up. The dialogue box showed that it was testing the connection for the inbound and outbound servers. Green checkmarks appeared and Dan hit the button that said *OK*. The dialogue box disappeared and his new Inbox appeared in the left-hand pane. He was about to close it down when the computer made a sound and a new email popped up.

Dan opened the email.

Hi, I'd be happy to hook you up. First I need to confirm that you aren't a police officer. Click the link to arrange a video call so I can verify your identity.

Dan hesitated. After a moment of thought, he forwarded the email to Lavinia.

Hi Lavinia, can you please forward this email to Jacob and see if he can tell me anything about the sender? They have a Facebook account where they're peddling 3D printers and liquid steel. Most disturbingly, though, someone running the page pretty much revealed themselves to be a Blood Dragon.

Dan hit *Send.*

SEVENTEEN

Driving the palms of his hands into his eyes, Jacob leaned his head back and let out a yawn. He stretched his arms out in front of him and glanced at the clock next to his bed. Three a.m.

Time for bed.

He finished typing an email to a woman from New Jersey who had clicked on a link in one of his phising emails. He'd gained access to her home computer and installed a key logger. From there he got access to her email and banking credentials. He wrote up his usual email for victims of his attacks, providing her with a description of how she had let him in, how it gave him access to her entire digital life, samples of her bank statement, and some texts she'd sent as proof that he was legit. Then he copied his standard paragraph about how to spot phishing campaigns, notes on the importance of using strong passwords to protect your digital life, and how to select them. He sent it from his friendly hacker account, pt3e@protonmail.com. It was short for "protect the third estate." Protonmail was his favorite email host. Based in Switzerland, they were like the email version of Swiss banking.

Jacob offered courses on internet security, but he'd long ago discovered that people learned best about its importance when they got hacked themselves. So he'd begun using common hacking techniques to hook people in and then take the opportunity to teach them without causing them actual harm. Most people wrote back to him, thanking him but wondering how they could trust that he still didn't have access. The odd person took it the wrong way.

He closed the rest of his applications, then checked his Inbox one last time. A single new message sat in his main Protonmail account. Lavinia had forwarded an email from the president's chief of staff. Jacob glanced at his pillow and grimaced. He selected the message.

Jacob, can you determine the sender's location?

Well, that would depend on how smart the sender was, he thought.

In Dan Nolan's message to Lavinia was a file attachment. Jacob read Dan's note and then opened the attachment.

Revealing the header information of the email, he scanned the jumble of text for the word "client" and found the sender's IP address right after it. Jumping to his browser, he went to whatismyipaddress.com and entered the code. Hangzhou.

Nice. Biggest city in the Zhejiang province. Over twenty-one million people.

Jacob glanced at his pillow again. Beckoning. He turned back to his screen with a frown, then continued to work to narrow down the location. Once he had the name of the internet service provider, he went to work trying to break in to their servers so he could search their logs.

He was lucky. Alibaba, the biggest internet company in Asia, didn't run the ISP. If they did, their security protocols would be strong.

The clock ticked forward while Jacob tapped away at his keyboard. With some help from Chen, he'd found his way in by 7:00 a.m. Searching the logs, he found the user. From there he located the user's business name and address.

According to Google, the Chinese company's name translated loosely to We Ship.

Original, Jacob thought.

Typing out the details, he replied to both Dan and Lavinia. He hit *Send*, snapped the laptop shut, and dove into his pillow while dragging the blanket over his head.

Sleep!

Lunch was the new breakfast for Jacob. He had to argue to get scrambled eggs and bacon from the menu, but the waiter relented on the promise of a big tip. Big, of course, was a relative term. He popped his laptop open and began tapping away at the keys.

"Do you ever look away from that thing?"

Jacob glanced up long enough to identify Lavinia towering over him.

"When I sleep. Although I'm waiting for Google to perfect the contact lens version of their Google Glasses product and then I can hack in my sleep."

Lavinia chuckled. "You never cease to amaze me, Jacob. Thanks for helping Dan with that email. I'm going to head down there to check it out, after the government event Tung invited me to."

"Do you want me to join you?"

"No, stay here in case I need your help. It could be dangerous."

"Yeah, danger isn't my thing. I got enough of that at the end of last year to last a lifetime. Seems to follow you around, doesn't it?"

"Lately, it does." She flipped her long brown hair over her shoulder and sat across the small table from him. "I'm going to get something to wear for tonight. I didn't exactly pack for a formal evening out in China. What about you? What are you up to today?"

"There's an electronics show in town this week. I'm going to check it out."

"How different for you."

"Yeah, it's like Christmas year-round in China for us nerds. There isn't another place in the world where new technology is this pervasive." He picked up his white linen napkin and dabbed his mouth. "You eating breakfast?"

"No, it's two o'clock in the afternoon."

Jacob glanced around, just now noticing there were no other patrons in the hotel restaurant.

"I just wanted to tell you that I'm going to go shopping and stop by the US embassy afterward. You know, to gear up."

"Gotcha. Want to meet up for dinner?"

She scrunched her face. "Jacob, I'm going to the government function tonight."

Jacob nodded. "Yes, tonight. Sorry, my days are a little fuzzy. I was up all night doing work for you."

A laugh escaped her lips again. "Thanks, Jacob. I'll see you."

"No, I'm done here. I'll go with you, just let me pay." He wrote a message on the back of the receipt, then left money to cover his bill.

"What are you writing?"

Jacob picked up the receipt. "For really tough stains on your shower curtain, try vinegar and water." He looked at her deadpan. "My tip."

"Please don't!"

He laughed. "I left money, too. Don't worry, I won't embarrass you."

The two left the restaurant together, took the elevator down to the lobby, then parted ways. Jacob pulled out his phone and checked the address for the electronics show.

He navigated the crowded streets, absorbing the unfamiliar smells and sights. While at six feet tall Jacob was slightly above average height in the United States, here he was a good half a foot taller than the average man in China. It was both good and bad. He could see above the crowd, but it also meant that he could be seen above the crowd.

He wasn't hiding from anyone in particular, but as a privacy advocate it was hard to be inconspicuous here.

Arriving at the expo, he was amazed at the size of the event. Rather than large expensive booths, the event was row upon row of tables with small vendors putting their goods on display. He saw a number of Apple iPhones that weren't made by Apple but still ran their OS.

There were many ingenious single function inventions on display. Tools to hack phone networks, a device that could listen in on a neighbor through a wall, but the one that captured his interest the most was a textile screen. It was a relatively heavy fabric that, when connected to a video signal, would transmit an image. The cloth was light gray and came in a sixty by ninety inch bolt. He imagined stringing a bunch of them together and hanging them in front of a building and making it look like something else entirely.

Jacob negotiated a fair price, along with the false promise that his company would be in touch with a bigger order. Slipping the folded bolts of fabric into his backpack, he continued on.

By the time he reached the far end of the room, vendors were beginning to wrap up for the day. A song had played moments before over an overhead speaker, and suddenly everyone was pulling boxes out from under their tables and packing up.

With bags full of one-of-a-kind purchases, Jacob headed back toward the hotel. He couldn't wait to play with his new toys.

EIGHTEEN

Upon entering the US embassy in Beijing, a stunning two-story building with both street-facing walls made entirely of glass, Lavinia put her bags through the X-ray machine, then waited while a security guard searched them. Retrieving her belongings she entered the main hall, where lines of people waited in front of a series of windows. There was a separate area for American citizens. Lavinia was shown to a private elevator with a glass door that looked thick enough to be bulletproof. When it came to a stop she stepped out into a less spartan-looking waiting area where American citizens cooled their heels in padded chairs.

"Lavinia Walsh?"

The woman's voice carried across the waiting room, and Lavinia stood and motioned with her hand in response. Her ID was checked before the woman beckoned her to follow through a secure door and into a private room where she was to wait for the ambassador.

It wasn't long before a tall woman with flowing blond hair slid open the glass door to her room. "Ms. Walsh, the president told me to expect you. I'm Terry Hamilton."

"Pleasure to meet you." Lavinia shook her hand.

"She asked that I provide you with whatever assistance you need. To that end—" she handed Lavinia a card "—I've written my mobile number on the back. I've arranged for you to meet my head of security, as I understand you need some weapons. First, however, she wanted me to notify her when you arrived. So I've done that already and she'll be calling us shortly."

As if on cue, the television at the end of the room turned on and the presidential seal came into view. After a moment it was replaced by Barbara Anderson, sitting at a conference room table with her chief of staff.

"Lavinia, you've arrived."

"Yes, safe and sound, Madam President."

"Thank you for your assistance, Ms. Ambassador."

"You're welcome, Madam President." Terry Hamilton backed out of the room and slid the door closed behind her.

"Lavinia, how are you doing?"

"Good, Madam President. I'm to attend a formal government function tonight. I was invited by Tung. Hopefully I'll get to meet the new vice president and the president. In addition, Jacob was able to track down a location from the email you sent, Dan."

"Dan filled me in on that," said the president. "What's your next move?"

"Jacob is pulling the details of the location for me. I'm going to head out there tomorrow to see what I can find."

"Be careful, Lavinia. Everything I've heard says that the Blood Dragons are dangerous." Lines formed around the president's mouth as she pursed her lips.

"I will. That's part of the reason I'm anxious to meet Liu Wei tonight. Apparently he's their leader."

"Don't give him any reason to put you on his radar,"

Dan advised. "If he's as dangerous as you're saying, you don't need to attract the attention of an army of enemies."

"I'll be careful. I don't plan to provoke him. I'll leave early tomorrow for Hangzhou. I'll case the building out and see if I can find a way in at night. I'll report back if I find anything helpful."

They signed off and the screen returned to the image of the presidential seal. Lavinia left the conference room and found the ambassador's office. She was waved through by her admin.

"You're done?"

"Yup, all done."

"That was quick. Let me show you to the equipment manager."

The ambassador led Lavinia along the hallway and back to the elevator. While the building was only two stories, she turned a key and the elevator passed by the ground level and descended to a secret basement. When the doors opened, an armed guard met them.

"Hi, Jimmy. We have a guest today."

Lavinia handed over her driver's license and signed in to a guest book. They were buzzed through a solid steel door and the ambassador led her to a small room on the left. Inside, a man sitting at a desk was cleaning a 9mm Heckler and Koch MP5 submachine gun.

"Hector, this is Lavinia. The president has requested that you dress her up."

He looked her over. "What do you normally shoot?"

"A Sig Sauer 1911 We The People," Lavinia said.

A smile crept across his face. "I love that gun. She's a beaut."

"My mother gave it to me as a gift when I was hired by the FBI."

169

"I like your mother. You and I are going to get along just fine." Hector waved his security card across a sensor, and the door behind his desk buzzed open. He pushed the door wide to reveal a huge storage room full of weapons and ammunition.

Lavinia high-fived Hector as she walked past him into the room. "Christmas!"

———

Pushing himself up on his elbow, Jacob slid into a sitting position against the headboard. He pulled his computer onto his lap, opened the screen, and began to work.

He opened a security-focused browser he was trying for the first time called Epic, and entered the name of the Chinese vice president who'd been assassinated. He spent the next few hours reading about various conspiracy theories. Most centered on the man who had run him off the road, Jang Dung.

From social media he found that the man's wife was suffering from congestive heart failure and wasn't expected to live much longer. A tragedy for their children, who apparently would now be raised by an uncle. The woman pleaded for friends and family to help their children after she was gone.

Studying Jang Dung's life, he saw nothing that would indicate he was political or angry. He seemed like a well-adjusted middle-class Chinese businessman who had enjoyed success under the Communist system. A family man. Why would he throw away his life and leave his children orphans?

Strange.

A news site showed a photo of the crash scene. Jacob

zoomed in on the burned-out red sedan, which he assumed belonged to Jang Dung. It was a Chinese-made electric vehicle. Noting the license plate and the make of the car, Jacob set to work.

More hours passed as he tried to get information from various sources. By late evening he had searches going on four screens spread out across his bed. It was ten o'clock when he finally got a hit on the car manufacturer. He was in!

Searching their network, he looked for the electric vehicle equivalent of an airplane's black box. In China, all electric car manufacturers sent detailed information back to the government. All without the driver's knowledge.

There it is!

Jacob accessed the central database for all electric vehicle driver data. He searched for Jang Dung's car. He found his file, but all of the data had been deleted. He randomly checked other vehicles as a point of comparison and all of their files were full of information.

Strange.

Biting his lip, Jacob tried another tack. It was another two hours before he found the data backup system. He cursed himself for not calling Chen earlier. He would have found it an hour ago if he spoke Chinese. Google Translate only took you so far.

Dang's vehicle information was also deleted in the most recent archive. He worked his way backward, day by day, back to the date of the accident.

Nothing.

Opening a search window, Jacob searched the entire backup drive for Dung's Vehicle Identification Number. He put a filter on the search, requiring that it was larger than ten bytes. A progress bar opened, starting at zero percent.

When it hadn't moved for ten minutes he put his computer down and crossed the room to the minibar. Grabbing a soda from the machine, he popped the top and took a large swig.

To avoid his equipment he lay down at the foot of his bed and closed his eyes for a moment. He wasn't sure how long he was out, but he was roused when his computer beeped. Lunging across the bed, he dragged the computer onto his lap and stared at the screen.

One record.

In a temp folder he found the data record for Dung's car and downloaded it to his local machine. In the service department's files he found the diagnostic codes for the model car Dung was driving. He opened both documents and began to analyze.

It was nearing midnight when Jacob hit pay dirt.

The green and yellow taxi ferrying Lavinia to the event seemed decidedly out of place. The Diàoyútái State Guest House, known locally as Diàoyútái Guóbīnguǎn, was a historic complex of buildings. It was part of a group of ten construction projects built in 1959 as a celebration of the tenth anniversary of the People's Republic of China.

The long, winding driveway was made of hand-hewn stone cut into large, smooth rectangles. On either side of the roadway were concrete railings with carved posts every ten feet. They approached a traditional Chinese archway painted pale blue, yellow, and gold with red trim. Lavinia gazed up through the side window of the cab at the intricate carving as they passed underneath. So much history!

When they pulled up to the main building, Lavinia

exited the taxi as quickly as she could in the hope that no one would see her arrive in the gaudy vehicle.

"Lavinia!"

Caught! Lavinia glanced up at the heavens for a moment, then turned. "Tung!" She smiled as she waved to him and made her way over to where he stood. "This place is beautiful!"

"Thank you. We're very proud of it. The government is a frequent guest of this heritage site."

"I can see why." Lavinia took his hand and he led her inside.

"Thank you for inviting me, Tung. This is a real honor."

He leaned in and spoke in a hushed tone. "Normally an American spy would not be welcome amongst this crowd, but the president has said that he would like to meet you."

Her eyes widened ever so slightly, but she maintained her poker face.

There was a heavy military presence, which made sense, given the president and vice president would both be in attendance. They were led to the Tongle Room at the back of the hotel. The ceiling and pillars were all a deep yellow and the walls were adorned with marble that was a mottled reddish yellow. The carpeting matched, a mosaic of red and gold. Lavinia found the room striking, although if you'd tried to describe it to someone, they would have expected it to be garish. It was a room you had to experience to appreciate. A true marvel.

There were in excess of twenty people milling about, although the guests of honor had not yet arrived. Women wearing black skirts, white jackets, and matching gloves glided about the room carrying trays of hors d'oeuvres. The smiles on their faces were as delicate as the crust of the pastries they carried.

Lavinia and Tung each accepted a tall glass of champagne. The fluted glass was intricately etched with traditional imagery.

Holding her glass without drinking from it, Lavinia surveyed the room as she spoke to Tung. "So the president wants to meet me? Why is that?"

"He didn't say, but I was asked to invite you. In China, one does what one is asked without question. The Party always knows best."

As if on cue, women in delicate dresses and men in tuxedos began to form two lines facing each other, starting near the entrance. Tung led Lavinia to the end of the line. As they passed a table with an array of flowers on it, Lavinia discreetly poured most of the champagne from her glass into a vase. She took her place across from Tung.

Music struck up and men in suits and equipped with earpieces entered the room and walked the length of the line. Lavinia assumed they were the equivalent of the Secret Service back home. The men circled around the back of the line and took up guard. When the last man was in place, the president entered with his wife, toasting the line with his own glass of champagne as he walked.

The new vice president followed a few moments later. He was accompanied by a young Chinese woman. Lavinia didn't recognize her, but it couldn't be his wife. She was far too young. The young woman looked up at Liu Wei with what Lavinia could only describe as reverence.

When the vice president had passed, the line broke up and people organized themselves into small groups. Everyone angled to get a moment with the president, except Lavinia and Tung.

It wasn't long before the president found them.

"Tung, may I have a moment alone with your guest?"

Tung bowed and backed away.

"Ms. Walsh." He addressed her in perfect English, extending a hand. "It's a pleasure to meet a friend of President Anderson's."

Lavinia shook his hand. "It's a pleasure to meet you. Thank you for the invite. The building is stunning." She gestured with her arms.

The president motioned for his wife to leave him, and he placed a hand on Lavinia's back to guide her behind a pillar. He leaned in close so only she could hear. "The vice president's death. It's not what it seems, I'm sure of it, but I cannot be seen looking for proof. I would like to ask President Anderson for your help in finding the true killer."

Doubt set in. Should she tell him what Jacob had found? That Jang Dung was innocent?

He leaned his head back and let out a hearty laugh, as if she'd told a joke. It looked so genuine that it took a moment for what had just happened to sink in. The crowd had gravitated toward them and inquisitive ears were within range.

Lavinia smiled and raised her champagne glass to her lips. She took a small sip and said, "Thank you, Mister President."

"You're welcome, Ms. Walsh." He spoke loudly now. "Has Tung been kind to you?" Other guests began to crowd them so the president guided her another few feet away.

"Yes, Mister President. Very gracious. We enjoyed a lovely meal at MeiZhou Dong Po."

He nodded. "I've eaten there before. Close to the American embassy. Very popular." The president walked a few steps, motioning for her to follow.

"Mister President, my colleague has found evidence that Jang Dung's car was hacked. He didn't have control of his vehicle at the time of the accident."

His eyes hardened and he pursed his lips. "You have proof?"

"Yes. But I don't know who the real killers are yet."

His eyes wandered over the crowd. They seemed to settle on Liu Wei. "How long will you be in China?"

"I'm not sure, really. I serve at the pleasure of the president. Tung tells me the two of you have met?"

"Just once, at the United Nations." He lowered his voice again. "I believe she's different than presidents past. That we can forge a new relationship between our countries and put history firmly behind us. Our countries' economies are intertwined, so what benefits one benefits the other." Then he added in a firm voice, "And vice versa."

Lavinia was mystified by the emphasis he placed on the words "vice versa." She stared hard into his eyes, also keeping her voice low. "I'm sure the president will give whatever assistance you request. I'll pass on the message."

"It's a good opportunity for her to demonstrate that I can trust her word over...others'."

"Why do you trust me to help you?"

"I'm aware of what you did four months ago. You put your life in danger to save the president. There are few people in this world who act when called upon."

"Good always wins," Lavinia said. "If it wasn't me, someone else would have been there for her."

"I wish I shared your optimism, Ms. Walsh. Don't get me wrong, I would like if what you said were always true. However, the former vice president was a good man and he didn't win."

Lavinia averted her gaze. His words reminded her of the conversation she'd had with Dan Nolan. Was she so naive?

He continued. "I trusted Liu Wei, but now I fear I was wrong. He played me for a fool. I can't explain here, but I was wondering if we could arrange for some time to speak alone. I'll have Tung schedule time and bring you to the palace for a private meeting."

"I'd be honored. Is there a message that I can convey to the president in advance of the meeting?"

He tilted his head and flashed a smile. She thought he wanted to say something more, but he checked himself. "No, not appropriate conversation for a night like tonight. The rest of this evening, I'd like for you to enjoy my government's hospitality." He raised his mostly empty champagne glass. "Enjoy."

With that, he was gone.

As the evening wore on, Lavinia found herself starting to tire of the mingling. At last a bell rang and people began to take seats around the two huge round tables. Each seated fourteen people, with the president at one table and the vice president at the other. Her observation of the two men's interactions that night led her to believe they did not like each other.

While everyone tried to get as close to the president as possible, it was relatively easy for Lavinia to take a seat next to the vice president. The young woman accompanying him sat on his other side, putting him between the two women.

"My condolences for the death of your predecessor," Lavinia said.

"It was a great loss."

"Have they had any luck finding the perpetrator?"

"Yes, a disaffected mid-level manager ran him off the road."

"You're referring to Jang Dung?"

"Yes. Had he not died in the crash, he would have suffered a fate ten thousand times worse."

While Dan Nolan's warning not to provoke Liu Wei

was fresh in her mind, Lavinia followed a hunch. "I find that interesting, because my sources tell a different story."

A dangerous look flashed across his face, but was gone as quickly as it appeared. "You have a source?"

"We are aware that Mister Dung's car was hacked remotely, and used as a weapon to attack the vice president."

"You have evidence of this?" The charm that he'd had on display so far that evening was gone.

"Yes, I do," Lavinia said.

After an extended glare, the vice president turned his attention to his plate, cut a piece of his steak, and placed it in his mouth.

"You will, of course, share this evidence with me?" he said while he chewed.

"I'm sorry, it's classified."

"I have the best military investigators in the world, Miss Walsh. I will find the people responsible for the murder of our beloved vice president and I will bring them to justice. On this—" he stuck his fork in another piece of meat and pointed it at her "—you can wager your life." He put the fork in his mouth and ate the piece of steak.

It was an odd choice of words. Lavinia held his gaze. Her knuckles were white, gripping her knife and fork. "I have faith that you will."

The vice president ignored any further attempts at small talk for the rest of the meal. When dessert was served, the woman accompanying Liu Wei excused herself and made her way to the bathroom. Lavinia waited a few minutes before following.

She paced the hallway and found the women's bathroom. It was just as opulent as the dining hall. The young woman stood in front of a mirror adjusting her hair. Lavinia approached and introduced herself.

"Hi, I'm Lavinia."

"Wang Juan." The girl smiled politely. Her English was perfect, just like the president's. If they were in New York, you'd think she was American.

"Does everyone here speak such flawless English?"

The girl laughed. "No, I went to Harvard."

Lavinia nodded. "It seems common that people here speak English. Back home, most people don't speak more than one language, unless it's Spanish."

"English is the universal language of business. You either learn it or you aren't relevant."

"I see. Are you Liu Wei's daughter?" Lavinia hoped she wasn't his wife or lover.

The girl laughed. "Liu Wei has never been married. His life is dedicated to China; he has no time to love anyone but his country."

"A friend, then?" Lavinia prodded.

"I am an admirer of what he stands for, you could say," the woman replied before turning her attention back to the reflection in the mirror. Their conversation was over.

Lavinia passed behind her, heading for a stall, when something caught her eye. She stepped back behind the girl. "Here, let me get your zipper. It's sliding down."

Lavinia pretended to fumble with the zipper before sliding it down three inches and back up to the top. As she did so she tilted her head to get a better look. She froze. On the back of the woman's left earlobe was the tattoo of a red dragon curled into a circle.

Lavinia stared at the ceiling, running the conversations from last night over in her mind. A rap at the door of her hotel room interrupted her train of thought.

Slipping out from under the covers she crossed the room to the door and peered through the peephole. Jacob waited outside, in his usual black jeans and black dress shirt. "What is your mission?" she called through the door.

There was a fit of laughter on the other side.

Lavinia threw on a sweatshirt and yoga pants, then pulled the door open and invited him in. In typical Jacob fashion he ran in and launched himself in the air in a sitting position and dropped onto her bed.

"Make yourself comfortable." Her hands were on her hips.

"So am I good or am I good?"

"I'll give it to you. You're good," Lavinia agreed. "That information came in quite handy, too."

"Really? How so?"

"I challenged the vice president's assertion that they'd caught the villain, telling him we had evidence that the car used in the assassination was hacked."

"What did he say?"

"I'll be honest, I was nervous at the look he gave me at first. Then he promised me that they'd quickly find who did it."

"Really? So he didn't deny it?"

"I think he saw that I was telling the truth, so he didn't waste time denying it."

Jacob grabbed the remote control and switched on the TV. He navigated to the local news.

"Do you understand Chinese?" she asked.

"No, but I can see the images, so I can tell if there's anything important happening."

Lavinia turned away from the TV and continued. "That isn't all, though, Jacob. He was accompanied by a young woman. I followed her to the bathroom and struck up a conversation. You'll never guess what I saw."

A smile spread across his face. "Oh, do tell!"

Lavinia frowned. "On the back of her left ear was the tattoo of a red dragon."

"Seriously?"

"Seriously."

"They seem to turn up everywhere we go." Jacob craned his neck at the TV. The vice president was being interviewed on the news. He was talking in Chinese, so they couldn't understand, but superimposed in the top right-hand corner of the screen were the images of two men.

Jacob grabbed the laptop beside him and attacked the keyboard. After a moment, he beckoned for Lavinia to come over.

"Look at this!" He read aloud: "'Chinese vice president claims two hackers were responsible for the death of the former Chinese vice president, not the man originally accused of the crime.'"

Lavinia's jaw dropped. "That was faster than finding Lee Harvey Oswald!" Biting her lip, Lavinia considered the news. "Jacob, you found some possible locations for where the guy who emailed Dan Nolan was from. I'm going to have to head out there. Can you find out where these supposed assassins lived and grew up? If I have to get on the road anyway, maybe I can look into their backgrounds on the same trip."

"China is a huge country." He frowned. "How does this help us?"

"Just find out where they're from or where they last lived. Maybe one of the locations will be on my way or I can circle back after following up on Dan's lead. It strikes me as suspect that within hours of my telling Liu Wei I have proof that the guy accused of killing the Chinese vice president is innocent, he comes up with new suspects in a matter of hours. That makes me wonder if he's involved in the assassination of the vice president himself."

"That's a pretty thin link, Lavinia."

"Yeah, well, most theories start out that way, don't they?"

"Just be careful of confirmation bias. That's how innocent people go to jail."

Lavinia stood and put her hands on her hips. "Look, we know that Liu Wei is the head of the Blood Dragons. His behavior surrounding the former vice president's assassination is, at a minimum, suspect. He directly benefited from the former vice president's death, by the way." She was counting the facts off on her fingers as she spoke. "We also have a potential link between the Blood Dragons and the social media campaign. So maybe all of this is related. It's up to us to prove it."

Jacob nodded, frowning.

He spent the next few hours researching the two men he'd read about in the news. He sent Lavinia to the all-night tuck shop in the lobby to pick up a paper copy of a map and some other supplies while he worked.

When he was finished, Jacob had plotted a series of locations on the map. The first star was on Guandong, where the Facebook contact who emailed Dan worked. Then he put stars on the villages where the two new assassination suspects were born and on cities the media linked the suspects to.

They sat down to plot a strategy.

NINETEEN

In a patch of the Atlantic Ocean off the coast of Venezuela, the sun-kissed water surpassed the critical threshold of seventy-nine degrees. The wind evaporated the warm water, forcing the newly warmed air to rise, while cold surface air rushed in to fill the void. A cycle of moving air was born.

As the tropical disturbance moved westward, it picked up wind speed. When sustained winds of thirty-nine miles per hour were reached the World Meteorological Society gave her a name. *Kate.*

Within days Kate entered the warmer waters around the Caribbean islands and was turbocharged to a Category Five hurricane. While her devastating winds of 170 miles per hour would cause unimaginable damage, they would claim less than ten percent of the deaths Kate would ultimately cause. The storm surge that would announce her arrival would be far more deadly, with waves exceeding twenty feet claiming lives without care for rank or station.

Kate was coming. With luck you would survive her wrath. Only luck.

There was no time for tears. In the rain and wind, who would see them anyway?

Alondra clutched her four-month-old child to her chest, her only girl bundled in a gray woven blanket. Her husband's calloused hand was clamped around her wrist as he led her from their flooded home. "Come, stay with me!" he called through the rain.

They'd thought they would be safe from the storm. He'd built their house himself out of stone and quality timber. He'd built it to survive rain and wind, but the storm surge had proven to be too much.

The wind was getting stronger, but aided by her husband's strength, they made their way toward the community center in the darkness. The water was waist high in places, so they had to slosh their way through it, fighting the furious undertow. Foreign objects littered the water, hitting their legs.

Alondra felt her husband stop and put a hand on her shoulder. "There!" he yelled into her ear, pointing across where there was normally a street. She saw the faint glow of four lightbulbs lining the roofline of the community center. He put his hand in the small of her back now, urging her along.

It seemed impossible that anything could outdo the clamor from the wind-driven rain, but they both stopped at the sound of an approaching roar. At first they couldn't identify the source, but in a horrifying moment they both saw it. A wall of water three times higher than the building they were approaching!

Newly motivated, they pushed through the waist-high water as the surge approached. Alondra felt a final push in the small of her back as her husband forced her behind a concrete retaining wall. Turning her back to the wall and pulling her daughter to her chest, she was horrified to see her husband being swept away from her.

"Gustavo!" She let out a hoarse cry, her arms drawing her child to her bosom.

How long she stayed there, she couldn't say. The love of life had disappeared and the water and wind battered her body. She wanted to give up, but the touch of her daughter gave her new strength.

Alondra had been praying since the storm began. Now she begged the Lord to forgive her for not folding her hands while she requested protection for the last of her family, but she needed her hands to hold her daughter tight.

The water level from the surge had crested and seemed to be dissipating. A prayer answered!

Somehow in the chaos she realized that her daughter was wailing. She sang a lullaby into her ear, but she knew the wind stole the words before they could make it to her child's ear.

With a final push, she crossed the distance to the community center's entrance. The doorway was set ten feet in, so as she came within the confines of the concrete walls of the alcove, the wind all but disappeared. With one weak hand, she pulled the door open and sloshed her way inside.

The building was flooded with a few inches of water, and two hundred fellow Puerto Ricans all stood within the main gymnasium. The lights in the building were still on, which seemed incredible, given the amount of water inside.

There was a large crash outside and the gym was plunged into darkness. A cry went up, the adults as loud as the children.

There was another crash as a section of ceiling buckled

and the branches of a tree broke through. Some ceiling tiles fell to the gym floor and water poured in. In the darkness, people scrambled to find safety in the damaged building.

Alondra knew the storm's name. Kate was searching for more victims.

TWENTY

Liu Wei paced the length of the control room, his black combat boots making a thud each time he took a step. None of his officers dared meet his gaze, for they'd never seen him in such a mood. With his arms clasped behind his back, he spun on his heel and retraced his steps.

Lavinia Walsh! Who is this woman?

Why was she investigating the assassination of the vice president? How had she discovered what really happened when his soldiers were the best technical hackers in the world? Did she know his full plot?

There was one truth. She had to be eliminated.

Stomping out of the control room, he marched the length of the polished concrete hallway to his office on the other side of the building. The glass door to his office opened as he approached and slid shut behind him. Dropping his large frame into the oversized chair, he turned on his computer.

He went to the steganography URL one of his Blood Dragons had found for him. A simple utility would encode a message into a photo that he could post to any photo-sharing site. His reader could then visit the site, download the photo, and decode it using the same utility. Email, phone, and text could all be tracked and read. The entire world could see and access the photo, but they would have no way of ever knowing it contained a message.

Invisible.

He entered his message: *Two objectives. First, it's time for the warning as discussed. Second, your president sent an agent to investigate the death of the former Chinese vice president. Lavinia Walsh must be eliminated.*

He clicked on the *Choose File* button and navigated to a photo of a sunflower on his desktop, which he selected before hitting the *Encode* button. The screen cleared, and his encoded image slowly appeared on screen, ready to download and post to the anonymous photo-sharing site.

After posting his image, he clasped his hands behind his head and leaned back in his chair. He stared at the concrete ceiling.

How had she known? More importantly, if she'd been sent to investigate, it meant that the American president knew or suspected that something was amiss. This presented risk. And opportunity.

Henderson was proud to be the youngest officer of the watch on the bridge of the *Wayne E. Meyar*, an Arleigh-class destroyer stationed as part of a naval task force in the South China Sea. The guided missile destroyer was part of a collection of ships on patrol to challenge excessive maritime claims and preserve access to the waterways as governed by international law.

Simply put, their job was to keep the Chinese Navy in

line. The Chinese had been constructing and expanding artificial islands in the South China Sea to try to extend their territorial claims. It was up to the US Navy to contain them.

Studying the monitors on the bridge, she traced a mark on the screen with her finger. "Vessel to port, Seaman. Distance and speed?"

The able seaman assisting her on deck studied his instruments. "Fourteen miles and thirty-five knots," he replied. He glanced at her for just a moment and looked away. "Shall I summon the commander?"

"Summon the commander."

"Aye-aye, summoning the commander."

By the time he arrived, two Chinese destroyers and a frigate had come into view.

"Sound the general alarm." The commander's voice was calm.

Henderson shifted her weight, then executed the order.

The ship came alive. All 158 souls on board jumped into action.

"Destroyer group approaching head on, Commander," Henderson informed him.

The bridge filled up as every hand on board the ship took up position.

The commander barked orders, which sailors repeated back as they executed. He communicated with the rest of the naval task force to coordinate their response. All eyes were trained on their instruments or the approaching collection of ships. They were well within sight now, and growing in size by the moment.

Henderson alerted other American vessels in the vicinity of what was going on and alerted High Naval Command. The entire military was watching now.

A Secret Service agent burst into the Oval Office. "Madam President, you're needed in the Situation Room." By the time she stood, five Secret Service agents had flanked her to lead her to the basement of the West Wing.

Formally known as the John F. Kennedy Conference Room, the 5,500 square foot room could be used to oversee military operations around the world. When she entered she could see that the twin eighty-inch television screens on the wall showed the identical image of the front of an American destroyer sailing toward three approaching ships.

The chairman of the Joint Chiefs of Staff, the secretary of defense, and the head of the National Security Council were all present. The chief of naval operations was on a smaller television on the side wall.

"What's going on?" President Anderson demanded.

"An Arleigh-class destroyer stationed in the South China Sea is on routine patrol and is being aggressively approached by a squad of Chinese destroyers," the chairman of naval operations replied curtly.

"Why are they doing that?"

"It's an intimidation move, Madam President."

"Are they going to attack?"

"I don't think so, Madam President. Not if they know what's good for them."

All eyes in the room were focused on the televisions. President Anderson stood watching with her arms crossed.

"Is someone going to turn?"

Just as she spoke, five short blasts of a horn were heard.

"That was the international signal for danger of a collision," the chief of naval operations explained. "They've been hailing their radios and demanding they adjust their course."

Chinese soldiers standing at their stations came into view as the ships continued to approach each other.

"Order our ship to turn," the president called out, her voice strong.

As the words left her mouth, the Chinese ships broke to starboard. The camera on the US ship turned to follow the Chinese military vessel as it passed beside the American destroyer. They were so close the agitated water between the two massive ships churned and splashed.

President Anderson took two steps toward the television. "What the hell was that?" She pointed at screens. "Why is President Xiu Ying Zhang doing this?"

All eyes were on the president, but she was met with silence.

Liu Wei stood at the command center, both hands grasping the hand railing as he overlooked the massive screen on the far wall of the amphitheater. A smile spread across his lips.

Message delivered.

Lavinia pounded on Jacob's door.

"What is your mission?"

"Jacob, open the door!" Lavinia demanded.

There was some muffled fumbling before it opened and Lavinia slipped inside. Pushing the door shut behind her, she slid the chain home.

"Someone was in my room!"

"What do you mean, you walked in on someone?"

"No, I went to check on the guns I got from the embassy and one is missing!" She was breathless.

"How many guns did you have? Was it in the safe? Because anyone can pick those."

"Jacob, shut up and listen to me! It wasn't the staff. I took four handguns and ammunition from the embassy. I have one on me all the time; the other three I'd stashed away. There's a false ceiling over the kitchenette in the room. I lifted one of the ceiling tiles and slipped them in the space—it's an old trick my dad taught me. One gun is missing."

Jacob's jaw dropped. Unable to find words, he began to pace. "Could it have fallen down the wall or something so you just can't see it?"

"No, I removed all of the ceiling tiles and stood on the countertop. One is missing. It had to have happened while I was at the government function. It's the only time I've been out of my room for an extended period of time since I visited the embassy. We need to change hotels."

"Okay, let me pack my stuff."

"No, leave everything. They may have bugged or put trackers in our clothes and our suitcases. We'll buy everything new."

"I would know if someone played with my electronics." Jacob put his hands on his hips.

Lavinia tilted her head. "You'd risk your life on that? Jacob, I know what our agency is capable of. If this was the Blood Dragons, then they have access to Chinese military technology. We have to assume the worst."

"Not leaving my stuff, sorry." He was pacing the room. "Clothes, shoes, suitcases, fine. I'm not ditching my computers. We'll find somewhere safe and I'll scrub them all down."

Lavinia shook her head. "Fine. Look, let's pack all of our clothes into our suitcases. We'll toss them in the dumpster behind the hotel. We'll go shopping for new clothes and stuff and then find a new hotel. There we can ditch the clothes we're wearing, you can scrub your equipment, and when we're sure we're clean we'll find a new place to stay. We'll have to pay for everything with cash."

"That rules out any mainstream hotels." Jacob frowned. "They require passports."

"Yeah, it does." Lavinia left the room, pulling the door shut behind her. She needed to pack.

TWENTY-ONE

Speaker of the House Bradley Tanner glided into the assigned breakout room in the United Nations building. A broad smile spread across his perpetually tanned face when he saw Olivia MacQueen and Chinese Vice President Liu Wei seated at the table next to each other.

"Pleasure to meet you in person." He reached out to offer his hand to Liu Wei, who extended a meaty hand that enveloped the American's.

Olivia MacQueen nodded at the speaker without getting up. It was a curious response, as she was known as a friend to Republicans.

Rounding the table, he took a seat across from them, speaking as he went. "So, I met with the big five defense contractors and they're thrilled with the way things are shaping up." He scanned their faces, expecting some validation. There was none.

"We're all on the same page here, right? Things haven't changed?" His smile was gone. "There's already money earmarked for both of you. You can't back out now."

"No one is backing out, Mister Speaker." Liu Wei spoke

in an even tone. "Money is not the primary motivator for everyone here, although I will take your donation." He allowed a small smile. "What I'm interested in is how the two of you expect to execute your part of the plan to replace Barbara Anderson." Tanner noted that he didn't refer to her by her title.

Tanner glanced over at Olivia MacQueen to see if she'd speak. She sat stoically, so he replied. "For weeks Olivia has been pushing the president's Puerto Rico agenda behind the scenes. The president leaves for the island tomorrow night, so your second provocation needs to happen while she's in the air."

"How do I get confirmation of her departure?"

MacQueen spoke up. "I'll reach out. The usual method."

"Will my attack elicit the required response?"

"It got all of us together today, didn't it?" Tanner smiled.

Olivia stood. "The president will want to keep the focus on the poor people of Puerto Rico. Don't worry, she's predictable and shallow. The day after your attack she'll give a policy speech on Puerto Rico and then, Mister Tanner, it's up to you."

With that she spun on her heel and was gone.

Liu Wei glanced at Tanner after she'd left and smirked. "If you think you're playing her, you're wrong."

Liu Wei returned to his hotel down the street from the United Nations building. He picked up his military phone and placed a call to President Xiu Ying Zhang.

"Mister President, you requested that I call?"

"How did your meeting with the Americans go?"

"It was fine, Mister President. A misunderstanding."

"What kind of a misunderstanding, Liu Wei? Your military provoked an American Navy task force. I didn't imagine that, did I? The Communist Party did not authorize such a policy. I run the military, not the vice president!"

Liu Wei dropped into the easy chair in the corner of his room, kicked off his shoes, and put his feet up. "The Americans send ships into our waters and try to dictate where we can sail, and you want to allow them to embarrass the great nation of China?"

There was danger in the president's tone when he responded. "You may have the support of the Communist Party, Liu Wei. But even in China, where we are one party, favor can be fickle. I am a man who would rather be betrayed by others than betray them. But I am not betrayed easily."

Liu Wei paused before responding. "You are not being betrayed, President Zhang."

The line went dead. Liu Wei tossed his phone onto the bed and finished his thought to the empty room. "You are being punished for your cowardice. For failing China."

He reached to the adjacent desk and grabbed his laptop. He powered it up and opened a secure communication channel. "Get the submarines ready. They need to be in position in the morning."

Olivia MacQueen sat on her bed, her back against the fabric of the padded headboard. She tapped at her keyboard, scrolling through the latest polling results. There was a beep as a new email arrived: *Lexus is away.*

That was the president's call sign. It was a two-hour

flight to Florida, where the president would switch to a helicopter for the trip to storm-ravaged Puerto Rico.

Opening the link Liu Wei had taught her to use, Olivia keyed in a message to the Chinese vice president: *Sixty minutes and away.* She coded the message into the photo of a sunflower and posted it to the agreed-upon photo-sharing site.

Rising, Olivia crossed the room to her walk-in closet. She stripped down, then selected a deep blue suit. Slipping it on, she stood in front of the full-length mirror and regarded herself.

President Olivia MacQueen.

———

Officer Henderson glanced at the picture of the USS *Stark* pinned to the central control panel on the bridge of the USS *Wayne E. Meyar.* The ship's commander had prominently affixed the photo there shortly after taking over responsibility for the vessel.

The commander had shared the Regan-era story of the USS *Stark* with his leadership team early in his tenure. The *Stark* had been in international waters, patrolling the Saudi Arabian coast near the Iran-Iraq exclusion boundary. A sole Iraqi fighter jet had approached the ship. Twice, Captain Glenn Brindel had ordered that messages be sent to the plane, asking the pilot to identify himself. The pilot didn't respond. Instead, unprovoked, he fired two missiles at the ship—one from twenty-two miles out and the other from fifteen miles. While only one missile detonated upon impact, both severely damaged the vessel. Brindel had reacted deftly, keeping the ship from sinking and protecting the lives of the rest of his crew, but thirty-seven Americans had died in the attack. An inquiry recommended that Captain Brindel be court-martialed for failing to protect his ship, although he was eventually just reprimanded.

The story served to highlight the almost impossible line between the call for action and the need for caution.

Henderson was the first to see the blip on the radar screen. "Submarines! Summon the commander. Sound the general alarm. All sailors to battle stations."

The general alarm sounded and the thunder of feet could be heard as sailors took to their stations all across the vessel.

"Get the commander of naval operations on comms." Henderson noticed the ship commander stride onto the bridge. "Commander on the bridge!"

Everyone saluted and the commander replied, "At ease. Status report."

Henderson briefed him. "We're tracking six submarines in the water within two miles, and eleven boats at sixteen nautical miles. Naval Command just joined on comms and we have an open line to supporting US naval vessels. The White House will be online shortly."

His hands clasped behind his back, the commander studied the screens in front of him. "This is either the start of World War Three, or the Chinese are trying to agitate us," he muttered. He addressed the commander of naval operations. "This is Commander Turner of the *Wayne E. Meyar* in the South China Sea. Sir, we are tracking six submarines at two nautical miles and eleven military ships farther off but operating in conjunction with the submarines."

"What's your assessment, Commander? Is your ship under threat?"

The commander stood still for a heartbeat, his square

jaw set, before answering. "Not at this time. There is no strategic value in attacking us."

"Please stand by for the White House," a woman's voice broke in over the communications line. Everyone went silent.

"We're here." The voice of National Security Advisor Ema Ricart filled the bridge.

"Madam President," the commander began.

Ema interrupted him. "No, the president is unavailable. We have the vice president here."

Henderson saw the commander frown. She could hear tension in the woman's voice as it came over the radio. She'd seen her once or twice on television but didn't know how to read her. It was fascinating to watch her commander deal with his superiors.

"Madam Vice President," the commander said in greeting.

The stern voice of Olivia MacQueen came in response. "Commander. The president is on a helicopter en route to Puerto Rico and is unreachable at this time. What's going on?"

"We're tracking six submarines at twelve nautical miles and eleven military ships farther off but operating in conjunction with the submarines. I do not interpret these actions as a threat to my ship at this time, although we have reinforcements in the region that are coming to our aid."

"How long have you served in the region, Commander?"

He snapped into rigid attention. "I've been commanding ships in this region for almost five years."

"In those five years, Commander, have you ever seen the Chinese behave like this?"

"No, ma'am."

"So what's your interpretation?"

"I believe they're sending us a message—"

"Which is?"

"Which is, that they have authority in these waters. It's not a secret that they've been building military bases, artificial islands, and solidifying their economic power in the region. Asserting their military independence in these waters is part of that. Which is why we'll hold course and not engage at this time."

The bridge was silent, save the gentle creaking of the destroyer as it cut through the water.

"As you were, Commander. I trust your judgment. We'll stay on the line with you. You have our full support."

A smile tugged at the edges of the commander's lips.

Officer Henderson had heard good things about the vice president, but this was the first live interaction she'd witnessed with her. The word around the military was that she was tough and a friend of the forces, which most in the military found impressive, considering their Republican bias and the fact that she was a Democrat.

Wang Jaun's concentration was interrupted when her computer beeped and a pop-up window informed her of an incoming email. The subject line made her fingers tighten over the keyboard. There'd been an update to the sole Instagram account she followed. The second update that day. She opened the email and clicked on the link.

The close-up image of a sunflower in a garden filled her browser. Dragging the image to her desktop, she navigated to the decoding site and clicked on the *Upload* button. She selected the file from her desktop and waited. A simple message was displayed in the decoded message box.

Order a more forceful incursion in two days.

The American vice president was ready to make her move.

TWENTY-TWO

"Madam President, I think you should reconsider this course of action." The hushed tone of the secretary of health and human services did little to hide his anxiety. "This speech, as written, would be highly destabilizing." He held his hands up as if to block her progress from the door to the stage.

President Barbara Anderson stopped, pushed her shoulders back, and drew herself to her full height. She was about to speak when her chief of staff, Dan Nolan, slipped his sturdy six-foot frame between the two political combatants.

If a dry joke were able to manifest itself as a smile, that's what Dan flashed before speaking in his quiet and confident voice. "Come now, Ron. Not the time or place."

Putting a hand in the small of the president's back, Dan directed her slightly to the right and led her toward the door.

"Thanks, Dan. I was about to say something I might have later regretted."

"Remember what our mothers used to tell us." The smile was back.

"Does this need to be said. Does this need to be said now. Does this need to be said now by me," she recited. It was Dan's oft-repeated mantra.

"Exactly."

Despite herself, the president laughed. "You're such a calming influence on the team, Dan. What would I do without you?"

"I'm not sure, Madam President, but I'm pretty sure you won the presidency without my help."

"Well, I appreciate you joining me for this trip. I know you'd rather be back at the White House monitoring things, but your presence on this trip is important to me."

A Secret Service agent looked to the president for confirmation that she was ready. Barbara Anderson gave a curt nod and the door was pushed open to reveal a boisterous crowd. Normally her entrance would be announced in grand presidential fashion with a band striking up "Hail to the Chief." Today silence was appropriate.

Mounting the steps of the hastily assembled stage in the school gymnasium, the president crossed to the podium. The media was front and center, where reporters stood with microphones in hand and camera operators with equipment hoisted on shoulders. Behind them, four hundred strong, were the desperate faces of Puerto Ricans who had endured deadly Hurricane Kate and the resultant storm surges. It was the third time in three and a half years that Puerto Rico had endured a natural disaster. The hurricane had made landfall three days earlier and while the winds, rain, and storm surge had since receded, there was ample evidence of Kate's visit.

As President Anderson stood behind the podium and looked over the crowd, a hush fell across the room.

"Three days ago, as you know all too well, a devastating

hurricane ripped through your neighborhoods. It has destroyed homes, damaged critical infrastructure, and worst of all, taken the lives of many of our citizens."

The president paused to look around the room again. Her gaze came to rest on a woman along the right-hand wall. Her white shirt was stained and torn, revealing her bra beneath. She balanced a young child on her hip. The child had four fingers in her mouth, self-soothing.

Looking back to the teleprompter, she continued. "I arrived today with the might of America behind me. As we speak, the USNS *Comfort* has arrived in port, bringing with it seven hundred medical personnel, five thousand units of blood, and a dozen operating rooms. Also en route are C-17 Globemaster III aircraft, carrying helicopters to aid in search and rescue missions. This is in addition to the Coast Guard helicopters already here or on their way. I want to tell the people of Puerto Rico we have your back."

There was polite applause from the crowd. Anderson knew they'd heard promises before, but when the entourage left, the people of the island had to fend for themselves. This time, it would be different. It had to be different.

"I believe this hurricane requires more than the people of America coming to the aid of Puerto Ricans. I believe that this natural disaster represents an inflection point in the history of Puerto Rico. I believe it is time that we revisit the status of Puerto Rico within America. This island cannot begin to heal and prosper unless there is great change."

Pausing again to allow the anticipation to build, the president could feel the people in the crowd leaning toward her, hanging on her every word.

"We must change the status of the Commonwealth of Puerto Rico. You are not Puerto Ricans, you are Americans!

You should no longer belong to a commonwealth, but a state...the State of Puerto Rico. I will put the full weight of the presidency behind this initiative, as I see no more important issue facing our nation than this!"

The room burst into deafening and wild applause. A smile spread across the face of the woman with the torn white shirt, who was clapping wildly while somehow balancing her baby on her hip.

Secretary of Health and Human Services Ron Wilson watched from the side of the stage, running his fingers through his neatly trimmed beard. "There'll be consequences for this, Dan. You of all people know that."

Dan Nolan stood with his hands clasped behind his back. His face did not betray any emotion. "The actions of great leaders always have consequences, Ron. Barbara Anderson is not a caretaker. She's a leader. A true leader."

"You know as well as I do what this means, Dan. As a commonwealth there are strict rules that govern the people. As a state they gain certain rights that could prove dangerous."

"Certain rights," Dan replied, raising his eyebrows. "You're referring to the right to declare bankruptcy? To begin anew?"

"Yes, that's exactly what I'm talking about. Their debt is held by investment funds. Funds that other Americans hold in their 401ks. If Puerto Rico were to declare bankruptcy, it would cause unprecedented damage to the economy."

"Something has to be done, Ron."

"Obama enacted PROMESA and they got massive debt relief."

"A drop in the ocean. You know as well as I do that it didn't go far enough. If I owe you a thousand dollars but can only afford to pay you ten, does it help me if you reduce my debt to five hundred?"

"Maybe they should have been fiscally responsible in the first place!" Ron's face was turning red.

Dan put a hand on the man's shoulder and turned him so they were facing the same direction. He led him away from the stage. "Ron, sometimes presidents come face to face with the people and what they see strikes a nerve. It brings to the forefront the fact that sometimes huge decisions with huge consequences have to be made, and the social good over the long term will outweigh the pain today. So now that it's out there, it's up to us to find a way to make it happen, to sell it."

"Dan, I don't think I can sell this."

"We'll find the answer together. You aren't facing this alone. We're all in this together."

"I'm afraid there is no answer, Dan."

There was a long pause. "There's always an answer."

Samantha Patel was at her desk working when she noticed people congregating around the television outside her office. While the headline *Breaking News* was an hourly occurrence on CNN, this looked different. Crossing her office, she slid the glass door open. "A.J., what's going on?"

The editor of the paper turned toward her and put a finger to his lips. All eyes turned back to the screen. Someone turned up the volume.

"We repeat, President Barbara Anderson is in storm-ravaged Puerto Rico today and announced that she would put the full weight of her presidency behind an initiative that would grant Puerto Rico statehood. This would be the most significant change to the territorial structure of the United States in sixty-two years. Smaller changes to US territorial boundaries have happened more recently, as in 2009 when six islands along the Rio Grande were ceded from Texas to Mexico and three islands and two banks were ceded from Mexico to Texas. Not since the addition of Hawaii in August 1959 has there been a change to the number of states in the country. Let's discuss this breaking news with our panel."

"Oh my lord," Samantha exclaimed. "How did we not hear anything about this before now?"

"Word is, it was an emotional response to the devastation she saw on the ground."

Samantha tilted her head. "That is so sexist. She's a woman, so it's an emotional response?"

"I'm telling you what people are saying," A.J. replied, raising his hands in mock surrender. "This came out of the blue. You know how leaky every administration is. No way this has been worked on for any period of time and not gotten out."

One of the commentators on the news broke in. "What happens to our flag? Do we add a fifty-first star? Are we going back to the circle of stars circa 1890?"

"Samantha, reach out to your sources inside the White House. We have some catching up to do."

As she stepped back inside her office, her desk phone rang.

"Hello?"

"Is this Samantha Patel?"

She fumbled for a pad and pen. "This is she. Who is this?"

"No names for now. I have a tip."

The voice was a woman's, but it was obvious to Samantha that she was trying to disguise it. Samantha glanced at the screen on the phone, but it read *Unknown Caller*. "What have you got?"

"There have been two incidents in the South China Sea between an American naval vessel and the Chinese Navy. The White House has covered it up because they didn't want it to interfere with the president's Puerto Rico initiative."

"Do you have any evidence of this?"

"Check the anonymous tip box on your website. I'll send you proof within the hour."

"Who else can validate your claims?"

"Everyone knows."

"Why are you reporting this?" Samantha probed. "What's in it for you?"

"A cynic, are we?" the voice mocked. "I'm a patriot. Left unchecked, this president will kill this country. The top priority isn't Puerto Rico, it's China. She's just too weak to face the obvious threat. Her attempt to hide the truth by distracting the American people with Puerto Rico is a dangerous game. One she shouldn't be allowed to play."

The line went dead.

Samantha didn't have to wait an hour. Within minutes, a series of files arrived.

A.J.'s head snapped up as Samantha stormed into his office, laptop in hand. "You aren't going to believe this!" Taking a seat at the round table in his office, she brought him up to speed on the call she'd just received. She kept one eye on her laptop, which was open to the tip line's internal portal.

"You have to wonder what their real motive is," A.J. warned. "The truth is rarely so straightforward."

"Yeah, I get that. I've put out some probing emails to my contacts inside the White House. We'll see what that yields," she said as she refreshed the web page yet again. "Here it is!"

A series of video clips began to appear in the web portal. Samantha downloaded the first video and hit *Play*. It was ten seconds long and looked like it was taken from a cell phone camera. It appeared to be from the deck of a US Navy ship and showed a Chinese military vessel running alongside it. The water between the ships was whipped into a frenzy.

"Look at the metadata for the file," A.J. instructed.

Samantha selected the file on her desktop and hit the *Command* and *I* keys on her Mac to reveal the video's metadata. "Date was yesterday and it gives me longitude and latitude at the time the video was taken, but whoever sent this deleted the information that could identify who the device belonged to."

In two steps A.J. was at his office door. "Get me someone from IT right away!" Sliding the door shut, he dropped back into his chair. "Open the next one."

There were eleven videos in all, and most were similar. They documented two encounters two days apart between an American military ship and the Chinese Navy. The final file was arresting. It was an audio file and it seemed to capture an exchange between the ship's commander and the White House.

A.J. raised his eyes from the computer to meet Samantha's gaze. His mouth hung open. "The president was unreachable while she was en route to Puerto Rico for her pet project. The vice president was left to deal with what could have been the start of World War Three!"

"There's a lot of interpretation in that statement, A.J.," she warned. "We need to verify that any of this is true."

"I recognize the vice president's voice, Samantha. You may not like it, but this is gold!"

"We need to verify the source." Samantha crossed her arms.

"Oh, I will. Don't you worry." A.J. stood and grabbed his jacket. "Begin writing the story. I'll be back, and I want to read your draft!"

Even in the dark, the view from the presidential palace was stunning. Liu Wei stood with his hands clasped behind his back, unable to suppress a grin. The president had summoned him in the middle of the night.

He already knew the reason for his late night summons. As promised, the American president had been goaded into following through with her flawed Puerto Rico policy. The deep fake video he'd created and shared with the Chinese president had been festering in his subconscious. The key phrase "and China will pay for it," had been a sheer stroke of genius. He had his brilliant assistant, Wang Juan, to thank for that one. She was his ultimate warrior. Equal parts beautiful, brilliant, seductive, and deadly.

"Liu Wei," the voice boomed from behind him.

Turning on his heel, the military man faced the president. He bowed slightly. "Xiu Ying Zhang, you requested my presence."

"You've heard the news?"

"I have. The president has gone public with her plan to

make Puerto Rico a state...and China will pay for it." He anticipated that adding the key phrase would serve to enrage the president.

"I was referring to your naval maneuvers, Liu Wei. Twice in the past week our navy engaged with the Americans in the South China Sea. Why?"

Liu Wei snorted. "The Americans determine where our ships can sail?"

"Antagonizing them is not the wish of the Communist Party, Liu Wei. Why would you bring us to the brink of war?"

"I have done no such thing!" His voice rose to fever pitch. "No one understands what our military is capable of more than me. No one in China understands better than I do how the Americans will interpret my actions. This is a game of chess. I suggest you leave the strategy to the master!"

The president drew himself to his full height. "The military is not your toy, Liu Wei, to play with as you wish. Movements on the battlefield are a form of language played by world leaders. Not their heirs apparent. There will be no more incidents. You will not provoke the Americans again. Is that clear?"

He felt pain in his stomach as he bowed before the president. "Yes, Mister President."

In his gut, Liu Wei knew that he had to accept this moment of private humiliation. No one would ever know the significance of this moment, but it was the beginning of the end of Xiu Ying Zhang's presidency.

TWENTY-THREE

Branches battered the windows of Lavinia's white Jeep as it sped through the forest. The trip was a series of skids and close calls that left Lavinia wary and her driver seemingly unfazed. Closing her eyes, she focused on the task at hand rather than where she was.

With relative ease, Jacob had found the villages where the two men now accused of assassinating the Chinese vice president had been born. The good news was that they were an hour apart. The bad news was that they weren't connected to China's extensive network of railroad tracks or highways.

Finding a driver to take her there had proven difficult. Fortunately with some off the record assistance from Tung, her Chinese attaché, she'd landed a retired military man as a driver. The challenge, however, was that his English was as good as Lavinia's Chinese.

The steady hammering of branches stopped and they broke into an opening. There was still no real road to speak of, just twin dirt tire tracks running through the grass, but the forest had given way to an open plain. Her driver accelerated and the car jounced along, tossing Lavinia about in the rear.

"Easy!" she called out.

Her driver was either ignoring her or had no idea what she was saying. Or both.

"Getting there alive is more important than speed," she said aloud, bracing herself with the frame of the front passenger seat.

They crested a small hill and the driver brought the vehicle to an abrupt stop. Down the hill to their right was a shantytown, with makeshift homes made of scavenged metal and wood. At the far end of the village was what appeared to be a rudimentary garbage dump that stretched three times the size of the village. She could see scattered columns of wispy black smoke rising around the outskirts of the dump.

Opening the door to her vehicle, Lavinia stepped one foot out of the Jeep and paused while she looked around. She could see young children playing in the streets. A soccer ball missing some of its leather patches was being kicked about with great enthusiasm. As she gazed, women of all ages began to come into view. This was the village of Yanzi, in Guanghe County in Gansu Province. One of the poorest parts of China.

Information on the village was sparse, but Jacob had worked his network and gotten some background. The biggest industry in town was a component recycling facil-ity...although there was no actual facility. Just piles of e-waste from Western countries.

While the process of melting circuit boards was toxic, it was profitable. The government was cracking down on illegal recycling efforts in and around the ports where scrap was imported into China. However, a resourceful young resident of Yanzi, who had escaped the town and gone to university, had created the business in an effort to save the town where his parents and siblings lived.

Trucks from mines in Gansu that delivered raw material for export were empty on the return trip. So the enterprising young man had bribed drivers to load their trucks with e-waste for delivery back to Yanzi. There the locals were more than happy to subsidize the income from subsistence farming by working for him. Over the past ten years he had become the richest man in the region.

With the right lens, you could argue he had raised an entire village out of poverty.

Setting her second foot on the ground, Lavinia closed the door to the Jeep and started to walk toward the closest grouping of women. They wore loose-fitting robes, mostly in white. The children wore a mismatched collection of First World hand-me-downs, although most were in bare feet. The group of women eyed Lavinia as she approached.

"Hi, does anyone speak English? I want to ask some questions."

The women began to chatter excitedly amongst themselves. One women beckoned for her to follow them into the village. Emboldened by the weight of the Sig Sauer hidden below the belt line in her Urban Carry Holster, she followed the women. As they made their way through the shantytown, the one thing that struck Lavinia was that aside from young boys, there were no men. No boys in sight who looked to be older than ten or eleven years of age.

A multitude of eyes followed her as she walked through the shantytown. She was led to a home where a woman sat in a rocking chair that no longer rocked. The woman stood and approached Lavinia. "Who are you?"

"My name is Lavinia." She shifted her weight. "I'm

investigating the assassination of the Chinese vice president."

"You're American?"

"Yes."

"It's strange for an American woman to be roaming the Chinese countryside investigating the murder of a Chinese politician."

"It is a little," Lavinia agreed, trying to flash a genuine smile but not sure she was succeeding.

The woman was five feet tall, slim, and elegant in her rustic surroundings. She glanced around. "Why don't you come inside where we can talk in private."

"Does anyone else here speak English?"

"No, just me. But we're sometimes watched, and I'm afraid that you stand out." Taking Lavinia's hand, the woman turned and led her into the rudimentary home.

Lavinia ducked to avoid hitting her head on the door-frame. Inside was a sparsely furnished single room. The ground was exposed dirt, with one corner covered with mats hand-woven from recycled milk bags. She presumed that was the sleeping quarters.

There were several tables fashioned from scrap wood, around which were an oddball collection of chairs. The two women sat across from each other.

"My name is Yayoi."

"I'm Lavinia, and admittedly a little out of place." The two women laughed. "Where did you learn your English? You don't have an accent at all."

"Princeton," the woman said. She seemed to enjoy Lavinia's surprise. "They say you'll meet grads from Ivy League schools in the strangest places. Go Tigers!"

"Really? That's surprising...somehow. I went to Northeastern."

"Not really. My parents gave me up for adoption when I was very young. They sold me to an American couple from New Jersey. I grew up in the town of Kingston, which isn't far from the school. I did my political science degree with a major in international economics."

"Which led you to a job here?"

"Not a job. More of a calling. I joined the Peace Corps out of university and I did a stint in India. I learned that the United States sold their garbage to countries like India and China, particularly their e-waste. It'd get shipped to poor towns like this one, and local kids would learn to forage for scrap. They'd melt circuit boards in open flames to try to recover the gold, not realizing that they were poisoning themselves."

"I'd never heard of that before coming here," Lavinia replied, frowning.

"I decided to return home and see if I could educate the people of my old town. Maybe make life a bit better."

Lavinia felt humbled. She glanced around at her surroundings. "You went to Princeton and now..." Her voice trailed off. She didn't know how to say what she was thinking.

"Now I live like this?" Yayoi motioned with her arms to the room. "You know, it was surprisingly easy. Although sometimes I feel like a fake. I still have my American passport. I could leave tomorrow and go back to the United States and get a job in Washington or New York. But I'm the only person here who has an out. None of these people have that luxury. That opportunity."

"You've made a difference?"

"I've made some progress. My house doubles as a school, if you can believe it. We were making strides until about five years ago."

"What happened five years ago?" Lavinia was leaning forward in her seat.

"They began raiding our town. The first raid was brutal. They took all of the men eighteen and older out to the fields and killed them. Lined them up and shot them in the fields, leaving their bodies to rot in the sun. They took the boys, aged twelve and up. Loaded them into trucks and took them away."

"Child soldiers?"

"Yes," she replied, closing her eyes and tilting her face up to the ceiling. "The raids continue. Every couple of years, they come back for the boys who have come of age. Anyone who resists is shot, so no one resists anymore."

"Is it the army?"

"It's an army within an army. They're loyal to the new Chinese vice president, Liu Wei."

"The Blood Dragons?"

"Yes."

"A few weeks ago I'd never heard of them," Lavinia confessed. "Now it seems I come across them everywhere." She reached into her pocket and felt the two photographs hidden away there. After a moment she removed them. "Yayoi, do you recognize either of these men?"

The woman studied the photos carefully, furrowing her brow. "Do you know their names?"

Lavinia repeated the men's names, pointing to each photo in succession. "These men have been accused of assassinating the vice president."

Yayoi let out a cry. She pointed to one of the photos. "That's Li Jie. He was taken in the first raid on our village. I don't know the other young man, but we aren't the only village that the Blood Dragons recruit from."

"Could Li Jie have been involved in the assassination? Is

it possible that he broke away from the Blood Dragons and went rogue?"

Yayoi shook her head. "No, impossible."

"Why do you say that?"

"Because Li Jie is blind."

Lavinia sat bolt upright in her chair. "I saw him being paraded on the news. He didn't act blind."

"He can see enough to walk around, but his vision is so bad that even glasses can't correct it. So he can't drive or read, but he could function enough day to day to subsist. But the legal definition of blind doesn't necessarily mean that you see nothing, it can also mean that you're severely impaired."

"Why would the Blood Dragons keep him around if he's blind?"

"Because he speaks perfect English. I know because I taught him. He was obsessed with learning, because he couldn't do much else. He was the best student I ever had. An incredible memory."

"So in other words, if Liu Wei needed someone to pin the assassination on, then he was the least valuable of his valuable assets?"

"Yes, that would make sense. But why would Liu Wei need someone to frame for the assassination?"

Lavinia sat silently as the realization set in on Yayoi's face.

"Why would Li Jie not defend himself?" asked Lavinia.

Yayoi looked suddenly tired. "Because his mother and sisters still live here. He knows that if he doesn't do exactly as he's told, then they'll murder the rest of his family."

Lavinia was bouncing around in the back of the Jeep again the next morning, but she hardly noticed. With Yayoi as her guide, she'd found the village where the second accused assassin was from. The story was similar, except that the boy was a gifted metal worker. His ability to recycle metals foraged from the waste piles was legendary. The word was that he'd been given a formal education as a mechanical engineer and was living in Hangzhou while he worked for the Blood Dragons.

Returning to Yayoi's village, Lavinia and her driver spent the night and were now headed to see what they could find about the second boy in Hangzhou.

After a few hours of off-road driving, there was an abrupt transition and they were on a modern highway four lanes wide. Closing her eyes, Lavinia tried to nap.

The lack of movement was what woke Lavinia up. Then an odd sound raised her to another level of consciousness.

Thunk, thunk, thunk.

The world came into focus and she found herself parked at a gas station. Her driver was at the side of the vehicle, pumping gas.

Lavinia rubbed her eyes with the heels of her hands and stifled a yawn. She glanced around at the buildings that surrounded them. They seemed to be in a sizable city.

When her driver returned to the car, Lavinia pulled out her phone. She missed having Yayoi act as an interpreter for her, but Jacob had built one into the phone he'd made for her. It was a chore, but she managed to confirm that he was taking her to a safe hotel for the night so she could catch her flight to Hangzhou tomorrow morning at Lanzhou Airport.

Once in her room, Lavinia contacted Jacob. Plugging in the flash drive he'd made for her, she booted up TAILS, the full operating system that she could plug into any computer and use for encrypted communication and web browsing that was erased once she shut the computer down. Running SIGNAL, which had end-to-end encryption, she was able to chat safely with Jacob online. She quickly filled him in on what she'd found during her foray into the jungle.

"I can't believe you're still alive!" Jacob marveled.

"I'm a big girl. I can take care of myself."

"I know, but sheesh!"

"So I'm in Lanzhou right now, but I'll be in Hangzhou tomorrow morning. I'm not sure where to look when I get there, though. We have the tip from Dan about the guy running the Facebook page and we have the second would-be assassin, both from this city. I guess I go after the Facebook lead first."

"Why don't you hang tight today and let me see what I can find."

Lavinia signed off, unsure about the best way to report back to the president without worrying about being hacked. She decided to reach out to her boyfriend, John Miller, and have him relay her message to the president.

Opening SIGNAL again, she initiated a video chat with John. There was a pause before his face appeared on the screen. He looked tired, but his face lit up when he saw her.

"It's great to hear from you," he enthused. "I've been worried."

"Everything is good here," she assured him, then briefed him on her findings so far. "I need you to pass this information on to the president."

"I'm not sure if I'll be able to reach her, but I'll try. There have been some developments here."

"Developments?"

"Yeah, developments. The news is still breaking, but a few days ago the president announced that she's going to convert Puerto Rico from a commonwealth to a state."

"Can she do that? Why is that contentious?"

"It'd require a Constitutional amendment, but she's vowed to put the full weight of the presidency behind the initiative. Then the next day a whistleblower revealed that the president covered up Chinese attacks on American naval vessels in the South China Sea so it wouldn't interfere with her Puerto Rico announcement. The Republicans in the House and Senate are calling for investigations."

"She'll be okay," Lavinia assured him. "She knows what she's doing."

"Lavinia, I'm not a politician, but from what I'm hearing, she's in trouble."

"Look, I can't worry about this right now. I need you to get my information through to the president, however you can manage it."

"I'll get her the information," he promised. "But Lavinia, be careful, please. I don't like the sound of these Blood Dragons."

"I'll be careful," she assured him.

"I love you, Lavinia."

"I love you, too."

Lavinia closed SIGNAL after saying goodbye and then shut down the computer. She unplugged the thumb drive with TAILS on it and pocketed it.

Hangzhou was an important manufacturing base and logistical hub for coastal China, in addition to being one of China's most beautiful cities. Home to twenty-one million people, it was an easy place for Lavinia to carry out her work.

Unfortunately, Jacob had given her eleven possible locations for their target's last known residence. Lavinia had spent the past two evenings breaking into the first six buildings on the list. Excluding two run-ins with dogs, the evenings were as uneventful as they were unproductive. She hoped that number seven would prove to be her lucky number.

It was eleven o'clock at night on a Friday and the streets in the industrial part of town were deserted. Lavinia walked past the target building on the opposite side of the street. The cracked sidewalks matched the building's facade, which looked to predate World War II. It was a relic lost in a modern city. There was no evidence of an alarm system and the main door didn't even have a deadbolt, just a simple tumbler lock.

Reaching the end of the street, she crossed at the corner and walked back in the direction she had come. She thrust her hands in the front pouch of her sweatshirt, fingering the lockpick set that was hidden there.

Tension wrench in one hand and a saw rake in the other, Lavinia dropped to one knee and inserted the delicate tools into the lock. Holding the tension wrench in place with her left hand, she quickly worked the saw rake back and forth until the tumblers fell into place and the torsion wrench rotated in the keyhole. She was glad there were no spool pins in the lock to slow her down.

Standing up, Lavinia pushed the door inward and peeked inside. Only silence greeted her. She stepped in and closed the door behind her. Reaching up to the front of her black knit beanie, she pushed on the clear plastic square that looked like a manufacturer's logo. A thin LED light turned on like that on a miner's helmet and lit the way while keeping her hands free.

She tugged on the leather tab of her Urban Carry Holster, and the Sig Sauer she'd borrowed from the embassy popped into her hand. With the gun pointed forward, she made her way down the long hallway. The floor squeaked with each careful step, making her cringe. If her adventures last night had taught her anything, it was that factories in this part of Hangzhou shut down at night.

The walls of the hallway were lined with photos of shipping containers over the years. A man was pictured posing in front of each container and the farther she progressed down the hallway, the older the man got. If this was a family-owned shipping container-manufacturing facility that had been in business for half a century, then this was probably another dead end. Lavinia holstered her gun and walked to the end of the hallway, ignoring the noisy floor.

She was about to reach out for the doorknob to the main facility when the final picture caught her eye. In the last two photos the now very old owner was accompanied by a young man. Lavinia studied the picture and gasped. It was the metal worker from the second village. This was where he'd worked before he was arrested for the assassination of the vice president!

She palmed her gun again before pulling the door toward her and peering inside. Her beanie light did little to brighten the expansive room. Glancing around, she listened for any sign of life. Nothing. She stepped inside.

A few feet in front of her was an unpainted shipping container. She followed the length of the container, which led to a full-sized opening at the back of the old building, connecting it to a modern facility. While the cavernous new building was darkened, there were security lights mounted on the wall about every forty feet, casting long shadows. She walked the length of the manufacturing building. It was full of modern metal cutting and stamping equipment as well as some welding stations. As she made her way back to the front, Lavinia discovered a paint room off to the side.

Returning to the old structure that faced the street, she found a staging area where completed shipping containers were lined up in front of a large bay door, ready for shipment. The remaining two-thirds of the old building was office space. Lavinia searched each of the offices but found nothing conspicuous.

The last door was locked. Lavinia considered passing it by and moving on to the next property, but after a moment's hesitation she removed her lockpick tools. She made quick work of the lock and pushed the door inward. The light from her beanie made something across the room glint. Narrowing her eyes, Lavinia entered the room.

There was a piece of corrugated metal on the floor, about two feet long by two feet wide, leaning against a machine the size of a table saw. The machine was a 3D printer, and sitting on the printer bed was the lower receiver of an AR-15.

To her right was a small computer desk, with a laptop sitting on it. Lavinia plugged her flash drive and an external hard disk into it. Booting up TAILS, she used the system tools to copy the laptop's hard drive to the external disk she'd inserted. When the files started to copy, she stood and crossed the room to inspect the 3D printer.

Behind the printer stand was a pail in which the corrugated metal had been put after being cut into thin strips. At the back of the printer, there was a feeder tube filled with more strips of corrugated metal.

Lavinia's eyes widened. This was how liquid metal was being smuggled into the United States. They were making shipping containers out of the material, shipping product to America, then cutting the containers up and melting them into spools to distribute on the streets.

It was strange that the lead from Dan's email exchange with the fake Facebook account holder had led her to one of the men accused of assassinating the vice president. If they were both Blood Dragons, perhaps it made sense, but what a coincidence!

The computer beeped behind her. Lavinia returned to the laptop, shut it down, unplugged her devices, and disappeared into the night, leaving no trace of her visit.

TWENTY-FOUR

The lights were making Bradley Tanner sweat so much, the makeup artist had to dab his face four times to blot it off.

"You gonna be okay, honey?" The woman's long brown hair had one bunch dyed pink and another blue.

"I'll be fine." Tanner tried not to breathe in the powder. Rising from his chair, he left the green room, heading for the stage. He made his way to the seat he was accustomed to taking on the set of Fox News.

He was greeted by Kimberly, the popular Conservative news host known for playing loose with the facts and entertaining her audience while she did it.

Following a brief introduction after going on air, Kimberly got right to the point. "Mister Speaker, what do you make of the president's stated primary objective of granting Puerto Rico statehood? Is this where our focus should be today, or should we be looking at China?"

"Well, you make a good point, Kimberly. The news yesterday that the president covered up Chinese provocations in international waters tells you everything you need to know about this president's fitness for office. President Anderson doesn't understand foreign policy, so when faced with the prospect of World War Three, she sticks her head in the beaches of Puerto Rico."

"Great imagery, Mister Speaker. That really drives the point home. Are you calling for an investigation into the cover-up?"

"Another great question, Kimberly. I'm tempted to call this one Watergate, but since that's taken, I'm going to go with China-gate. The president deliberately misled the American people so that she didn't have to face an existential threat to this country's liberty. I believe we need a special prosecutor to look into this and find out what the president knew about these attacks and when she knew it." Waving a finger in the air, he added, "And exactly when did the president come up with this Puerto Rico playbook, because it didn't come out of left field; it came out of the North Atlantic Ocean, if you catch my meaning!"

"Is it too early to be talking impeachment, Mister Speaker?"

"As I've said before, Kimberly, if ignoring a threat to this country's very existence out of fear isn't an impeachable offense, then I don't know what is, quite frankly!"

Bradley Tanner wanted to share his secret information on the air that very moment, but he knew the timing wasn't right. If he could remove the president for dereliction of duty, then revealing his secret at the right time would be the knockout punch that would eliminate Olivia MacQueen. It would also leave the Oval Office to him.

When the time was right.

Olivia MacQueen sat with her hands folded in her lap. Off camera, in the wings, she could see her lead Secret Service agent scanning the studio for threats. That was his steady state. Alert.

She'd watched Bradley Tanner's interview an hour before, and was ready for her own contribution to the turbulence that had whipped up since the story broke yesterday. She'd spent hours with Rasha, preparing for this television appearance. There was a fine line to walk, but she was ready.

"I have with me today Vice President Olivia MacQueen, to discuss the latest developments," said Lisa. "Madame Vice President, thanks for joining us."

"Thanks for having me." *Smile. Remember to smile.* Her life coach reminded her again and again that she came across as too serious and intense. It was constant work for her, but she'd gotten good at projecting a persona since entering politics.

"So as you know, Madam Vice President, Bradley Tanner was on our show earlier and he's talking impeachment. What are your thoughts on that?"

"It's a little early to be talking about impeachment, Lisa. As you know, the president wrote extensively about Puerto Rico before ascending to the White House. So it's natural that she'd want to support the people of Puerto Rico in a time of need."

"But you aren't saying that she shouldn't be impeached?"

"Lisa, our founders created a framework that allowed the coequal branches of government to hold the Executive Branch in check. I believe in our institutions and that whatever happens, the final outcome will be a just one."

"You have to agree that the actions of the Chinese Navy are unacceptable?"

"Fair."

"They are tantamount to a declaration of war and our president was derelict in her duty by not responding."

"I'd refer to the actions of the Chinese as a provocation."

"Okay, a provocation, then. Which the president ignored, and worse still, hid from the American people."

"I'm sure that the president will have a conversation with Chinese President Xiu Ying Zhang."

"Should the president be impeached over this?"

This is it! Olivia thought. The moment. "You know, Lisa, to this point we haven't even had contact with China yet. Had the president's inaction resulted in deaths or damage to one of our ships, then perhaps you could argue that impeachment was the right next step. But at this point, it's just been provocations. I'm sure the president has a plan to address this before it gets out of hand."

The setup was there for the world to see. When the Chinese attacked tonight, she'd be able to fall back on her words and support impeachment. The game was in play.

Dan Nolan's bare feet made no noise on the Berber carpet of his hotel room as he paced across the room, lost in thought. His hand rubbed his chin.

He'd always distrusted Olivia MacQueen, but watching her interview made his blood boil. You couldn't interpret any of what she said as a defense of the president. Her responses were vague and indirectly supported an investigation of the president. It was unprecedented, absurd! Where he'd seen red flags in the past, now there was a five-alarm fire.

Snatching up his cell phone, he dialed Lawrence's number from memory.

"Hi, Dan," came the amicable investigator's voice. His likable demeanor was one of the reasons he was so effective. When people talked to him, they'd just offer up information voluntarily.

"Lawrence, any developments with our little project?" He was careful not to say anything that might give away his investigation of the vice president. You never knew who might be listening.

"I'm on it right now, actually."

Frowning, Dan realized that this call was fruitless. What could Lawrence say on an open line? "I'm en route back from Puerto Rico. I'll be in Washington tomorrow. Maybe we can catch up?"

"Can do. Just give me the sign."

Dan thanked him and hung up. He was pacing again.

The president needed to respond to Bradley Tanner and put Olivia MacQueen in her place.

Lawrence had left his beloved Oldsmobile at home and rented a black Honda Accord. Having met the woman in black face to face, he had no desire for a repeat performance, and she knew what his car looked like. The Secret Service had stepped up patrols around One Observatory Circle, so he also had to station himself much farther out. He'd selected a park half a mile away.

It also meant that surveillance had to be done remotely. To solve that problem, Lawrence had ordered a ProDrone from a company in Japan. It was a drone that had two fixed-axis claws that could carry and deliver a payload. He'd used the drone in the dead of night to place battery-controlled WiFi cameras around the back of the residence and in the woods across the street. The cameras had to be switched out every two days to recharge their batteries.

One of his men had followed the vice president from her appearance at Fox News back to the residence. Lawrence had watched her arrive on camera an hour ago, shortly after Dan called. Nothing unusual since.

He was checking the array of video feeds on his three iPad Pros when there was a tap at the driver's side window. Snapping his head toward the sound, he came face to face with the barrel of a gun. A gloved hand motioned for him to open the window.

Lawrence tapped the button for the power windows and with a silent hum the window retracted. He raised his hands. Standing beside his car was the woman in black. In her hand was a Heckler and Koch USP pistol.

"Hello, Lawrence. I know who hired you. Pack up your shit, and if I find any evidence that you're watching or following me, there will be repercussions. Are we clear?"

Lawrence cleared his throat. "Yes, ma'am."

The woman backed away, the gun still pointed at him. When she reached the tree line she disappeared into the woods. A moment later he heard the quiet hum as an electric motorcycle peeled off.

Lawrence started his car and drove around town until he was sure he wasn't being followed. He found another place to park, still a half mile away from the vice president's residence, but on the opposite side of his last location. He launched his drone and retrieved all of his cameras.

He didn't know who the woman in black was. A

member of the Secret Service? The vice president's life coach? Certainly, the vice president couldn't be sneaking past the Secret Service and driving around on a motorcycle. Whoever she was, she knew his name, and by implication she'd know where he and his family lived.

The operation was over.

TWENTY-FIVE

Lavinia picked at the pasta dish she'd ordered through room service. She was normally an adventurous eater, so when she was out of the country, ordering was not usually a challenge. This hotel, however, wasn't great. The white chunks might be chicken. Then again, they might not be. She pushed them to the side of her plate.

Having been in China for over a week now, Lavinia was frustrated with her progress. She had learned *things*, but not necessarily the *things* she wanted to learn.

She had opened Jitsi Meet, the secure VOIP application recommended by Jacob because it played nice with TAILS. She paced her room, checking the screen to see if there was a message from Jacob each time she passed it.

Aloud, she recounted what she knew. "Liu Wei runs the Blood Dragons. The Blood Dragons are at least involved in smuggling liquid steel into the United States, if not completely responsible. That likely means they were also behind the social media attacks." She chewed her lip. Hopefully Jacob would be able to confirm that when he called. The two men accused of assassinating the vice president were both Blood Dragons but were probably innocent of the assassination. If they were innocent, then Liu Wei might have actually killed the vice president.

There were still two missing links. Could they prove that the vice president's car was hacked by the Blood Dragons, and could they directly link them to the social media attacks on President Anderson?

Her computer let out a stilted buzz, paused, then did it again. Lavinia answered on the second ring. "Jacob! How are you? Are you safe?"

"Good, I'm good. Yes, no problems at the hotel. Not the nicest accommodations I've ever enjoyed, but no one's breaking into my room, so that's a win. Where are you?"

"I'm in a hotel. Worse than the one you're in, if that makes you feel any better."

"A bit. Actually, yes it does." He gave a sly smile.

Lavinia had never seen him look so stressed, but it was nice to see him maintain his sense of humor.

"Let me link in Chen. He's been helping me."

"Is that secure?"

"Yeah, by default all of our communication is running through the TOR router, so it's impossible for anyone to intercept the call."

"I'll take your word for it." She waited a few moments and then Chen's face appeared on screen. They all exchanged greetings.

"Okay, we're all here. Lavinia, Chen and I went through the files that you pulled from the warehouse. That computer was being used by someone to run Facebook groups masquerading as Americans. There were sixty-six different user accounts, some of which Facebook had shut down for suspicious activity. Some were active and some had been created but weren't live yet. So he was one of a large network of people operating fake Facebook accounts."

"So that directly links the Blood Dragons to the social media attacks and to the flood of liquid steel in the US. That's perfect!" said Lavinia, clapping her hands together.

"It does. Nothing on the drives links them to the assassination plot, though. But you proved that one of the suspects is legally blind. I can confirm that the other one was working out of the warehouse where you stole the drive. From the email activity on the drive, Chen found references to him and he's an engineer. An expert in 3D printers. He invented the process that allows the printers to use liquid steel to print guns, but he is definitely not a hacker. In fact, the guy who was running the social media attacks out of that location is a really bad excuse for a hacker. He thinks he knows more than he really does. I would have never been able to track him down as easily as I did if he knew what he was doing."

"So dead end as to who hacked the vice president's car, then?"

"Yup, I'm afraid so. For now, at least."

"Well, we know that Liu Wei is up to something. The question is, who is he acting for? Is he doing this at the behest of the president or is he undermining him?"

"Can't help you there."

"I think I need to have a conversation with my attaché back in Beijing. Jacob, if I call him, I'm assuming they can track me?"

"Don't use the actual phone. Run the VPN app on your phone first, then use the app called Burner. It'll give you an unlimited number of phone numbers to call from. No one will be able to call you back that way, and it'll ensure that you're untraceable."

"Okay, I guess that's all for now," Lavinia said.

"Are you coming back to Beijing?"

"Let me talk to the attaché first. I'll let you know what I'm doing over SIGNAL." That was the encrypted messaging app on her phone.

Lavinia hung up the call and turned off her computer. Sitting back in the easy chair in her room, she crossed her arms over her chest and bit her lip.

A short time later, Lavinia pulled out her phone and followed Jacob's instructions. She enabled the VPN, then used the Burner app to call Tung.

He answered on the fourth ring. "Lavinia, so nice to hear from you!"

He sounded genuinely pleased. Lavinia was still wary of the man, unsure if she could trust him. How high up did the conspiracy go? Who was Tung really loyal to?

"Hi Tung, nice to speak with you again. Thank you for inviting me to the state dinner. I enjoyed getting to know the president and the vice president. The president in particular."

"President Xiu Ying Zhang was very pleased to get to know you, Lavinia. He explicitly mentioned you to me the next day and asked that I convey his personal welcome to China to you."

"That's very gracious, Tung." Lavinia paused before plunging ahead. "Listen, I don't know how to broach this topic, so I'm just going to put it out there. When I spoke with Vice President Liu Wei, I told him I'd discovered that the man first accused of killing the vice president was in fact innocent." She could hear the sound of Tung moving the phone from one ear to the other.

"Yes, I heard this," he said simply.

"I was shocked to see on the news the next day that they had two new suspects."

"Liu Wei is in charge of the military and the military investigations unit, as you know. He maintained that post when he took over as vice president."

"Yes, I'm aware. Look, I've been doing some more digging. The former vice president was assassinated by someone who hacked into Jang Dung's car and remotely used it to crash the vice president's car. The two men who were arrested, well, one of them is legally blind and the other is a metallurgical engineer. Neither of them had the skills necessary to hack Jang Dung's car."

There was a long moment of silence as Tung absorbed this information.

Lavinia pushed on. "Tung, is it possible that Liu Wei was behind the assassination to allow him to ascend to the vice presidency?"

"I'm sorry, Miss Lavinia, but I must go."

The phone went dead.

Wang Juan sat across the table from the intelligence analyst.

"Play it again."

Lavinia Walsh's voice filled the small office. "Tung, is it possible that Liu Wei was behind the assassination to allow him to ascend to the vice presidency?"

"Make me a copy of this message."

The analyst saved a copy of the message on a flash drive and handed it to Wang Juan. She went directly to Liu Wei's room.

TWENTY-SIX

The Honda Accord's tires screeched in protest as they were forced to take the turn too tight and too fast. The acrid stench of burning rubber filled the car. Lawrence stomped on the accelerator despite roaring through a residential neighborhood.

The moonlight revealed a stop sign ahead and he jammed on the brakes, but he was going too fast. Halfway through the intersection he gave up trying to stop and floored the accelerator again. Approaching his street, he braked hard and squealed around the corner. The front end of the car rocked upward as he hit the curb to his driveway, followed by the rear of the vehicle.

He jolted to a stop and threw the car into Park. Lawrence pushed the door open, jumped out, and slammed it shut. He popped the trunk as he rounded the vehicle and removed the canvas duffel bag with his drone cameras. A dog barked as he threw them over his shoulder and jogged to his backyard.

Lawrence paused to grab a shovel from the shed. He dropped the shovel and bag over the chain-link fence at the back of his yard. It backed onto a long-abandoned quarry, but there was a hundred yards of forest at the back of his yard before it broke into a clearing. He followed the shovel and bag over the fence.

Dodging trees, he ran through the woods toward the clearing, careful not to turn an ankle on the uneven terrain. The bugs that had assailed his face disappeared as he burst into the open. The dark of night was pushed back by a quarter Moon. He began to dig. By the time the hole was large enough to cover the entire duffel bag, sweat had broken out on his brow. He placed the bag inside and covered it up with dirt, stomping it down and then spreading a layer of dead leaves across the freshly turned soil and patting them down with his feet. He repeated the procedure until the ground was level. Spreading the remaining dirt in the woods, he then took handfuls of leaves and covered the entire area.

He used his hands to clean the dirt from his shovel as he walked back toward his house.

Tossing the shovel over the low-lying fence, he vaulted over, then returned the shovel to the shed and went around the side of the house to slip through the front door. He washed his hands in the bathroom by the door, then went to his home office.

Powering up his computer, he sent a group text. It was two words: *Vacation time*. It was one of their internal codes, and it meant that an operation was immediately suspended.

He opened the Contacts app on his computer and looked up the address for one of his employee's cottages and jotted it down.

Dropping to his knees, he pried the baseboard from the wall. There was a hole the size of a model car in the drywall, just above the two-by-four bottom plate. Reaching in, he removed a Ziploc bag. Inside was five thousand dollars in twenties. He pushed the baseboard back into place.

Crossing the bungalow, he opened their bedroom door. His wife was asleep on her side with her hands folded under the pillow. The faint amber light from the smoke alarm lit her face. *Angelic.*

Crossing the room, he sat on the bed next to her. She stirred. "Honey, wake up." He put a hand on her shoulder.

Turning to face her husband, she said, "Hey, you're back."

"We need to leave. Right now. Pack up the necessities for you and the girls, but we need to go."

She sat up and slid back against the padded headboard, her eyes wide open. "What's going on? Is it work?"

"It's work." He nodded.

Lawrence watched as she slid off the bed without a word and crossed the room to turn on the light. She went to the walk-in closet and returned with three suitcases. He was amazed. As the wife of a private investigator, she knew there was a time to ask questions and a time to act. Now she acted. He'd never loved her more than at this moment, but it did little to assuage the guilt that washed over him.

Together they packed, slipping into the girls' bedroom and emptying their drawers of clothing and stashing it in the suitcases. When they were done, Lawrence loaded them into the trunk of the rental car.

They each woke up one girl, slipped on her shoes, and wrapped her in a blanket. They stood and caught each other's gaze for a moment, each holding a child in their arms. With sad eyes Lawrence held his wife's gaze and mouthed the words, *I'm sorry.*

His wife mouthed her response. *I love you.*

Once they were in the car with the girls belted in and covered in their blankets, Lawrence spoke. "I can't tell you everything. I may be overreacting, but there was a threat from one of the most powerful people in the world, so I'm taking it seriously. I'm taking you to Connor's family cottage. It's empty this time of year, but no one will be able to find you and the girls there."

"We'll need to pick up a cell phone so I can call you."

"Yeah, we'll get a pay-as-you-go phone on the way. I'm so sorry about this, honey."

"I knew what I was marrying." She gave him a wry smile. "When this is over, I get my new kitchen."

Lawrence smiled.

It was a statement, not a question.

Lawrence rubbed his eyes with one hand while the other gripped the steering wheel. He reached down till his fingers brushed the warm can of Red Bull. He raised it to his lips and drained what was left. Crushing the can, he dropped it on the floor of the passenger side of the car.

He'd slept with his wife for three hours before slipping out of bed and getting back in the car. It wasn't nearly enough.

Rush hour. Damn!

Staring straight ahead, he wondered what his next stop should be. He reached down and turned on the stereo. He scanned channels before stopping on a news station. After listening to a report about the local garbage strike, he snapped the radio off.

Damn!

The name of the upcoming exit gave him an idea. He

signaled and worked his way over to the right-hand lane. Pulling into the exit lane, he left the freeway.

Lawrence parked the Honda Accord in front of a modest two-story home. He pulled out the phone he'd bought at a gas station and dialed his friend's number. "Hey, Henry, sorry to bother you at work."

"Lawrence, how's it goin'? People don't get called to the office unless there's an emergency. Are you okay?"

"Yeah, I'm okay. Listen, can I use your computer?"

"Now?"

"Yeah, I'm in front of your house right now. I can't explain, Henry, but I can't go home right now."

There was a pause. "I can go home at lunch to let you in," he offered.

"No, I can get in, don't worry about that. Is there a password on your computer?"

"Nope."

"Okay, I might need it for a few hours, but I'll be gone by the time you get home."

"Whatever you need," Henry said.

"Thanks, Henry, you're a savior. I'll explain another time."

"No problem. Keep safe, Lawrence."

Lawrence hung up. He pushed his door open, stepped out onto the sidewalk, looked left and right, and made his way to Henry's front door. He had the lock popped in under thirty seconds and was inside. He went straight downstairs to the computer he and Dan had used only a week ago.

Opening the desk drawer, he found a blank pad and a pen. He set them on the desk next to the computer and moved the mouse to wake up the screen.

Over the ensuing hours, Lawrence researched Olivia

MacQueen's history. Her personal Facebook account was private. He could read her LinkedIn profile, but he couldn't find any other personal social media accounts that he could attribute to her.

Out of university she did a year and a half in the Peace Corps. Three months of training in the US followed by fifteen months in Bangladesh. He came across a photo of her and a group of Americans in front of a Peace Corps banner.

From there she did law school, was a staffer for two members of Congress, then got her first job at a Washington-based firm as a Constitutional lawyer.

An unremarkable career chronology, until she entered politics.

Lawrence spent the next hour finding the names of as many people from the past that he could connect to her. He then analyzed that list to see if he could find more recent connections and track them back to her.

He wanted to figure out who the woman in black was. It had to be someone from Olivia MacQueen's past, someone who was so close to her that they'd be willing to threaten Lawrence's family.

Over the next three hours, Lawrence spoke with a dozen people from the vice president's past, posing as a reporter writing a puff piece on the vice president. All were thrilled to share anecdotes, and all of them insisted that the vice president know they gave her glowing reviews.

Washington. Typical.

Going back to his notes, Lawrence tried another tack. He listed her connections in reverse chronology and checked them against her LinkedIn network. It was amazing that LinkedIn let you see any user's network, even if you were not connected to them.

It seemed that just about anyone who came into contact with MacQueen stayed in her orbit. There were just three people over her career that he could find who didn't. He'd hoped to find a short list of people from her distant past that she kept in touch with, and maybe among them he'd find his woman in black.

The list of non-contacts included one woman and two men. The woman was in the Peace Corps with MacQueen. They'd both started and ended their assignments at the same time. Comparing that to the other members listed in the photo, they were the only two who were in Bangladesh for fifteen months. Everyone else was there for three years.

Checking MacQueen's list of contacts, he confirmed that the woman, Victoria Thomson, was not a connection.

Odd.

Victoria Thomson was the vice president of Human Resources at a telecommunications firm in Washington. Lawrence found her office and placed a call. Unlike most of his phone calls that day, he got through to her on the first try.

"Ms. Thomson? My Name is Colin Pencilton. I'm writing a piece on Olivia MacQueen's life before politics and I'm reaching out to her former friends and colleagues. I understand—"

"I'm not a friend of Ms. MacQueen's."

The phone went dead.

Barbara Anderson spun in her chair, her fingers gripping the leather arm, as Dan Nolan burst into the Oval Office. He was out of breath.

"Madam President, we have a problem!"

"What's going on?"

Dan crossed the room and in an instant was beside her, tapping on her keyboard. He went to CNN and clicked on the top story. The headline read *"China will pay for it!"*

There was a video report from a reporter with a link that read *full video*, which was almost an hour long. It was a speech by the president to the Economic Club of America. It included a twenty-minute Q&A at the end, as she wandered the stage in her signature peacock blue suit. During the speech the woman spoke about allowing Puerto Rico to declare bankruptcy and to start again. "We must all give a little now to allow Puerto Rico to become a successful part of the United States in the future."

There were other controversial remarks as well. She claimed that a new round of tariffs on China would pay for almost all of Puerto Rico's restructuring.

President Anderson sat staring at the screen with her mouth open. "Dan, that isn't me!" she exclaimed.

Dan looked at her hard. "I don't know how a video like this is possible, Barbara. Deep fake videos are a new technology. They take a subject sitting in a chair and can make it look like they're saying something they're not, but to make it look real they can't change body movements. Having someone walk around and engage with the audience is impossible!"

The president's eyes were glued on Dan. It wasn't lost on her that it was the first time since she'd won the presidency that he hadn't referred to her as Madam President. He was as scared as she was.

"Dan, I don't know who did this."

"Only a state actor could pull something like this off. It's like Stuxnet—everyone knew that we did it because it was so sophisticated only a government would have the resources to produce it."

Stuxnet was a virus that infected computers all around the world, but only activated when it recognized centrifuges that had been purchased by Iran. It made the centrifuges speed up to dangerous levels for one hour every twenty-six days, then slow down to one tenth the required speed. The result was that the nuclear material being developed was flawed and the centrifuges themselves developed cracks. It was the most sophisticated virus in history and the start of the cyberwar era.

Turning back to the screen, Dan said, "Play it again."

They watched the video three more times. Together they identified a few inconsistencies. The woman picked up a pen with her right hand, although she didn't write anything. Barbara Anderson was left-handed. The shoes were wrong. They appeared to be a knockoff of the brand she favored.

"Dan, get the FBI to open an investigation into this. We need the press secretary and her team working on a response. A denial!" She shook her finger at Dan. "This is unacceptable and we need to react right away!"

Dan left the room, typing madly into his phone as he went.

TWENTY-SEVEN

Lavinia's hand was wrapped around the grip of her embassy-issued Sig Sauer. Her eyes darted left and right in the back of the Jeep, branches whipping by. She was haunted by an unmistakable feeling of déjà vu.

She spoke into her phone so it could translate. "How far are we?" Lavinia had taken to calling it her Lego phone whenever she was in front of Jacob. The device spoke to her driver in an electronic woman's voice.

She leaned forward in her seat with the phone extended so the man could reply. He spoke and Lavinia looked at her phone expectantly, waiting for it to translate. The woman's voice returned. "Who knows? We're in a forest, not on a highway."

Lavinia frowned.

The front windshield splintered like a web and a cloud of red mist covered Lavinia's head and shoulders. The Jeep veered to the left and Lavinia braced herself for impact as they ran into a tree.

There was a thunderous crash. The back of the car rotated so that it was in line with the front of the vehicle before it flipped and flipped and flipped. How may times, Lavinia would never know, but it seemed to last forever. When the vehicle came to rest on its tires, Lavinia opened her eyes. Her driver was dead. A bullet had hit him smack in the nose, and his body had been battered in the crash.

You couldn't escape the smell of gasoline.

Undoing her seatbelt, Lavinia tried the door. It wouldn't open. Sliding across, she tried the door on the other side, but it wouldn't budge either. She pulled her arm into her shirt-sleeve and brushed the glass off the seat. Reaching into her pocket, she pulled out her wallet and jammed it to hold the door handle open. She leaned back on the seat and kicked with both feet. The door opened a few inches. Sitting up, she threw the door open and got out of the vehicle.

Glancing back inside, she looked for anything critical. Her backpack had all of her personal items in it, so she grabbed it just as a bullet ricocheted off the door of the car, narrowly missing her. Lavinia ducked and scurried behind the destroyed vehicle, dragging her backpack behind her. Her gun was drawn and in her right hand while she searched every pocket on her with her left. Her fingers grasped a matchbox.

Reaching for the gas cap, she unscrewed it and dropped it on the ground. She grabbed a nearby tree branch, which was about two feet long. Stepping away from the tank, she lit the match and jammed it in the jagged end of the stick. She moved it toward the tank.

There was a *whoosh* when she was still six inches away from the open tank as the fuel vapors ignited, and she dove away just as a fireball erupted from the tank. Rolling a few feet toward the woods, she came to a stop and looked back at the Jeep.

The vehicle was engulfed.

Huddled over, Lavinia reached behind her for her backpack and threw it on while she ran through the woods. When she was behind a tree as wide as her body, she peered back. She saw a man pop up for a moment and peer over his rifle at the car. He disappeared again, but Lavinia had what she needed.

Running ninety degrees to the sniper's position, she stayed low as she went. The foliage was thick and provided ample cover. About a hundred yards in, she banked another ninety degrees and made her way parallel to the sniper's last position. When he came into view, she slowed and dropped into a crouch below a fallen tree. There were two men.

Without hesitation, Lavinia sprang from her hiding place and ran toward the two men, both arms extended, the gun in her right and supported by her left. The men were peering over a fallen log toward the burning car.

Eighty yards, seventy yards, sixty yards... Lavinia counted in her head.

One of the men turned his head toward her. In full stride, Lavinia fired. Then fired again. His head snapped back and he fell to the ground. As the second man reacted, she continued to pull the trigger till her magazine was empty.

She stopped thirty yards away. Both men lay dead.

After staring for a stunned moment, she started to walk, glancing all around. Her hearing pricked up, now sensitive to the minutest sound in the jungle.

When she arrived at their hiding place, what she found was a well-fortified snipers' nest. There was a makeshift kitchen with cans of food packed away in a wooden crate set up as a locker. Camouflage netting draped over the fallen trees that had been arranged in a *U* formation. Boxes of ammunition were piled up against one of the walls.

She checked the back of each man's left earlobe. They both had red dragon tattoos.

Crouching again, she studied the woods around her. Reaching down, she picked up the sniper rifle closest to her with one hand while using the other to fill the pockets of her camouflage pants with five round magazines.

There had to be something around here important enough to protect. Which also meant she wasn't alone. She knelt behind the barrier and put the rifle up to her shoulder, pivoted toward the way she had just come, and gazed through the scope. It was logical that the unprotected side of the snipers' nest must face another snipers' nest.

Leaning against the fallen tree, she studied the woods. Nothing moved. Amazing, considering how many shots she'd fired.

Lavinia performed a three hundred and sixty degree search using the scope. Through the foliage, she caught sight of a building. It was about two hundred yards off the road that ran through the woods and would have been invisible from the ground.

Lavinia slung the rifle over her shoulder and moved off toward the building. She reloaded her Sig Sauer.

As she moved through the woods, her training at the Terrorist Training Academy came back to her. Last month, John had asked her if she wanted to take a vacation together. As a joke, she'd suggested the training course, but they'd ended up doing it. They'd had a ton of fun, but today it might just save her life.

Lavinia arrived at the edge of the tree line. Twenty-five yards away lay what appeared to be an abandoned Second World War-era airplane hangar. There was no sign of life.

Lying down, she trained the rifle scope on the forest and

searched the edge of the woods on either side of the hangar for movement. Nothing.

She raised herself to a crouch and brushed the dirt off her hands. Rifle over her shoulder, she supported her pistol and made a break for the building. She reached a steel door on the side of the building without incident. Reaching over, she turned the knob.

Unlocked.

Her hand still on the doorknob, she took a deep breath. Pulling the door open an inch, she froze and cringed at the sound of metal grating against metal.

Oh my lord!

She peered through the crack into a cavernous room. The lights weren't on, but daylight spilled in through large windows at the end of the building that stretched from the apex down to the top of the first story.

The door groaned as she opened it wide enough to slip inside, gun first.

The huge building was deserted.

Staying close to the wall, she began to examine the perimeter of the building. She could see a pile of rubble across the expanse, but she stayed disciplined and made her way slowly around the building. Against the back wall were stacks of metal-framed chairs with padded seats and plastic seat backs. They looked brand new and very out of place.

As she approached the pile of rubble it came into focus. There were large wooden frames like you'd see on the set of an amateur theater. The frame itself was painted black and on the face was a vinyl covering of blue with white lettering with the words "Economic Club of America."

It was odd. Lavinia pulled out her Lego phone and took a photo. She completed a search of the building and found nothing else. Going to a window at the far end of the building, she peered out, looking for activity.

Still nothing.

What is this place?

Moving the length of the building at a brisk walk, she checked the window kitty-corner to the one she'd just looked through. Raising the rifle, she put her eye to the scope and searched the tree line. She was halfway through her survey when she caught sight of movement. As she moved the scope back, a group of six men came into view. Three of them carried rifles like the one Lavinia was holding. The other three men held pistols.

There must have been four snipers' nests, one at each corner of the land surrounding the building. The building was empty now, but did the security detail mean someone was coming back?

There were too many of them for her to take out. She might get one or two before the others scattered, but that was the best-case scenario. The door she'd used to enter the building made a ton of noise, so she couldn't sneak out that way, even though it faced away from the soldiers.

Lavinia ran the length of the building to the windows on the other side. The frame was made of wood and the glass was held in place by some sort of gummy material that had long since hardened and been painted over many times. Reaching into her thigh pocket, she removed a military knife. Slicing away the hardened material, she cleared enough of it that she could remove the pane of glass. She lowered it to the floor, then slipped through the hole and onto the grass on the other side. Reaching back inside, she retrieved her backpack and the rifle.

Making a beeline for the trees, she was sure to keep the building between herself and the soldiers. Once safe in the woods, she headed toward the forest road. How was she going to get out of here on foot?

She found the road and, staying about twenty feet away from it to be hidden from any vehicles that might happen along, she started walking, wondering how long she would survive with no water or food.

She'd gone half a mile when she noticed something white in the distance. Gripping her gun more tightly, she kept the muzzle pointed ahead. As she got closer she could see that it was a car. Closer still, and it was clear that it was abandoned.

The car was just off the forest road, parked between some trees so that it didn't block the way. The vehicle was a BMW and it looked new. There was no way it'd been there long.

Lavinia peered through the window. The key was in the ignition and there was a rucksack on the passenger seat. Through the back window, she saw a mess of electronic equipment strewn across the floor and seat, partially covered by a jacket. Lavinia caught a glimpse of her reflection in the side-view mirror. Her face and shirt were splattered with the blood of her driver. She was disgusted but couldn't spare the water to clean it off.

The fact that the key was in the ignition suggested that they planned to send someone back to get it. Lavinia tried the handle and the door opened easily. Picking up the rucksack, she unzipped it and looked inside. There was a single canteen full of water and some military food packs.

For completeness she turned the key. The car was dead. No surprise.

She took a look around before turning her attention to the back seat. She took the jacket and tried it on. A little large, but it covered the blood on her shirt. Sifting through the equipment, she found a dozen WD Passport backup drives. Lavinia opened her own backpack and the rucksack and rifled through all of the items there. She consolidated what she felt was most important into one pile of critical items, including the backup drives.

Retrieving the keys, she went around back and popped the trunk. It was lined with plastic, like you'd see in a mafia movie. There was a pool of blood in the plastic lining at one end of the trunk. Lying inside was a shovel and a pair of construction gloves.

Lavinia studied the ground around the car. About ten feet away was a patch of freshly overturned dirt. Lavinia put on the gloves and grabbed the shovel. She started to dig.

She was down about six inches, just her fourth shovelful, when she hit something. Getting down on one knee, she choked up on the shovel with both hands and cleared the dirt away. Blue cloth. She continued to clear the dirt till her worst fears were confirmed. It was a leg. The urge to throw up was accompanied by a tinge of fear that ran down her spine.

Based on the size of the disturbed plot of dirt, Lavinia moved to where she thought the head would be. She carefully cleared the earth away, very quickly hitting a human head. She worked carefully around it, uncovering a decomposed face and long blond hair. Clearing away part of the chest so she could get a good shot of the woman's clothing, Lavinia took a photo. She then re-buried the body and returned the shovel and gloves to the trunk.

Slipping back into the woods, Lavinia continued her trip through the jungle. She needed to find someplace safe before nightfall.

A bright orange glow filtered through the trees. A chill ran through her as a breeze tickled the nape of her neck. Having walked for hours, Lavinia was facing the prospect of having to survive a night in the jungle when a horse-drawn cart happened along. She poured the last of the water from the canteen into her hand and washed her face. Ditching the rifle, she hid her Sig Sauer in the holster at the small of her back, then ran to catch up to the cart. When she was alongside it she flagged the driver down.

While the middle-aged man didn't speak English, he welcomed the haggard American onto his cart. Eager to avoid being seen, she motioned that she wanted to sleep and he pointed to the cart and handed her the blanket he was sitting on.

Lavinia settled into the cart, which was full of sacks of rice. She hefted a few aside to make herself a place hidden from view. She pulled the blanket over her and tried to rest. At the Terrorist Training Academy, they were taught that the most important weapon when in enemy territory was sleep.

She must have been more tired than she realized, because she fell asleep right away. The temperature had dropped by the time she woke, and the farmer was unloading his sacks of rice. Lavinia got up and helped him.

After thanking the man, she set out to scope the town she found herself in. It was anything but modern, but certainly better than the alternative she'd faced a few hours ago. Using what was left of the water in her canteen, she rinsed off her face again.

Her phone was dead, so she used a combination of hand signals and sounds to try to convey her need for somewhere to stay. The farmer understood and led her to a hotel where

Lavinia found a room. In her entire life, she'd never been so happy to strip down and have a shower.

After she'd cleaned off, with her phone plugged in, she called Jacob.

"Where are you?"

Lavinia laughed. "I wish I knew." With a sense of urgency, she recounted her adventures. Jacob interrupted her here and there with questions, but for the most part he listened in anxious silence.

"Can you connect me to those drives?"

"I wish I could. All I have is my Lego phone." The shower had restored her sense of humor.

"It's not a Lego phone," Jacob shot back. His tone was not amused.

"Seriously, Jacob. I have no idea what's on the drives. However, I have to assume it's related to the Blood Dragons, given what else was in the car."

"Do you know who the woman you found was?"

"No. The body was pretty decomposed, although I'm pretty sure she was Western."

"How are you going to get back here?"

"I don't know. I'm going to have to get creative, because I don't have a ton of money."

"Can you get access to a computer there? Does the hotel have a business center?"

"If you could see this place, you'd know the answer to that is no. It's a trade hub, but it's still pretty rural. I need to get my bearings and find a path back to Beijing. How are things back home?"

"A little crazy," Jacob admitted. He filled Lavinia in on the video of the president that was making the rounds. "It's caused quite a stir."

"Is it really her? Could it be an actor?"

Jacob was silent for a moment. "Deep fakes are getting more and more convincing, but the video was an hour long. She was walking around stage and taking questions."

"Could the video of the president be a deep fake?"

"That's the thing," Jacob said. "To have someone sitting down and speaking is one thing, but to have someone walking around stage then taking and answering questions... well, that's a whole other level. No one's ever done that before."

"What about *Rogue One*, the Star Wars movie where they brought dead people back to life to reprise their roles? Remember Princess Leia at the end?"

"Yes, that's true."

Lavinia could almost hear him thinking.

"You'll have to watch the video when you get access to a computer. I think you'll understand when you see it," he said.

"Has the White House commented?"

"They issued a vehement denial in a formal statement, but the next press conference isn't scheduled till tomorrow."

"I need to get back there fast," Lavinia declared.

The parking garage had become familiar ground for Lawrence. Today he parked two stories down and took the stairwell up. He sat in the shadows, anticipating Dan's arrival. His eyes darted from place to place while he waited.

It was twenty excruciating minutes before the now familiar headlights from Dan's car appeared on the top level of the garage. When Dan stepped out of his car in the darkness, Lawrence brushed past him on his way to the electrical room. Once closed inside, Lawrence began to vomit information.

"Dan, the vice president is crazy!" Even in the darkness, he could tell that Dan was taken aback.

"Lawrence, what happened? What's going on?" There was concern in his voice.

"Listen to me. The second voice in the room? Rasha Brown? They're the same person. Rasha Brown is Olivia MacQueen!"

"I don't understand. She's pretending to be her own life coach?"

"She's not pretending, Dan, they're the same person. She has multiple personality disorder."

In the green light from the ceiling-mounted smoke detector, Lawrence could just make out the stunned look on Dan's face. "I'm telling you, she's mentally ill!"

"How do you know this?"

"Olivia MacQueen was in the Peace Corps after college. She crashed out after a year and a half of her three-year commitment."

"That doesn't prove anything," Dan reasoned.

"You have to let me finish," Lawrence said, his voice urgent. "There was a woman, Victoria Thomson. They joined the corps at the same time and they both finished at the same time. I found her."

"What did she say?"

"She wouldn't talk to me at first, Dan. It took hours to earn her trust, but she finally opened up. They were in Bangladesh. The two of them became fast friends. Got an apartment together and everything. One night a couple of guys broke into their apartment and attempted to kidnap Olivia. Victoria came home and foiled the attack. You can imagine how an attack on two American women would go over, and Victoria Thomson got a lot of local media attention for her bravery. A few days later the two of them were in their apartment and MacQueen's alter ego came out. She thinks it might have been the first time she manifested, but the person that came out said her name was Rasha Brown and she was Olivia's protector. She told Victoria that she had to leave Bangladesh because she was taking attention away from Olivia. That Olivia had a higher purpose in life."

"You're kidding!"

"No, and listen to this. Victoria told her that she was staying, but she was scared so she crashed at a friend's apartment. The next day Olivia MacQueen filed a false report claiming that Victoria had been sexually abusing her while she slept and that she was so afraid for her safety that she'd made Victoria find somewhere else to sleep. There was no way to refute the claim."

"So what happened?"

"Their superior didn't know what to do, so he sent both of them home halfway through their commitment. Victoria was appalled that her reputation had been ruined, but she didn't know what to do. So she just went home and tried to put it behind her."

"And she opened up about it to you, twenty years later?"

"It wasn't easy, Dan. I had to swear to her that it would never go public. If it did get out, she'd deny it."

"Did she say what Olivia's higher purpose was?"

"No, she didn't know and she didn't try to guess. But she's made it to vice president—it's not a stretch to say that she feels she's destined to be president one day."

Dan was silent.

"That's not all. The woman in black? It's Olivia MacQueen also."

"The woman on the motorcycle?"

"Yes. She caught me surveilling her residence two nights ago and she threatened me and my family."

Dan looked aghast. "Is your family safe?"

"I took my wife and daughters out of town. They're safe, but I can't hide them forever."

"Lawrence, I'm so sorry I brought this on you and your family."

"Dan, you couldn't have known. This woman is one step away from the Oval Office. If anything happened to the president, she'd have her finger on the nuclear button!"

In the dim green light, Lawrence could almost see Dan turning the puzzle over in his mind. Lawrence looked into Dan's shadowy eyes. "What's the next step?"

"I don't know."

TWENTY-EIGHT

Her hands shook with rage. She hurled her phone across the room, and it exploded into pieces against the wall. Startled programmers raised their heads from their screens and stared at her.

Wang Juan barely noticed. She stood and marched out of the room, heading straight for Liu Wei's office. Barging in without following the normal protocol made him snap his head up from his screen.

"What's wrong?" His voice was stern.

Without speaking, Wang Juan took control of his keyboard and navigated the security system. She pulled up the video she'd just watched and opened it to full screen, then stood back with her arms crossed against her chest.

Video of a sniper and his spotter in the jungle came into view. The spotter turned his head before his face exploded in a torrent of blood. Then a hail of bullets rained down on them, and their bodies fell to the ground.

While the hangar had been used to create the deep fake video, the renovations to the building had been done so they could create a secret facility for Liu Wei's army of hackers.

The surrounding forest had been wired with security cameras, in preparation for the new facility. So while they weren't being monitored by live personnel yet, the report from the other snipers had led to a review of the video.

The look of shock on Liu Wei's face was unmistakable. His eyes were glued to the screen. She watched him, waiting for the moment. In reality it took forty-seven seconds, but the wait felt like forever. The figure of Lavinia Walsh, gun drawn, came into view.

Liu Wei gasped.

Wang Juan switched to a different camera. While it was from a distance, there was no mistaking it. Lavinia had found the car that had broken down and was digging. She found the body of the reporter.

"I have sat by submissively," said Wang Juan. "I have done what you've asked. You know that I am more dangerous than any of your soldiers. It's my turn. Let me put down the girl."

Liu Wei sat back, considering.

Wang Juan continued. "We released the video and now an American knows the truth. She can tie us to it and reveal our plans. Time is of the essence. Send me after her!" Her voice hopped back and forth over the border of self-control.

Liu Wei stood. His military background had bred him for moments like this. Forever the tactician, he explained the necessary next steps to her. A taut smile pulled at the edges of her lips. Wang Juan spun on her heel.

She had to pack.

TWENTY-NINE

Not one for breakfast, Dan always preferred to be at the office early. Despite what was going on at the White House, an old university friend had reached out and insisted they meet. They'd chosen to have breakfast at a Waffle House restaurant. As he waited, Dan stared at the menu, but the words didn't register. His mind replayed the video of President Anderson addressing the crowd at the Economic Club of America.

The president swore the video was fake, but it looked so real. The Economic Club of America didn't have a website or anyone who would come forward to confess to being a member. A fact the White House had seized upon in their official response. However, commentary programs had dominated their panel discussions with expert after expert asserting that the video had to be real. The quality was too pristine. Even Hollywood, with a multimillion dollar budget, would struggle to produce a video that real.

Sure, there were hints of inconsistencies. But for a president with a marginal grip on power, her administration was now even more fragile. They needed some time for things to stabilize.

"Dan!"

His head snapped up to find Richard Lauderbach approaching his table. The two had attended MIT together. Dan accepted the man's outstretched hand and motioned for him to sit.

"Dan, it's great to see you. It's been what, twenty-five years?"

"Yeah, about that. Too long, for sure. Listen, Richard, as you can imagine, there's a lot going on at the White House and I need to get back. What can I help you with today?"

A look of understanding crossed his face. "Yeah, sorry to take your time. We've had a couple of things cross my desk at NASA. You know when you see dots connecting, and it sounds crazy, but after 9/11 you feel like you should report anything?"

Dan folded his hands on the table and leaned forward.

Richard continued. "I don't want to raise this through NASA because it's probably nothing and I don't want my superiors to think I'm a conspiracy theory nut."

"Yet you're here, so whatever it is, it's obviously bothering you."

Richard nodded. "We have a satellite, the Lunar Reconnaissance Orbiter, orbiting the Moon and mapping every inch of its surface. It can get as low as thirty-one miles and image the surface in stunning detail. But about a month ago, it developed a blind spot. That in and of itself isn't particularly concerning, as it could be a lot of things. Software glitch, solar flares, damaged hardware. Lots of things."

"Yes," Dan prompted.

"Did you watch the Chinese Moon launch?"

"Yeah, you know me. I've been a space nut since I was a kid."

"Well, the rocket they used was massive. I mean, super massive. Far beyond anything they would need to put a lander on the Moon." He was waving his arms to emphasize. "So four days later they land. Do you know where they land?"

Dan shook his head. "Right where Apollo Eleven landed?"

"No. Smack dab in the middle of our orbiter's blind spot." Richard sat back, his eyes locked on Dan.

Dan looked at the ceiling for a moment, considering. "Can we see it with any of our telescopes? Do we only have one satellite around the Moon?"

"The laws of optics make it impossible to see the surface of the Moon in any great detail from a land-based satellite... and no, even Hubble couldn't see it."

"What about other satellites?" Dan repeated.

"Yeah, about that. There are four. All of them have developed the same blind spot. All around the same time."

Dan sat back in his seat. "You're kidding."

"I'm not."

"What did the Chinese put on the Moon?"

"My bet? It isn't just a rover."

"Do you think it's some kind of weapon?"

"Well, that's the thing. Normally I'd say that isn't possible. You'd need to develop something that could be launched from the Moon, make the trip to Earth, then survive reentry. That'd be a tall order."

"So not a weapon, then?"

"Not something that has to survive reentry," he replied with a cryptic smile.

Dan shook his head.

"Look at this video." Richard unlocked an iPad and placed it in front of Dan.

Glancing at Richard, Dan hit the *Play* button in the middle the screen. An object came into view. It was a satellite. A moment later something that looked like a drone from a science fiction movie entered from the edge of the screen. A long pole on the front separated into four pieces and opened up like the mouth of an alien. The four jaws were joined by some kind of mesh. Like an alien swallowing its prey, the space drone crashed into the satellite. Its main thruster came alive and forced both items down into the atmosphere.

"What was that?" Dan queried.

"That is what the dots look like when they're connected."

"Wait a minute. Are you saying that China put some drones on the Moon that can attack American satellites? What are they going to take down? Our television satellites?"

"Yeah, I thought of that, but clearly that wouldn't be the target. What about our GPS satellites?"

Dan considered it. "That would be annoying to most of the world, but that's a lot of expense and trouble to inconvenience the American public."

"Our military relies on GPS satellites, Dan. Our ships, our planes...and our nuclear missiles."

Dan felt the blood drain from his face. "Without our nuclear deterrent, there's nothing to prevent..."

"Exactly."

After a moment of thought, Dan asked, "Based on the size of the satellite, can you estimate how many of those drones they landed on the Moon?"

Richard nodded. "Did that already."

"And?"

"I'd estimate between fifteen hundred and two thousand."

Dan stood and ran from the restaurant without ordering breakfast.

Dan raced down the hallway toward the Oval Office, dodging interns and bureaucrats. The Chinese had to be behind the deep fake video of the president. The Moon lander, four satellites all unable to see what the lander is doing, and deep fake videos undermining the president. If he'd learned anything in his life, it was that there was no such thing as coincidence.

The hallways were abuzz. People were milling about, everyone in a rush. Dan skirted a group of people congregating in the hallway as he reached the Oval Office. The door was open and Dan could see the president, vice president, the head of the FBI, and others. He marched in.

"Madam President, I need a moment."

Barbara Anderson stood, relief washing over her face. "Dan, come in."

The director of the FBI and the vice president both turned their gaze expectantly on Dan.

"Dan, the vice president claims that you hired a private investigator to follow and spy on her. The investigator has fallen off the grid. Tell them they're crazy. I'm outraged, quite frankly."

Dan locked his gaze on the vice president. He knew the sentence for lying to the FBI was a maximum of five years per offense. Plead the Fifth? Silence would implicate the president.

He turned to face the president. Dan's voice broke as he addressed her. "Madam President, against your explicit orders, I did hire an investigator to follow the vice president."

All activity in the room ceased.

Olivia MacQueen smirked. The FBI director's mouth dropped open. The president sat down. The moment stretched for an eternity as silence ruled the room. The reprieve was broken as the FBI director motioned for an agent behind him.

"Dan Nolan, you have the right to remain silent..."

Bradley Tanner shook hands with reporters and thanked them for coming. He mounted two steps in front of the Capitol building and turned to face the throng of reporters. A hush fell over the huge group as they strained to catch every word of the House Speaker's address.

"Thank you all for coming. Today in the House I'm going to put to a vote the opening of an investigation of President Barbara Anderson. The House Intelligence Committee will be charged with looking into allegations of abuse of office, domestic espionage, dereliction of duty, and obstruction of justice."

He paused and let that sink in. Tanner did his best to keep his face serious, but he'd been waiting for this moment for months. He couldn't wait to confront Olivia MacQueen with the fact that he knew about her multiple personality disorder diagnosis and that once the president was impeached, he would have her impeached on the grounds that she was unfit for office. But there was a task at hand.

"You've heard me over the past week express my

concerns about the president's questionable focus on domestic issues when we face a growing and persistent threat from China. With the news today that chief of staff Dan Nolan has been arrested on charges of domestic espionage, we need to find out what the president knew and when she knew it. In addition, I call upon the FBI director to appoint an independent council to also investigate these serious allegations."

Tanner paused again. Taking a deep breath, he continued. "It's a little early to talk about impeachment and I want to encourage all members of the House to show restraint while the mechanisms of our democracy go to work to uncover the truth of the deceit in the White House. I will not be taking any questions right now. After the House session concludes today, I will be happy to answer your queries."

There was a roar from the crowd as reporters tossed out questions. The Capitol police interceded and separated the Speaker of the House from the crowd as he mounted the steps of the Capitol building.

Vice President Olivia MacQueen closed the door to her office and went to her desk. She sat down and crossed one leg over the other. Seated in front of her was House Speaker Bradley Tanner.

"Mister Tanner. Big day." She smiled.

"Yes, big day. You've spoken to the Cabinet?"

"Yes, I've had a private conversation with each of them since the news broke this morning. There are some wavering, but it won't take much to get them on our side, if need be."

"I've already formally requested the appointment of a special prosecutor and as you've probably heard, I intend to request that the House Intelligence Committee open an investigation and that they begin to draft articles of impeachment."

"Good. There may be some further developments that speed up the process."

"Oh?"

"I got a message from our friend today. There will be more news tomorrow."

"I'm not privy to it?"

"No, you're not."

Tanner frowned. He stood and circled his chair, putting it between them. "I'm as much a part of this as you, Olivia. I don't think it's right to withhold key information from me about our strategy."

"You just need to play your part, Bradley." She used his first name in kind. "When the president is impeached, the House will move to appoint me as president and I'll be sworn in to replace Barbara Anderson."

A smirk spread across his face. "I'm afraid, Olivia, that isn't going to happen."

Olivia MacQueen smiled. "Really? Why is that?"

Bradley Tanner drew himself to his full height. "I've become aware, Olivia, that you suffer from multiple personality disorder. You will be impeached after President Barbara Anderson is impeached, on the grounds that your condition makes you unfit to be president. In fact, you could be removed right now."

A change came over Olivia MacQueen's face as she slid her chair forward and took control of her mouse and keyboard. The monitor hanging on the wall behind her desk came to life. She opened a video and clicked *Play*.

The image of an examination room came into view. A woman in a white lab coat sat on a chair adjacent to a young girl in a sweatshirt, faded jean shorts, and oversized shoes with a hole in the toe and they spoke about an abortion. The woman patiently answered her questions.

"Will I go to jail?" the girl asked.

"No," the female doctor assured her, taking her hand in her own.

"They made it illegal last year. My pa said it was against the law. My pa would kill me if he knew."

"Well, as you are aware, this place is secret. We don't keep any records, so if you don't tell anyone then no one will ever know."

Olivia MacQueen closed the video and regarded Bradley Tanner. His mouth was agape.

The voice of Rasha Brown came forward, emanating from the body of Olivia MacQueen. "Your daughter, I believe. Performing illegal abortions in your home state of Alabama. Much more where this came from, Mister Speaker. So, let's talk about how events will unfold in the coming days."

THIRTY

It was eleven o'clock at night when six men dressed in business suits strode through the employee entrance of the Zhongnanhai, the Chinese equivalent to the White House in Beijing. They bypassed the regular security procedures, avoiding metal detectors and an X-ray machine normally used on all visitors to the complex. They moved unimpeded.

The men crossed the campus to the presidential residence in unison. They piled into the elevator and when the doors slid open on the second floor, they were met by two ceremonial armed guards standing at attention.

The lead man, the only one wearing gloves, reached inside his suit jacket and removed a Sig Sauer with a wicked-looking silencer. The guards' eyes opened wide but they couldn't react before the man shot each of them in the chest. Both guards fell to the floor, grasping at their wounds. The man in charge approached and put a single bullet in each of their heads.

Standing before the president's bedroom door, he turned sideways and raised his foot back, poised to kick.

With one deliberate blow, the twin doors flew inward. The six men entered the room.

President Xiu Ying Zhang and his wife both sat bolt upright in bed, surveying their attackers. The lights were snapped on and, guns drawn, two of the men in suits went to each side of the bed surrounding the terrified couple. The man in charge raised his gun and shot the president in the head before turning the gun on his wife.

Turning, he removed the silencer and dropped the Sig Sauer on the floor. On the bottom of the pistol grip was a bar code and the words *Property of the US Embassy: China.*

Liu Wei picked up his phone.

"Yes?"

"It's done."

"They're both dead? The gun planted and surveillance video replaced?"

"Yes."

"Notify the authorities. Make sure that our people assist the investigation in any way that they can."

"Yes, sir."

He hung up, held the receiver for a moment, then placed another call. "The president was attacked and has been injured. Details are scarce. Wake up the key Communist Party members. We must meet immediately and await information as it develops."

Again, Liu Wei hung up, then placed a third call. "In ten minutes, send the security video of the assassination to the phones of all members of the party. Announce that the president is dead."

Liu Wei sat down at his desk and played the video that

his Blood Dragons had created. The first camera angle was the actual video from above the elevator door and showed the two guards being gunned down. Two single shots from a distance. The second camera angle was from the adjacent hallway. In it, Lavinia Walsh came into view and put a single bullet into the head of each of the dying guards. She then raised her foot and kicked the door open.

THIRTY-ONE

President Barbara Anderson was in the Situation Room with the director of the FBI, the director of Homeland Security, the head of the Defense Intelligence Agency, and six other intelligence agencies.

With her arms folded across her chest, the president listened as they gave their briefing. She found the conference room stuffy, as the air filtration system was being repaired. It felt symbolic.

The director of the Defense Intelligence Agency was speaking when all hell broke loose. The door opened and a page entered the room, approached the FBI director, and handed him a message. Conversation in the room stopped and all eyes turned on him.

With his usual calm, the director of the FBI addressed the room. "The Chinese president has been assassinated."

There was a collective gasp. When silence returned he spoke again.

"That's not all. They've implicated DIA agent Lavinia Walsh in the murder."

Barbara Anderson stood and pounded the table. "That's preposterous!"

"There's security video," the FBI head continued. "One moment while we bring it up." He was fiddling with his phone. A tech person knocked, then entered. The FBI director waved her over and the two spoke. The sound level in the room rose as people typed, spoke into their cell phones in hushed tones, and chatted.

"Okay, folks, we're ready." The FBI director motioned to the screen. The executive seal on the main television disappeared and video from a security camera appeared.

Barbara Anderson watched as two well-aimed shots struck both guards and they fell to the ground with mortal injuries. The video feed switched to a second camera, this time from an adjacent hallway. The figure of Lavinia Walsh came into view. She stood over the two men before pointing her gun and executing them both with single head shots.

There was another collective gasp.

The woman then kicked in the door and entered the bedroom.

All eyes turned to Barbara Anderson.

Dan, her rock, was being held by the FBI. She hadn't heard from Lavinia in a week. She felt utterly alone.

The president stayed standing and addressed the room, looking directly at the FBI director. "I believe that video," she pointed at the TV, "is as fake as the one of me addressing the Economic Club of America. I want an investigation and I want every intelligence agency to make it a priority. I am being attacked on social media by...no one can tell me who. I'm being attacked by the Republicans, and I'm being attacked by the Chinese..." She trailed off. "This is a setup! I'll repeat, I want every resource in this government focused on proving that these videos are fake!"

"Madam President," the chairman of the Joint Chiefs of Staff said. "Liu Wei has been named the new president of China and he has just declared war on the United States for assassinating their president. I presume that you want to respond in kind? That you will ask Congress for a war resolution?"

The president stared him down. "Perhaps you haven't heard me. China cannot be at war by itself. This video is fake." She pounded the table. "Prove that it's fake and get me the person who created it, while I de-escalate with the Chinese."

The room emptied, with the exception of her admin, who was taking notes. "Get me the attorney general and the deputy pardon attorney."

Night had fallen on an exhausting day in Washington. The Oval Office was packed with reporters, television cameras, photographers, and high-ranking officials from the Democratic and Republican parties. Behind the Resolute Desk stood Olivia MacQueen, the chief justice of the Supreme Court, and a very unhappy Bradley Tanner.

The chief justice held out a Bible. "Madam Vice President, place your left hand on the Bible and raise your right hand."

Olivia MacQueen followed his instruction.

"Repeat after me. I do solemnly swear that I will faithfully execute the office of President of the United States, and will, to the best of my ability, preserve, protect, and defend the Constitution of the United States. So help you God."

Olivia MacQueen repeated the words, led by the chief

justice. Her enunciation of every syllable was deliberate. When she had finished, the chief justice addressed her directly.

"Good luck, Madam President.

THIRTY-TWO

Lavinia's Lego phone rang. Reaching to her bedside table, she picked it up and put it to her ear. It was Jacob.

"Lavinia, I assume you haven't heard the news."

"I'm in the heart of China, Jacob. There isn't a lick of English anywhere."

"The president has been impeached."

Lavinia sat bolt upright in bed. "What?"

"Yeah, she's been impeached for ordering you to assassinate the Chinese president."

Lavinia simply stared, unable to comprehend what she'd just heard.

"Jacob, what are you talking about?"

"China has declared war on the United States because you shot the president and his wife. They're playing a video of you taking out the two presidential guards."

"Jacob, that's crazy! You know that I'm in the middle of nowhere!"

"I know, Lavinia, but the video looks totally real. President MacQueen has issued an international warrant for your arrest. She's offered a $100 million bond for your apprehension. Dead or alive!"

Lavinia's face went cold. "The president can't order the killing of an American citizen," she offered weakly.

"Yeah, well, she's making an exception for you and no one is challenging her. Wherever you are, you need to get out of there."

"Where do I go?"

There was a long pause. "I don't know."

"How long ago did this happen?"

"Liu Wei just went on television a short while ago. They released the security video of you to the media in the press conference. If you're in a city you need to leave now, before people see the video."

"This is Liu Wei's work. He's behind this. Jacob, I need to find a place where I can finish my investigation."

There was a pause. "I have an idea, but I don't want to share it over the phone. Do you still have your TAILS flash drive?"

Lavinia got up and went to her backpack. She reached into the left-hand pocket and felt the drive there. "Yeah I have it."

"Okay, get to a computer and call me."

"Jacob, this is crazy. I have very little money left on me. I won't be able to use credit cards or go to a bank. How am I supposed to survive? If I'm being accused of assassinating the Chinese president, no country will take me in!"

"Trust me, Lavinia, I know a country that will give you asylum. It's possibly the only country in the world, but they know a little bit about being the little guy taking on the world. Call me when you can."

"I can't promise when that will be."

"I'll be next to my computer, waiting."

Lavinia studied all of her belongings. The twelve backup disk drives could be immensely valuable or worthless. They took up valuable space and could be damaged if she found herself in another firefight. Should they go with her?

As she paced the length of her room, a myriad of thoughts raced through her mind. If she hid them in the hotel room they'd be safe, but if they did have something valuable on them, then there was a chance that she couldn't get to them in time to be able to use them. Hedging her bets, Lavinia took six of the drives, wrapped them in a plastic bag from the garbage bin, and looked around the room. Crossing over to the love seat, she removed the cushions and felt in the gap where the back and seat met. It was deep. Lavinia pulled out her Swiss Army knife and made a slit in the material at the end of the crevice. Her fingers could feel the wooden frame inside the couch. She slid the six drives into the crack until they disappeared from her touch. Safe.

Packing her remaining things, Lavinia slipped her fatigue pants and blue top back on. She'd washed them in the bathtub last night with hand soap and hung them to dry while she'd slept. They were wrinkled but clean. She put on her shoes, threw on the jacket she'd taken from the BMW, and headed for the door.

In the lobby she took a local newspaper up to the front desk. The owners were a pleasant middle-aged couple. Their smiles indicated that they hadn't heard the news yet. Lavinia paid for the paper and her bill, then motioned with her phone that she wanted to take her picture with them. Just a friendly tourist looking for a moment.

Holding up the newspaper discretely at chest height, she snapped a selfie of the three of them. At least she could prove that she was nowhere near Beijing the morning after the murders, and now she had witnesses.

At the local market, Lavinia spent the last of her money. She bought a tarp, a few bungee cords, and a rugged duffel bag, which she loaded with food and bottled water.

The town was encircled by low mountains. At the top of the southern mountainside was a paved two-lane road. Lavinia would enter the woods headed that way, hoping people would think she was going to hitch a ride. In reality, she would follow the terrain and hike to the opposite side of the small town and set up camp to await Jacob's arrival.

When she was packed, Lavinia hiked up toward the road. She made sure that the locals saw her go.

From her vantage point twenty feet up in a tree, the view was amazing. The valley below was lit by silver moonlight. In the Terrorist Survival Course she'd taken, they spent two days on outdoor survival skills. Their first task had been to build a place to sleep in the safety of a tree.

Lavinia had scoped the area before nightfall and found a sturdy tree with two thick branches that were healthy and about level. She'd foraged for thick fallen branches that weren't rotted and laid them across to form a platform. She cut her backpack into strips to make string to tie every second branch to the live tree branches. The platform was more than wide enough to hold her.

She threaded the tarp that she'd bought in town down between the two outermost branches and then wrapped them back upward. With the remaining straps made from her backpack, she tied the metal loops along the length of the tarp together to form an enclosed sleeping area. By sliding underneath it, she would keep from rolling off the side of her platform. That done, she hung the sturdy travel bag off the foot end side of the platform. In it were all of her food and other important supplies.

It was late enough now that Lavinia ventured down the slope and back into town. She kept close to the buildings so she'd be hidden in shadow. When she arrived at the food exchange, she peered through the windows to make sure it was empty. Removing her lock pick, Lavinia popped the lock and was inside in seconds.

The building was modern for this transition town in the mountains. It had basic amenities and was decorated with handmade crafts. Lavinia had seen an office computer through one of the windows when she'd helped the farmer who'd given her a ride into town unload his rice. She quickly located the small office and sat down at the keyboard.

She groaned. They keys were in Chinese. She hadn't thought that through. Removing the TAILS thumb drive, she plugged it in and hoped it would boot up in English. The screen went dark and the now familiar lines of code scrolled across the screen while it initialized the computer.

Relief flooded through her when the screen came up and everything was in English. The position of the keys was very similar to her own computer, so she booted up the chat program and tried to call Jacob. A message popped up: *Offline.*

Damn!

It had never occurred to her that she'd need to use it in a place where she didn't know the WiFi password. She clicked on the network finder and saw four networks. With relief she saw that one didn't require a password. Connecting, she called Jacob.

He answered immediately and his voice boomed around the room. "Lavinia, I'm so glad you're okay!"

Her eyes opened wide and she put a finger to her mouth. She tested keys until she found one that lowered the sound.

"Jacob, I don't know if the owners live upstairs or what. We have to talk quietly," she whispered, leaning in to the screen.

"Got it! Are you safe?"

"Yes, I've built a shelter in the mountains. I have enough food for a few days. I can always come in at night and steal some more if I have to."

"Okay, first of all I need to get to you and then we'll have to find our way to Sealand."

Lavinia frowned. "The place where they have killer whale shows?"

Jacob rolled his eyes. "No, the Principality of Sealand. In World War II the British built a series of platforms in the ocean to help patrol for German submarines. One of them was seven miles from the coast, which is four miles past the boundary for international waters. The forts were abandoned in the 1950s. On September 2nd, 1966, Roy Bates of the UK moved his family onto the platform and claimed it as a new micro-nation."

"A micro-nation? Is that a thing?"

"It most certainly is. And you, my dear, have formally requested asylum and emergency citizenship with the Principality of Sealand. And it was approved by Prince Michael himself."

"How many people live there?"

"Well, at least one person at all times. Google it."

Lavinia typed *Sealand* into the browser and it produced an image of two concrete pillars supporting a metal platform. "Jacob, if the American government finds out I'm there, I don't think they'll have any trouble taking Sealand. I don't think Prince Michael would want the trouble."

"Prince Michael knows a thing or two about standing up to bullies, Lavinia. You can read about their history later, but trust me. If he grants you asylum, you're good."

"So our plan is, you're going to meet me in the forests of Northern China, then we're going to find a way to get to the North Sea, and then to Sealand, where I'll be protected by the military of Sealand? Which has one member?"

"When you put it like that, sure, it doesn't sound like much of a plan. Who else do you want to ask for asylum? Russia?"

Lavinia sighed. "When will you get here?"

"I'll leave in the morning. Give me some landmarks."

The two discussed plans for how to connect when Jacob arrived. Lavinia thanked him and signed off, shutting the computer down and removing her thumb drive. Since she was there, she took a loaf of mantu bread and a six-pack of bottled water. With barely a sound, she left the building and slunk back to her mountain hideaway.

THIRTY-THREE

Alice furrowed her brow. The Iranian minister's dialect was so difficult to understand that it required her full concentration to translate. Speaking in her practiced monotone, she relayed the spirit of his message to the gathered body.

The American delegation had walked out in protest, as soon as the Iranian minister had called for the destruction of Israel. Amazing that the Iranians were focused on that, with China and the United States on the brink of war.

When the verbose man stopped speaking, there was scattered applause from sympathetic Middle Eastern countries. Alice sat back in her seat, drawing a deep breath.

Perfectly fluent in nine languages, she'd been something of a linguistic prodigy growing up. Words came so easily to her. It was a gift and a curse. It had allowed her to achieve her dream of working at the United Nations, but the pay left something to be desired. New York was not an inexpensive place to live, and her salary required that she live in a cramped apartment shared with two other translators.

Scanning the list, she looked for her next assignment.

Bang! Bang, bang, bang!

Alice tore off her headphones. "Are those gunshots?"

Everyone in the room full of women stopped, their expressions the same.

Alice ran for the door, placing one hand on the frame and one on the doorknob. Opening it a crack so she could peer out allowed the sound to pierce the room. Reverberating.

Bang, bang, bang, bang!

Pushing the door shut, Alice turned the lock and spun toward the other women. Without a word being spoken, they began to pile chairs and desks in front of the doorway. When they were done, they retreated to the back of the room, most of them holding hands. The women huddled together. Fear transcended nationality.

One woman was on her cell phone, speaking in hushed tones with the 911 operator.

After what seemed an eternity, there was a resounding rap at the door. "UN police!"

The lock was undone and the door forced open, the desks screeching as they were forced out of the way. Six armed men entered the room while others watched the hallway.

"All American translators, follow us. Everyone else shelter in place."

Alice stood, along with eight other women, but looked back at the others behind her. "We can't leave them!"

"We have our protocols, ma'am. You come with us willingly or I'll carry you kicking and screaming. It'll be faster if you come of your own accord, though."

Glancing back at the remaining women, she met the gaze of a woman in a headscarf. *Go,* she mouthed.

Alice turned and followed the soldiers.

There were seventeen of them in total. The soldiers

guided them down several hallways in military fashion. They led them to a secure elevator. The glass door was as thick as a bank vault door. Obviously bulletproof. The soldiers packed the women into the elevator. One entered with them, pressed the button for B5, and secured the door. They began to descend.

When they reached the bottom, the doors slid open and the soldier led them down a secure hallway. A woman and man dressed in battle fatigues herded them through the huge steel door into a panic room. It looked like it had been built in the seventies, with cherry wood-paneled walls and harsh fluorescent lights.

More and more people arrived. She heard one of the soldiers speak into her walkie-talkie.

"Everyone confirmed, sir."

The device crackled. "Lock it down."

The remaining soldiers all entered the room, locking the door behind them.

Air began to stream in through vents, located high in the walls. Everyone heard them start up.

"Secure air system," one of the soldiers assured them.

After a few minutes, Alice began to feel her eyelids droop. Glancing around, she saw that some people had dropped to the floor and were sitting cross-legged. One man collapsed, hitting the floor face-first, a tooth flying from his mouth and skittering across the floor.

Alice dropped to the ground, her back against the wall. Her last thought before everything went black was, *I always dreamed of working at the UN*.

———

Olivia MacQueen strode into the Situation Room with her

head high. She took a seat at the head of the table. The chairs around her filled up with members of the intelligence community, Homeland Security, and other White House staff. When the door was closed, she called the meeting to order.

Liu Wei's decision to frame Lavinia for the president's assassination sped up the process of putting both of them in power. However, he had not responded to any of her messages since. She didn't like the sudden silence.

"Someone tell me what's going on."

The chairman of the Joint Chiefs cleared his throat. "Madam President, there's been an attack at the United Nations."

The skin around her lips tightened. "An attack? What kind of an attack?"

"Sixteen Chinese nationals entered the UN building and began shooting indiscriminately. Security followed protocol and evacuated all American personnel to the safe room in the basement. It appears that one of the air canisters that supplies the room with oxygen was replaced with sarin gas."

Olivia's mouth dropped open. "What?"

"Everyone in the room was dead within minutes."

"How many victims?"

"Eighty-three."

"All American?"

"Yes, Madam President."

President MacQueen stared at the chairman. "Who's responsible?"

"Madam President, the Chinese have declared war on the United States. This attack was in retaliation for the assassination of the Chinese president by Lavinia Walsh. Now, let me share our proposed responses."

Olivia MacQueen stood without a word and stormed out of the room.

"Madam President?" the chairman called after her.

Olivia walked as fast as she could in her spiked heels back to the Oval Office. Once inside, she closed the door behind her and leaned against it.

"Rasha, what do I do?"

Her voice changed as Rasha took control. "Get a grip! Liu Wei has double-crossed you. The asshole wants a war. So give him a war!"

"War? I can't take the country to war!"

"Every president worth their salt has taken the country to war. It's how you cement your power."

Olivia crossed to her desk and sat down at her laptop. Selecting her video conference software, she maximized the screen so she could stare herself down. "I didn't guide you to this point so you could be weak!" Rasha Brown admonished the image on the screen. "I've navigated every minefield, outsmarted every politician, taken down anyone in your way. I won't let you be weak in the face of success!"

"People will die," Olivia said in a childlike voice.

"Yes, people will die. But not you. We have fifty times the nuclear weapons China has—they can't compete with us. They won't. This attack on the United States is the best thing that could have happened to us, don't you see? We're teetering on legitimacy, but this—" she pointed at herself in the screen "—this will cement our place in history!"

The image on the screen seemed to morph. The chin lifted, the eyes relaxed, the mouth opened slightly. Reaching into her desk, Olivia removed a folder containing her Daily Presidential Brief, a pad, and a pen. Closing the drawer, she stood, straightened her skirt, and strode back to the Situation Room.

When she reentered the room everyone stood, following her with perplexed looks. The president took her place at the table. Setting her materials down, she spoke in an even voice. "Now, let's hit back!"

A roar of approval engulfed the room.

THIRTY-FOUR

Jacob rolled into the small town in his Jeep just as the sun was setting. Navigating along the dirt road of the main street, he found what looked like a safe parking spot. He exited the vehicle, slung his oversized backpack on, and pocketed the keys. His black combat boots stirred up dust on the road. Jacob scanned the street, looking for the landmarks Lavinia had described. Getting his bearings, he rounded the vehicle and disappeared into the darkness.

He hiked up the hill, watching where he placed his feet to avoid turning an ankle on the uneven ground. Within minutes he reached the tree line and entered the woods. Ten feet in, he removed a flashlight from his pocket and snapped it on.

For the first time that day, Jacob felt fear creep into his thoughts. "Lions and tigers and bears, oh my!" he whispered, quoting Dorothy in *The Wizard of Oz* as he placed one foot in front of the other. In the darkness Jacob's mind began to play tricks on him, as he thought he heard rustling behind every tree he approached.

Get a grip!

Rubbing his eyes with his left hand, he suppressed a yawn, but didn't stop moving into the woods.

There was a rustle nearby and a rush of adrenaline washed away his fatigue. His muscles tensed and he came to an abrupt stop. He felt a tap on his shoulder and he broke into a run, almost leaving his skin behind.

He heard a laugh above him, slowed his run, and circled around the tree he'd just passed. Looking up, he aimed his flashlight toward the sound. "Tree dweller?"

"No safer place to hide," came Lavinia's voice.

Following the sound with his light, he found Lavinia. She dropped a handful of pebbles.

Jacob put his hands on his hips. "I'm your ride out of here, remember?"

Lavinia looked down at Jacob where he stood with his head cocked to one side, looking indignant. "Sorry, I couldn't resist," she called down. "Come on up."

Jacob paced around the tree, studying the pattern of branches before deciding on a path. He gripped the flashlight between his teeth and started to climb.

Pausing, he slipped the flashlight to his left hand. "These hands were made for typing, Lavinia," he complained. He popped the flashlight back into his mouth and continued to climb.

Sliding toward the end of her platform, Lavinia made room for him to join her. It took longer than Lavinia would have expected for his hand to appear, lit by the flashlight he held between his teeth. The light danced between the tree trunk and the gaps in the platform as he struggled to haul himself up.

"Getting down is easier," Lavinia promised.

He pulled himself up and rolled onto the platform. Lavinia shifted out of his way. "Yeah, I just roll off the edge," Jacob replied. He surveyed his surroundings, playing his light across the entire platform. "Nifty place you've got here."

"Keeps me safe from the bears."

Jacob flashed her a horrified expression.

"Thanks for coming, Jacob. You're a lifesaver." Lavinia put an arm around him and pulled him in.

"Well, I've been to jail for you. What's a little trip to the jungle in China?"

Lavinia leaned her shoulder into his and gave him a light bump. "It's a forest. You did go to jail for me, didn't you?"

"I did, and if it weren't for your boyfriend I'd probably still be there!" He waved his hands in the air for emphasis.

"He's a good guy," Lavinia agreed.

"Have you talked to him?"

"Not in a few days, no. Conditions haven't been right." She motioned around with her right hand. "So catch me up. What's going on?"

Jacob rubbed his chin, lost in mock thought. "Aside from you being the most wanted person in the world?" He began to count off against his fingers. "The Chinese have vowed to avenge the death of their president. Liu Wei has taken over as the Chinese president. The American and Chinese navies are on alert in the South China Sea. President Anderson has been impeached and removed from office, replaced by Olivia MacQueen. Quiet otherwise."

"How did I supposedly kill the president?"

"Your missing gun from the embassy."

Lavinia's mouth dropped open. "I forgot to report that to the ambassador!"

"I'm not sure that would have made much of a difference. The question right now is how does Liu Wei retaliate?"

"Tung must be devastated," Lavinia mused. "He seemed like a good guy. He was afraid of Liu Wei; he said as much to me."

"I remember you told me that. At the state dinner."

"What's his end game? Why frame me for this? Does he want a war?"

"If he does, then he wants a short one."

"That's what doesn't make any sense, Jacob. They have less than three hundred nuclear weapons to our six thousand."

"Who's going to use a nuclear weapon in battle, though? It's just like we learned last year, remember? Even a small regional nuclear war would spell the end of human civilization," Jacob reasoned.

"So what's his end game?"

"Well, if he wanted to become president of China, he needed to assassinate the existing president. You were getting in the way with your investigations, so by framing you he achieved both."

"But he's promising to retaliate?"

"He can't *not* retaliate."

"Exactly. By choosing this path it has to lead him to war. You know, Dan didn't trust the vice president at all. This has worked out pretty well for her, too."

"Are you suggesting she's involved? A conspiracy?"

Lavinia paused for a long time. "No, I don't have any evidence of that. But I can't help but feel that she's involved somehow."

Jacob stifled a yawn.

"We should get some rest. Turn off the flashlight and let's try to sleep."

Lavinia fastened the tarp over them using the bungee cords. Secure for the night, she closed her eyes and felt safe for the first time in days.

Lavinia woke Jacob before sunrise so they could steal into town to recover Jacob's vehicle. Once in the safety of the Jeep, the two got on the road and discussed their plan.

"So how do we get to Sealand? Aren't there like six countries between here and there? And without a passport, if that weren't a tough enough excursion."

"Private jet."

Lavinia wrinkled her brow. "Private jet? Where does the money come from to pay for that?"

"We have a private benefactor."

"Who?"

"Someone sympathetic to your cause."

"Jacob, who is it?" She tilted her head and stared at him.

"Trust me, Lavinia. Money isn't an issue."

"I have a gun." She smiled and pretended to pull it from the small of her back. The sun was up now and the wind was rushing through her long brown hair. She felt her sense of humor was back.

Jacob seemed to consider. "Okay, I'll tell you. It's Aaron."

Lavinia turned her head so fast, she felt a twinge. Rubbing her neck, she asked, "You spoke to him? How is he doing? Where's he living now? Is he still hanging out with Martin?"

"Yes, good, classified, and yes." Jacob fished for his sunglasses. "Honestly, though, Martin is still pretty messed up."

Lavinia could understand. Last year she'd inadvertently teamed up with Aaron and Martin to stop a terrorist attack on the United States. At the time, Martin was an NSA analyst and Aaron was a hacker. Martin's wife and Aaron's friend were killed in a terrorist attack. Aaron and Martin had been fast friends ever since.

"Aaron is fronting us some money? That's incredible!"

"He says hi, by the way, and that he misses you."

Lavinia felt her emotions catch in her throat. Her eyes blurred. The gravity of the situation was starting to sink in. The entire world was looking for her. If President Barbara Anderson had been removed from power, then it was conceivable that her own government would believe that she'd actually assassinated the Chinese president. There wouldn't be a friendly government in the world, save perhaps Sealand. She'd traded only intermittent messages with Aaron since her adventures with him last year, and here he was coming to her rescue with no questions asked. She cleared her throat. "I'll reach out and thank him when we get to Sealand. What's our plan?"

"We need to cross the border into Russia. Aaron has arranged for a flight from a small private airport in a mining town in Southern Russia. From there we go to Latvia, where we'll transfer to Belgium. From there we'll sail to Sealand."

"How do we get across the border? I don't have a passport."

"Open the front zippered pocket of my backpack."

Lavinia undid her seatbelt and reached behind her. Opening the zipper, she stuck her hand in and came out with a thick white envelope. Opening the flap, she saw a wad of Russian money. Slipping it back inside, she asked, "How much is this?"

"A lot. Like, a lot a lot."

"Aaron sent this?"

"He wired me the money. I had to pick it up at a local bank in Beijing before I left to get you."

"Won't they be able to trace that to you and then to me? Russian money would be a hint that we're going to Russia."

"Oh ye of little faith," he chided her. "He sent it to my numbered Swiss account. I hired a local hacker to go and pick the money up for me."

Lavinia glanced at him, the greenery whipping by in the background. "You're good."

"I am so." Jacob grinned like a schoolboy on a snow day.

"So we drive to Russia, bribe the border guard, fly to Latvia, then on to Belgium. There you've chartered a boat to take us to Sealand?"

"Not quite a charter."

Lavinia had a flashback to the night last year when she and her father had to use garbage can lids to paddle a small fishing boat he'd stolen to meet an American submarine. They'd almost died. "You got us a real boat, right?"

Jacob looked at her. "Trust me."

Lavinia stared ahead, suddenly worried again.

"Hey, in my duffel bag there's a small black case. Can you pull it out?"

Lavinia took off her seatbelt again and got on her knees on the front seat. She unzipped the duffel bag and rifled around inside. Coming up with a cube-shaped black case, she removed it and brought it up to the front seat. A zipper ran around all four sides of the hard-sided nylon case. When she opened it, she found what looked like a very expensive drone. "What's this?"

"Our eyes."

"For what?"

"We have three hours of forest road driving ahead of us before we hit a major highway. With this baby flying above, we can see if there's any trouble ahead."

"Will it be able to keep up with us?"

Jacob laughed. "Can we keep up with it, is the right question. Her top speed is 179 miles an hour. Her range is about thirty minutes and I have three backup batteries. So we won't have coverage for the whole drive, but a good chunk of the way."

Lavinia placed it in her lap and pulled out the controller. Turning the device on, she familiarized herself with the controls.

"You got it?"

"I've got it."

"Let me slow down so you can launch." Jacob dropped his speed.

Lavinia launched the drone and navigated it out of her window. She'd expected it to drop behind them when it hit the wind, but instead it raced forward and up.

"This thing's powerful!"

"Bought it at the electronics market. Thought it might be useful."

Lavinia took the drone up to a hundred feet and set a sensor so that it would track their speed and hold its distance just ahead of them. The high-definition camera gave her an incredible view of the road before them.

Lost in thought as she monitored the screen, Lavinia turned the news Jacob had given her over and over in her mind.

A green military Jeep pulled into the village Jacob and Lavinia had just left and parked in front of the food-processing plant. The passenger side door was thrown open and a long slender leg clad in tight-fitting fatigues emerged, followed by a second. Wang Juan stepped out of the vehicle and onto the dusty road. Glancing around the modest downtown, she surveyed the shops and market.

She made her way down the street and entered the market square. Removing a photograph from her pocket, she approached a fish vendor and held the photo up for him to see. "Have you seen this woman?" she asked in flawless Mandarin.

The fisherman squinted at the photo and shook his head, before motioning to his wares and asking if she was interested in making a purchase.

Wang made her way through the square, flashing the photo to each vendor. It wasn't long before she found success. The woman barely looked at the photo before nodding so hard that her hat slipped out of place. Pointing to the forest, the woman explained that she'd seen her leave for the woods the day before last. Wang followed with her eyes, pointing her own hand to confirm the spot where her mark had entered the woods.

Without thanking the woman, Wang turned and strode toward the spot, whistling for her three support soldiers to follow her.

As they approached, she drew a pistol in her right hand and a military knife in her left as she led the three soldiers, who had their assault rifles pointed forward. In unison, they flipped their safeties off. The soldiers flanked Wang Juan, each of them entering the forest at a different point. Knowing that they had her covered, she alternated her eyes between the trees and the ground.

They climbed the embankment to the top and stood at the edge of the minor highway. Looking back over the village set in the valley, she scanned the area. "Why would she let herself be seen leaving?" Her question was not directed at any of her companions in particular. "Unless she was trying to lead us away. You." She pointed to one of the soldiers. "Get a drone in the air and search the woods that way." she pointed toward the opposite side of the town. "We'll see if we can find her on the ground."

In short order, one of the men had his drone high in the air. Wang Juan led the other two through the woods. They were halfway across the valley when she got a message. He'd found something.

The drone hovered over the area of discovery. Wang Juan and her team jogged to the site. It wasn't long before she found footsteps in the dirt, although they were too big to belong to a woman. She crouched to study the boot print. It looked fresh. Her eyes followed the trail. It stopped up ahead, backtracked, then circled a tree.

Wang raised her eyes, searching upward. She saw what the drone had found. A platform. Circling the tree herself, she found a path up, holstered her gun, and began to climb. Motioning to the soldier closest to her, she made eye contact so she knew he saw her.

As she approached the platform, Wang removed her pistol again and continued to climb. A few feet now. She coiled her legs under her and prepared to spring if necessary. Listening intently, she heard nothing but the sounds of the forest below her.

Exploding upward, she broke the plane of the platform with her gun drawn.

Empty.

Clambering onto the platform, she found a tarp secured

to it with bungee cords and some torn strips of nylon, but no sign of her mark. The bungee cords looked new. It had to be Walsh!

Wang Juan removed a military walkie-talkie from her belt. "Get the drone back in the air and the video feed sent to my phone. Check the roads in all directions."

THIRTY-FIVE

John Williams, aka Jocko, watched as the Navy SEALs' commanding officer mounted the hastily constructed platform. It was amazing, what you could do with milk crates, sheets of plywood, and some black paint.

The weathered commanding officer stood with his arms folded behind his back and addressed the crowd. His booming voice made a microphone unnecessary. His presence in Mongolia was a sign of how important the raid they were about to embark on was.

"Two days ago, a group of Chinese nationals, on orders from President Liu Wei, attacked the United Nations building, killing eighty-three Americans. They were gassed to death with a chemical known as sarin gas. I don't have to tell any of you what a terrible way to die that is." He stared down the room. "SEALs, we have been asked to do the impossible. Again." He punctuated the word with a pause. "With limited time to plan, a high risk of failure, and no appetite for anything other than success, this is what we train for! I'm going to hand the briefing over to your unit leadership, but I made the trip out here because I want you to know that we're behind you. This is a larger scale raid than the one that killed Osama bin Ladin. It will be more dangerous and the stakes are higher. I ask one thing from each of you. Do America proud."

Jocko replaced the CO on stage and assumed his traditional briefing pose. He gazed at the two platoons in front of him. Eighty men. Helicopter crews, soldiers, and support personnel. All ready to give their lives. Ready to exact a pound of flesh for their country.

"Soldiers, the target of our mission is China's most notorious prison, known as Qincheng Prison. This facility is used to hold political prisoners. In fact, there are two innocent Americans serving life sentences there, after being wrongfully convicted of being spies. Our mission is to find and rescue the two Americans, kill all of the prison guards and staff, and release all prisoners and provide them food, weapons, and money to facilitate their escape. Based on what is known about Qincheng Prison, our enemy casualties will match those suffered in the attack on the United Nations building. Once our objectives have been achieved, we are to retreat back to this base, refuel, and return to the East China Sea before going on to our base in Japan."

Jocko launched into the details of the raid, describing the role of each team and soldier in minute detail. Transporting such a large number of soldiers deep into Chinese territory, executing a raid, then getting out in one piece was unprecedented. Not since World War II had a mission of this scale been undertaken.

They had to be perfect, or at least some of the men in front of him would not go home.

When the briefing was complete, Jocko met with the leadership team.

"Sergeant Peters, are your men ready?"

"Yes, sir. We'll create a secure environment for our boys. The Chinese guards won't be able to get more than a smoke signal in or out of the prison."

"Sergeant Boesch? Any questions?"

"One question, sir. If a chopper goes down, we can spread our personnel out across the remaining helicopters. What if two go down? Will there be any choppers waiting in reserve?"

Jocko looked at him. "This isn't the goddamn LA bus system. Don't let two get shot down."

Boesch laughed. "Yes, sir."

The beating of the helicopter's rotors made conversation in the cabin impossible, so no one spoke. No one needed to. Everyone knew their role.

Sergeant Peters glanced out of the helicopter's side window. Five other specially modified Black Hawks flew in formation low over enemy territory to evade radar. Their flight time was an hour each way, given the need to zigzag to avoid cities in the populous country.

He loved the pre-drop calm. Everyone in the helicopter was relaxed but focused. When the doors opened a hit of adrenaline would surge and jolt the heart like a defibrillator, and then it'd be go time.

His hands lay idly across the bag of jamming equipment in his lap. He was on one of four teams that would set up a perimeter of electronics to jam all phone, internet, and video equipment in and around the prison. When their job was done, the other choppers would fall out of their holding pattern and the soldiers would spring into action. They'd breach the perimeter and the attack would be on.

If all went well, they'd take out all of the guards in the prison and be in complete control within eight minutes. The two Americans would be found and extracted, and then their communications experts would make a general announcement to the prison telling them they were being set free by America. Merry fucking Christmas in the middle of June!

It seemed like just minutes later that his chopper began to descend. The pilot announced their arrival over the comm system.

Peters felt a bolt of electricity explode through his body. He leaned forward against his restraints, taking a quick inventory of the equipment around him. *Let's do this!*

There was a bump as the helicopter landed and the side door slid open. Peters jumped to the ground, his equipment in hand and on his back. He regrouped with the other soldiers, peripherally aware of the helicopter taking off again just seconds after it had landed. All twelve men aboard had exited with trained efficiency. Together they jogged the hundred yards through the forest to their assigned positions.

He and his partner reached the base of their assigned wall, dropped their duffel bags, and slipped off their backpacks. They assembled the jamming equipment with precision, then waited for the signal.

It came.

"Go virtual umbrella!"

After turning the equipment on, the two men retreated a hundred yards and lay down in the brush, their rifles trained on the prison wall. Anyone who might try to mess with their apparatus would be taken down.

"Go hard landing," came the order.

The SEALs in helicopter Red Two felt their chopper accelerate and then dive. As the prison came into view, its lights went dead. The mechanical team had done its work. Right on time, as always.

Jocko was the first to set foot inside the prison, his assault rifle bursting into action before his lead foot hit the ground. A trio of guards had come to greet them and Jocko mowed them down in seconds. The rest of his men fanned out to secure the courtyard they'd landed in.

Four other helicopters made similar landings within the walls of the sprawling prison, each spilling out eleven soldiers.

The sound of gunfire and the smell of propellant ruled the night. Jocko's wing of the prison fell quickly. Within minutes they'd secured the southwest quarter of the building. The chatter over his earpiece indicated things were not going so smoothly on the far side of the building.

"Melrose and Watson, stay here and guard the choppers. We're going to help on the north end."

Jocko took seven men with him. Glancing at the map, he led them down a wide corridor. The prison had been built in the 1980s with help from the Russians. The design was spartan at best. Not a lot of nooks to take cover in.

The sound of gunfire came from around the corner ahead. Jocko signaled for his men to stop. He called into his microphone, "Chopper Red Two at southwestern corner of hallway A2. Sound of heavy gunfire. Can we help?"

"Chopper Red Three here. We're pinned down from the guard tower. Taking heavy fire. Help appreciated."

Jocko pulled a dentist's mirror from his thigh pocket. *Gotta love low tech.* Slipping it around the corner, he got a view of what was going on. The good guys were pinned down from above. The right-hand side of their hallway featured a series of alternating glass and concrete wall panels. The guards had shot out the glass and had the soldiers pinned in place. A well-placed grenade and there would be mass casualties.

He huddled with his team. Jocko sent two men back the way they'd come to the last window. They needed to kick it out, make their way along the prison courtyard, and launch a grenade into the guard tower.

"Help is on the way," he called into his microphone.

"Hurry!"

Jocko and his men went to the edge of the hallway and waited. Gunfire continued to ring throughout the prison, making it hard to determine what was going on. When an explosion sounded above and to their right, they burst around the corner and pointed their guns toward the blown-out windows. They were met with silence.

The two groups of soldiers met up and after brief greetings, moved quickly down the hallway.

"There must be an armory in the far wing. The resistance we encountered there was well armed. These aren't ordinary prison guards."

"I agree with that."

"Do we go after the American prisoners or take out the armory?"

"Red One has the armory. Let's find our prisoners and get them on the chopper."

They found the main cellblock and disposed of the two guards at the door. Sliding the bars aside, they entered. Two soldiers stayed back to guard the doors while the other fifteen went cell to cell looking for the Americans.

"Got them!" came a cry halfway into the block. There was the sound of a cordless reciprocating saw cutting away at the lock. The soldiers retreated with the two stunned Americans in tow. The other prisoners made a ruckus as they ran down the cellblock, but the soldiers ignored them.

They burst out of a door marked as a fire exit. Two helicopters sat waiting in the courtyard. Before they could take a step toward the choppers, they heard a whistling sound.

"Mortars!" Jocko called out, pushing his men back inside. Everyone ducked close to the base of a wall, anticipating a blast.

An explosion came, but it didn't hit the building. Getting up and running to the door, Jocko looked outside. Both choppers were on fire. The pilots had exited their vehicles and stood by, watching the scene in shock.

Not good!

There was more whistling followed by another massive explosion.

"If that's three choppers down, we're in trouble," he said aloud to no one. "You three, take the wall and find out where those mortars are coming from and take them out. You six, take our targets to the nearest chopper and evacuate."

"What about the rest of us?" one of his men asked. "That's three choppers down, which means twenty men don't have a ride."

"We finish the mission, then I'll take nineteen men with me and we'll play hide and seek."

"For how long?"

"For as long as it takes."

There was a pause. "I'm with you, sir."

Jocko glanced around at his men. "Let's get this done."

When the last of the guards was eliminated, the communications team turned the power to the prison back on and made a general announcement to the prison population: "On behalf of the American government, we are granting you a chance at your freedom. In the courtyard by the main entrance you will be issued a backpack with four days' worth of food, money, and a weapon. Good luck."

Jocko and his men handed each prisoner a backpack as they left through the main prison gate. Smoke from the burning helicopters hung low across the ground. Some of the former prisoners left in groups, while others made off by themselves. When the last man had left, the remaining American soldiers regrouped.

"Everyone listen up," Jocko called. "Peters and Boesch raided the kitchen. We have enough food to last a long time. Let's make ourselves invisible until the good guys can come back for us. It may be a long time before that can happen. But we're SEALs. We can do this if we stick together and remember our training. Hooyah?"

"Hooyah!" came the response. The men shouldered their packs and left the prison, making for the hills.

———

The image of three smoldering Black Hawk helicopters was burned into President MacQueen's mind. *Failure!* The words rebounded through her mind. *You're a failure! You're not cut out for this!*

Rasha took over. *Cut it out! You're in command, so act like it!*

Olivia MacQueen glanced from the screen to the military brass around the room. "Someone want to tell me what the hell is going on? Was this part of the strategy? Leaving burning helicopters behind?"

The head of the Joint Chiefs of Staff gulped. "An inconvenience. The SEALs torch any equipment that's damaged to protect our technology. No soldiers killed, just minor injuries."

"How many men left behind?"

The general looked at the screen, avoiding her penetrating gaze. "Reports are that twenty men will have to make their way on foot. They'll retreat into the hills and hide until we can extract them."

"When will that be? This mission relied on surprise and the fact that no one in their right mind would have attempted such a raid. You'll never get a helicopter in there to extract them, soldier!"

"They're SEALs. They're trained for all eventualities. They'll survive until we can get them out. And we will."

"I'd better not see video of the Chinese military parading around a bunch of American soldiers. Am I going to see that?" the president snarled.

"No, Madam President."

THIRTY-SIX

"Jacob, stop!"

Lavinia put one hand on the dash of the Jeep while balancing the drone's controller in the other as Jacob stomped on the brakes. When they'd come to a standstill, he looked over at Lavinia. "What is it?"

She held up the video screen so Jacob could see. "Checkpoint around the bend. There are six soldiers, from what I can see. What do we do?"

"Do we go on foot?"

"To Russia? It'd take us two years to walk that far."

"We can go back the way we came. It's the only way we can keep the car."

Lavinia thought for a while, staring at the trees on either side of them. "No, we do both. Go on foot and keep the car." She quickly filled him in on her plan.

"I get to be the bait? That's your plan?"

"We could switch roles."

Jacob held up his hands. "These hands were made for typing. We had this conversation."

"It's settled then."

Lavinia got out of the car and headed off into the woods.

Jacob counted to a thousand as instructed, then put the Jeep back into gear and brought the car up to speed just below the limit. As he rounded the corner, a military vehicle parked diagonally across the road came into view. He'd need to drive on the shoulder to get around it.

He pulled up to the row of guards. There was an unnatural smile on the lead guard's face.

Jacob tried to act natural. "Hi there, just passing through."

The soldiers looked at each other before one of them came forward.

"Who are you?"

"Just a tourist. I'm a little lost, I have to admit."

"Out of the car."

Jacob feigned confusion. He looked left and right, then back at the guard. "Me? You mean me? Oh, because this isn't a car, it's a Jeep."

The man removed a pistol from his holster and pointed it at Jacob. "Out of the vehicle, funny man."

Jacob's eyes went wide. He raised his hands, then reached down with one hand and pulled on the lever to open the door with two fingers. His eyes locked on the soldier, he moved one hand slowly to undo his seatbelt.

The man led Jacob to the front of his vehicle. "Keep your hands up. Get on your knees."

Jacob complied and the man circled behind him, his gun trained on Jacob's head.

There was a rustling in the woods behind the soldiers. All six of the men turned their heads to follow the sound. All but the one behind Jacob pointed their assault rifles in the direction of the sound.

Jacob could just make out a red mark on the back of the men's earlobes. *Damn, these guys are everywhere!*

The rustle returned.

"Lion?" Jacob offered helpfully.

The soldier behind him barked an order and three of the men disappeared into the woods, pursuing whatever was making the sound. When they were gone, the soldier turned his attention back to Jacob.

"A tourist in this region? That seems unlikely." He continued to circle around Jacob and stopped in front of him. "Have you ever seen this woman?" He removed a photo from his pocket and held it up to Jacob.

He gulped. It was a photo of Lavinia.

When Jacob didn't answer, the soldier continued. "How about this man?" He put the photo against his chest and slipped it behind a second photo, then jammed it in front of Jacob's eyes. It was a photo of Jacob.

The soldier's head suddenly exploded in a cloud of red. Two more shots rang out and the other two soldiers dropped to the ground. Lavinia came running from behind the men. She emptied her magazine into the tires of the military vehicle and continued running toward Jacob's Jeep. She expelled the magazine while in full stride and slammed in a new one.

There was the sound of voices from the woods across the road.

Jacob got to his feet and ran for the driver's side door.

Lavinia slid across the front hood of the Jeep and landed by the passenger side door. Throwing it open, she jumped in and commanded Jacob, "Go!"

While Jacob jammed the gas pedal to the floor, Lavinia turned in her seat and stared hard out the rear window. The other soldiers hadn't returned to the road yet. Turning back to face forward, she pulled her seatbelt on and looked over at Jacob. His hands were shaking on the wheel.

"Are you okay?"

He turned to face her. There was blood splattered on his face. "Fine, I'm fine. Absolutely fine."

Lavinia placed a hand on his shoulder. "Let's switch, Jacob. I'll drive."

"No, I'm good," he said as he turned his head back toward her.

Lavinia reached across and cranked on the wheel to put them back in their lane. "Jacob, it's okay. Let me drive."

He nodded and pulled onto the shoulder. The two switched places. Lavinia put the vehicle back in gear. "That drone sure came in handy. I can't believe he sent so many of them to investigate the sound. That was fun, flying it through the tree leaves to make it sound like someone was running through the woods."

Jacob was silent.

"Jacob, it was the only way. These people have murdered innocent villagers. If they catch us, we'll get the same treatment, believe me."

"I know. He was a Blood Dragon."

"You're sure?"

"A second before you blew his head off I could see a red tattoo behind his ear." He spoke in a deep monotone.

"Get some rest, Jacob. I'm good to drive."

Jacob used a shammy from the glove compartment to wipe the blood off his face, then fell asleep as the adrenaline wore off and his body crashed.

Lavinia drove in silence and was relieved when they made it to a real highway. In order to have full employment, the Chinese government supported huge infrastructure projects. They would build entire cities that would lie vacant for years until people eventually populated that part of the country. They were known as ghost cities. This highway was no exception. It was five lanes wide in each direction, but there was no traffic at all.

Taking advantage of the silence, Lavinia turned the facts over in her mind.

They knew that Liu Wei was the leader of the Blood Dragons, which meant he was in on both the social media attacks and the flood of liquid metal into the United States. There was now little doubt that he'd murdered both the vice president and the president and framed Lavinia for the latter to get her out of his way.

She could still see no logical end game. Unless he was a psychopath and wanted to start World War Three. But who would stand with him? China had no chance of winning a nuclear exchange with the United States. He'd done all this just to achieve power?

Jacob stirred next to her. When he sat up, his black hair stood up on end where he'd leaned against the window.

"Welcome back to the land of the living, sleepy boy."

Jacob rubbed his eyes. "I can't believe I slept!"

"I think you were in shock," Lavinia offered.

"That was pretty awful."

"Jacob..."

"I know," he cut her off. "We didn't have a choice. Where are we now?"

"We're half an hour from the Russian border."

"I thought it was cold," he replied, rubbing his shoulders.

"I'm glad you woke up, because you're the only one in this car who knows the plan when we get to the border."

"Yeah, don't worry. Aaron has us covered. I should probably be driving, though."

Lavinia pulled over, happy to surrender the wheel. The ground was dusted with a light layer of snow. The wind bit at her face as she rounded the front of the vehicle. They weren't dressed for this weather. She dropped into the passenger seat and pulled the door shut.

They drove for half an hour before Jacob pulled over again.

"I think you should get in the back area and I'll cover you with the blanket and our bags. If we happen to get the wrong guard, there's still a chance he'll check my passport and let me pass."

"There's a right guard? He bribed one guard?"

"Don't worry, we've got it covered. It just doesn't hurt to be careful. After all, you are wanted internationally for the murder of the Chinese president. One can't be too cautious."

Lavinia shot him a look. "How do you know if you have the right guard?"

"We have a secret passphrase."

"Which is?"

"I ask him if the vodka in Russia is good. If he replies, 'In Russia the vodka is always good when it's cold,' then he's my guy."

Lavinia sighed. "This is what you get when hackers play spy." Getting out of the Jeep, she closed the passenger door and climbed into the back storage area. Jacob covered her with a blanket and then piled their bags on top of her.

Hopping back into the driver's seat, Jacob put the Jeep back into gear.

In the back, Lavinia positioned her ear so that it was covered but she could still hear what was going on. After what seemed an eternity, she felt the vehicle slow and then stop. A few moments passed and they crept forward again before coming to an abrupt stop.

"Hi there!" Jacob said cheerfully. "Is the vodka in Russia good today?"

"Papers."

Wrong guard! Lavinia swore under her breath.

"Sure, papers, one sec." Jacob rustled through the glove box. "Your English is perfect," he complimented. "You must love the vodka here."

"Why you talk about vodka? Papers, now!"

There was more rustling. Lavinia assumed Jacob was removing his American passport from the glove box and handing it to the man.

"Why you coming to Russia? What is your business here?"

"No business, just vacation."

"Vacation? Here? In history of world, no one take vacation here. Nothing but mines and trees for two hundred kilometers. Why you here?"

Jacob gave no answer.

"Unlock your doors. I search."

Lavinia could hear the passenger door behind Jacob open. The temperature in the car dropped. A few moments passed and the door was slammed shut. Lavinia held her breath, her hand gripping the handle of her Sig Sauer 1911.

The tailgate was lifted and she felt a gust of cold wind rip through the vehicle. She braced herself for the blanket to be pulled away.

"Petrov, why you make a career of that car?"

"This is the first car we've had in a month!" the man replied in a gruff voice.

"Let them go. Is your move. You're just trying to waste time because you lose at chess. I check the car."

Lavinia felt about a hundred heartbeats race by before the welcome sound of the tailgate being slammed shut came.

"I am Vladamir," a new voice addressed Jacob.

Jacob's voice cracked in reply. "Is the vodka in Russia good?"

There was a pause. "The vodka in Russia is always good...when it's cold. My American friend. You have something for me?"

There was silence, then the man spoke again. "I have to search car. Or my friend, he wonders. Unlock the doors again."

The door behind Jacob was pulled open and a cold blast of air penetrated the car's interior again. Lavinia could hear some rummaging around. The door slammed shut, then the tailgate was lifted again. Lavinia gripped her gun, the butt braced on her knee. The blanket was pulled back and she found herself face to face with a Russian man. He wore a heavy wool coat and a fur hat. A smile broke across his face and he waved to Lavinia. Then he dropped the blanket and slammed the gate down

"You're good to go." It sounded like he pounded a hand on the hood.

The car started to move again. A few moments later Jacob announced, "That was our guy."

"Can I come out now?"

"Yeah, they can't see us anymore."

"I'm glad it wasn't Petrov that pulled the blanket up. How much money was in that envelope?"

"Enough for him to let you into the country."

Lavinia scrambled over the back seat and then between the front buckets and dropped into the passenger seat. She pulled on her safety belt. "Lord, that was close!"

"You're telling me. When the first guy lifted the tailgate, I thought we were goners."

"I was afraid I was going to have to shoot him."

"I'm glad you didn't. You're already wanted by the Chinese. We don't need to add the Russians to that list."

"How far are we from the airport?"

"Not far. It's twenty minutes past the border."

"Are we going to have to smuggle me onto the plane, too?"

"No. It's a private jet. Aaron has paid off the staff there. It'll take us to Latvia. At that point we'll be in the European Union and we can take a plane to Belgium without showing a passport. It's just open travel across the EU."

"God bless the Eurozone."

"Yeah. From Belgium we're off to Sealand."

Lavinia stared out the window. The terrain here was fully covered with snow. It reminded her of the time she'd spent in Canada when she was a kid. Reminiscing made her reflect on how she'd gotten into such a mess.

———

Wang Juan stood with her arms crossed. Three body bags lay on the ground in front of her. One of the three remaining soldiers stood in front of her holding a consumer drone, telling her about the American man they'd stopped. He matched the photo they'd been sent. They were convinced that he'd killed their three colleagues, but she knew better. Lavinia Walsh had ambushed them. It was so obvious that she'd used the device to break the six soldiers up so she could defeat them.

Lavinia Walsh was smart and dangerous. Willing to kill. The two women had much in common.

THIRTY-SEVEN

The commander of the USS *William P. Lawrence* was on the bridge when the instrument panel went haywire.

"Sir, ships on our scopes."

"How many ships?"

There was a pause. "Hundreds, sir."

The commander paused. "Hundreds? Sailboats? Fishing boats?"

"No, sir. It looks like two-thirds of the Chinese Navy has set sail!"

"Get me the naval commander on the line!" he barked.

"Aye-aye, sir!" came the steady reply.

Putting his binoculars to his eyes, he stared ahead until a line of ships came into view. It looked like a video from D-Day as the Allies sailed across the English Channel. He zoomed in on a ship in the middle. It was a Renhai-class destroyer. If the convoy had a destroyer then it would surely include an aircraft carrier.

"Sound the alarm!"

President Olivia MacQueen stood at the edge of the table in the war room, her arms crossed. "What am I looking at?"

The naval commander replied, "You're watching the Chinese Navy deploy its fleet into the South China Sea."

"Why? What's their plan?" she snapped.

"It's early to say, but they must think we're going to attack. We'll have to monitor their path."

"Are they going to attack the homeland?" she asked.

"Good luck, if that's their plan. We'd destroy the entire convoy before they've crossed the Pacific. Our ships can hit them from more than a thousand miles."

"I want some scenarios to be prepared to repel them," she ordered.

The military men around the table glanced at each other before the head of the Joint Chiefs of Staff spoke. "Madam President, scenarios to repel what? There is no chance they're going to attack the United States."

Unfolding her arms, she drove her fists into the table with a thud and leaned forward. "You don't know Liu Wei, but I do!" she snapped. "If he's deploying two-thirds of his fleet, then there's a reason for it. They aren't on a kamikaze mission. He's a military planner from a family of military planners. There's a reason for it," she repeated, "so stop questioning me and get me some battle plans."

The men looked at each other, but when no one spoke they all turned and filed out of the room.

Olivia MacQueen sat down in the empty Situation Room and crossed her arms. Rasha was firmly in control.

Liu Wei stood at the head of the command center. The twenty-foot video screen showed a world map with a cutout of the South China Sea. Electronic representations of Chinese naval ships were in red while the paltry American presence in the region was in blue.

It was the largest deployment of a military navy since World War II. Yet it was just the first wave. In a move that was sure to perplex the American military, the two hundred ships he'd just deployed would break for the Pacific Ocean and toward the United States.

Their first target would come as a surprise. At top speed it would take six days to get to Alaska. There they would establish a land base from which they would begin the invasion of the United States. An attack the world would have thought impossible.

The arrogant Americans would not panic, believing their land-based missiles would destroy the Chinese armada. But in three days Liu Wei would unleash a devastating weapon that would leave his enemy blind.

Liu Wei's father was a household name. A brilliant and beloved man. But China would never forget Liu Wei. The one who delivered China its *mingyun*. Its destiny.

Every seat in the Situation Room was filled, but the room was silent as Olivia MacQueen took her place.

"You may begin."

"Madam President, thank you for joining us at this late hour."

"No hour is too late when the safety of the United States is at stake, General."

"Yes, Madam President," the four star general mumbled. "The two hundred ships that left port two days ago have all broken for the Pacific Ocean. So we have to assume that their target is California. At top speed, they could reach California in about six days. With two days passed, they are four days away. In the meantime, their remaining hundred ships have clogged the South China Sea, forming a blockade. This makes any attack on the Chinese mainland difficult. We'd be limited to guided missiles. We have a few thousand in the region, given that we've scrambled a substantial portion of our navy."

"How long until we can attack their ships?"

"In about three days; they'll be in range of our land-based missiles."

"As soon as they're in range, destroy them."

The general shuffled the papers he was holding. "Yes, Madam President."

"What about our missing SEALs? Do we have a plan to recover them?"

"Not yet. They've made contact. They're all safe at the moment, they're just staying invisible. The Chinese military has been searching the area, but so far they've managed to stay out of sight."

"We need to find a way to get them out of there before we sink the attacking ships," MacQueen said. "What of Lavinia Walsh?"

"She's disappeared. We think she's hiding in the forests of Northern China. The Chinese are very motivated to find her, given what she did. So it's just a matter of time till they do."

"Good."

"What's the plan when they find her?"

Olivia MacQueen stared right through the general. "Let them execute her."

There was a collective gasp in the room.

"The woman is a traitor to this country." MacQueen

stood and turned to face the room. "Whether she went rogue or she was working under instructions from Barbara Anderson, we may never know. Whichever it is, she is at the center of the crisis that I now have to clean up!" She stared down the room. "Don't second guess me. I'm the only hope this country has to fix this."

The sound of Liu Wei's boots announced his arrival when he entered the command center. The entire room stood and turned to face him.

Reverence!

Everyone in this room knew the plan. They knew what was about to transpire. They were witnessing history.

"Activate the Nest. Launch the bats."

That was the order everyone had been waiting for. Anticipating.

An image filled the enormous screen at the front of the command center. The video was taken from a camera on the rover that had been dropped on the surface of the Moon. The lunar lander was shaped like an upside-down pinecone. A countdown clock appeared on the screen and the anticipation in the room rose as it got closer to zero.

When the countdown ended nothing happened for a handful of seconds. Then suddenly there was a large puff from inside the spacecraft, and hundreds upon hundreds of black objects were shot out of the holes in the pinecone-shaped lander. It looked like it was shooting watermelon seeds out into space.

The image held for a few minutes before the screen cleared and was replaced. In the distance was Earth, but in front of the camera was what looked like a sea of bats. In